THE BURGLAR

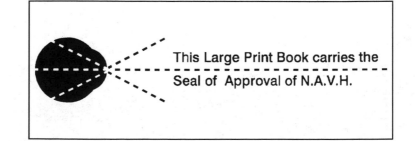
This Large Print Book carries the
Seal of Approval of N.A.V.H.

THE BURGLAR

THOMAS PERRY

THORNDIKE PRESS
A part of Gale, a Cengage Company

Farmington Hills, Mich • San Francisco • New York • Waterville, Maine
Meriden, Conn • Mason, Ohio • Chicago

LIBRARY OF CONGRESS CIP DATA ON FILE.
CATALOGUING IN PUBLICATION FOR THIS BOOK
IS AVAILABLE FROM THE LIBRARY OF CONGRESS

ISBN-13: 978-1-4328-5921-3 (hardcover)

Published in 2019 by arrangement with The Mysterious Press, an imprint of Grove/Atlantic, Inc.

Printed in Mexico
3 4 5 6 7 8 23 22 21 20 19

For Jo, Alix, and Ian

1

A young blond woman ran along a quiet tree-lined Bel-Air street at dusk. She kept her head up and her steps even and strong. The street was in the flat part of Bel-Air just north of Sunset, a neighborhood with big old houses built as mansions by movie and television people in the 1950s and '60s. Mansions still occupied giant parcels sectioned into lawns and gardens, but over time the old owners had died, and the new owners had noticed that the houses were not the newest styles and not as large as a house might be. For years they had been in the process of demolishing the old homes to build new ones that looked to them like clearer embodiments of wealth and potency.

The runner's name was Elle Stowell. She wore a dark blue T-shirt that said YALE on it and black running shorts. On her feet was a pair of distinctive running shoes of a brand worn by female runners who lived in neighborhoods like this one. They cost hundreds of dollars and were superbly made, but their real purpose was to give their wearer an edge that was more sociological than athletic. They were a credential, proof that the runner belonged here.

Elle was small, an inch over five feet tall. Her size and her pretty face made her seem younger. She was very fit, her body thinner and more long-muscled than an Olympic gymnast's because her daily routines relied more on running and swimming than on jumping and upper-body work.

Elle Stowell needed to be physically exceptional but needed not to look physically exceptional. She had to be able to show up in neighborhoods like this one looking like the daughter of the couple down the street. She often put on a shirt with the name of a university so she would appear to be a student home for a visit and running near her parents' house.

She had a light complexion and blue eyes, and she spent lots of money on styling and dyeing her hair to duplicate the golden look of the daughters of the rich. She acknowledged that she did not compare with her best friend, Sharon, who could walk into a restaurant and cause the conversations at tables to trail off, or her friend Ricki, who was a model and appeared to be an elongated ink drawing of a goddess. If pressed, Elle might have admitted she was cute.

A week ago she had driven through this neighborhood looking for the right house, and then three days later, she had walked her friend Elizabeth's little white French bulldog through here on a leash. At each house where a dog lived, the dog would charge to the fence and bark at the French bulldog, warning it to stay away forever or face dire consequences. When she had finished the walk, the bulldog felt flattered by the attention, and Elle knew where there were dogs and where there weren't. At the place she was going there weren't.

Elle needed money right now, but she didn't like working after dark, when the danger increased. Her work required her to look rich and be where rich people lived, but she was careful to tone down her appearance to avoid being kidnapper bait — no sparkly jewelry, no watch or rings, no daydreaming, particularly at night. She never let her alertness lapse, and she listened for cars overtaking her from behind. Even if there was nothing to be afraid of, no attention was welcome. Her only accessory was at her waist: a black fanny pack which contained a few small tools and a lot of empty space.

She reached the block she had chosen and ran straight to a house that was undergoing a thorough renovation. She was sure that, when completed, it would look a lot like an old gray stone bank. It had a long front porch with four pillars that appeared to hold up the front end of the roof but were only ornaments. At this stage of construction the house was surrounded by scaffolds: three levels of steel piping with walkways consisting of two ten-inch-wide boards laid side by side every three or four yards.

Elle veered in front of the building, already pulling on her surgical gloves, and hoisted herself up on the temporary chain-link fence, stepped on the chain and padlock that held the gate shut, and jumped to the ground inside the fence. She went to the scaffold on the side of the house, pulled herself up onto the first level about six feet up, and walked along the scaffolding, feeling a slight springy bounce of the boards under her feet. It occurred to her that if her 105 pounds made the boards bow a little and rebound upward, a carpenter who weighed twice as much must have a pretty bouncy walk.

She kept turning her head to look over the tall concrete fence a few feet from the scaffold. She kept looking in the windows of the house next door and seeing things that pleased her. There were no lights on in the rooms she passed. In the kitchen, the timers on the oven and the microwave, and the lighted green dots showing that the refrigerator was working, were the only signs that the power was on.

When she reached the back end of the board walkway, she shinnied up a vertical pipe of the scaffold. She was hot from running, and the coolness of the metal felt good on her legs, which were doing most of the work of pushing her body upward. She reached the second level and kept going to the third. The top level of the scaffold jutted about two feet above the eaves of the house, so she had an unobstructed view of this side of the peaked roof, a bit of the terrain beyond, and the tree canopy that shaded the quiet street for a distance on both sides. Dusk had now faded to darkness, and she could see strings of streetlights going on throughout the neighborhood.

She spent a few more minutes looking at the house next door. That house was not under renovation. She could see enough of it to verify that it was still in pristine shape from its own rebuilding a year or two ago.

She could also see that the swimming pools — one big irregular-shaped pool and a long strip of water near it for swimming laps — were covered with black plastic sheeting. The nets were off the tennis courts. Days ago she had already verified that no dog was present, the cars were locked in the garage, and the newspapers and mail had been stopped.

Elle knew a lot about houses and about the ways people in rich neighborhoods thought about them. At the moment when the people living next door had learned that the house on the lot where she was standing right now was going to be razed and this monstrous building erected in its place, they had undoubtedly begun to make plane reservations. They had gone somewhere to wait out the long period of construction. If they were rich enough to afford a massive house in Bel-Air, they didn't have to sit in it and listen to the sounds of bulldozers, saws, cement trucks, nail guns, and foremen shouting at their crews in Spanish. They had, as rich people could do, sidestepped the unpleasantness. Right now they might be in the South of France or on the New England coast or touring Iceland.

Elle bent down, picked up the end of one of the boards forming the walkway of the scaffold, propped it on the scaffold's railing, and eased it across the empty space to rest on the railing of the balcony extending from the house next door. She wiggled the board to be sure that it was solidly and evenly resting on the two railings. Then she opened her fanny pack to take out a bungee cord, wrapped it around the board twice, and used the two metal hooks to secure it to the scaffold so the board would not move.

She lifted herself to the level of the railing, set a foot onto the board, and then began to walk. For Elle, walking on narrow footholds at great heights was not a pleasure, but she had learned to do it as a teenager in gymnastics. A ten-inch board was much wider than a ten-centimeter balance beam, and she wasn't expected to do any tricks on it. She kept her attention on the board and walked over it without allowing her mind to interfere.

She got over the railing to the balcony and looked in the French doors. The view was limited because of gauzy white curtains and the lack of light, but she could see this was a bedroom with an empty bed, a dresser with nothing on the surface, and an open empty closet. The ceilings were at least twelve feet high, and when she looked back at the scaffolding she had just left, she estimated that the level of the French doors where she stood was nearly thirty feet above the ground. She took out her small flashlight to look for signs of an alarm but spotted none in the bedroom. Most contractors didn't think doors and windows at that height were worth wiring.

She examined the lock on the French doors, then selected the right bump key for the lock on her key ring, inserted it and turned it just far enough to get the pins under pressure, hit the door with her shoulder, and turned the key farther as the pins jumped. The door swung inward.

The room was big and luxurious, but it wasn't the one she wanted. This was a room a family might keep immaculate and waiting for grandparents or other guests — close to the rest of the family but far enough away from them to preserve everyone's nerves. It had a bathroom with a telephone — an indication the intended visitor was elderly — its own balcony, a good television set. She went through the doorway to hunt for the master suite.

When she got to the master suite she found the door locked, as she had expected. This room took a different bump key, but when she stepped inside she felt hope. She had been putting off working for a while, so she was experiencing a shortage of cash. The picture of a woman on the man's tall dresser caught her eye. The woman was dark-haired, wearing a dark blue strapless evening gown and a necklace. She was very attractive. She seemed to be in her late thirties at the time of the sitting, so she was now probably in her fifties. The necklace was exquisite. It was a chain studded with diamonds, made to suspend a circular sapphire cradled in a nest of diamonds. There had been wealth here. Maybe it was still around.

Elle considered. She had been hoping to find a bit of cash for her immediate needs and then move on. When people went away, they often left some so they could replenish their wallets with American money without having to go to a bank when they got home. But if a woman had serious jewelry, she would not have taken it with her to Europe or Asia. She would have left it locked up in a safe-deposit box at a bank or in a hiding place at home.

Elle had to make a quick choice: look for the envelope of cash inside a book or taped under something, or look for the jewelry in false containers and safes. She had to move. She had seen nothing to worry about yet, but she knew that it was best to do things

15

rapidly in case there were security devices installed that she had not seen.

People were not always very smart about hiding things. It had astounded her at times that people still hid things between the mattress and the box springs of a bed, but they did, so she had to look there before she moved on. What she found this time was a Colt Commander pistol. She released the heavy mattress and let it cover the gun and went on. She found the safe in the man's walk-in closet. The space was big enough for a drive-in closet if the owner could have driven a car up the stairs. The safe was built into the wall behind the row of suits, but it was not a very formidable one.

The safe reminded her of the safes in hotel rooms. Its display had only four lighted squares for the numbers. She sat down, made herself comfortable, and began to work the combination. To a novice, ten thousand possible digits would have seemed a daunting number, but Elle was optimistic. She was a rapid typist, and her decision to go after the jewelry was final.

There were some combinations that were more likely than others. She hit four 0s, four 1s, four 2s, all the way through 9. She hit 1234, 4321. The address of the house was 1477. If the owner used birthdays, the final two numbers would be the year, which had to be 99 or less, and because there were only four digits, the first pair had to be a single-digit month and a single-digit day. Colored stones were often given because they were birthstones. A sapphire was the birthstone for September, so maybe the first digit was 9.

She set the second digit as 1, then went upward on the final pair of numbers from 1 to 99. When nothing happened she made the second digit 2 and repeated the process. When she made the second digit 4 and then ran the final two up to 70, there was a click, then an electronic sound like something spinning, and the safe popped open. The sight made her draw in a breath. She opened the blue velvet case and recognized the sapphire necklace from the picture. Behind the blue velvet case was a black velvet case, and when she opened it she saw a sparkle of diamonds. She turned on her flashlight. Yellow diamonds. She put both necklaces into her fanny pack, then looked farther inside the safe. There were papers that might be worth something, but not to her. She turned off the flashlight. She had done enough, and she sensed it was time to go. As she closed the safe, she saw that the four numbers were blinking on and off. She didn't want the owner to come into his closet and instantly see that his safe had been opened and his wife's necklaces stolen. Any delay in discovery was good for Elle.

Elle decided that the blinking probably meant that the safe had been opened but not reset. She pushed the door shut and then hit reset, then 0000. The blinking stopped, but she had an uneasy feeling.

Elle went back along the empty hallway to the guest room with the French doors and stepped out to the balcony. From here she could see for a distance. Far down the street she could see a pair of cars. They were black-and-white with numbers painted on their roofs, and the lights above the windshields were spinning red and blue. They were moving fast, but she heard no sirens. They were on their way to a crime in progress.

Elle grasped the board on the balcony railing with both hands and hoisted herself up so her knees were on it. She didn't have anything to hold on to to rise to her feet, so she crawled quickly along the board to the scaffold on the other house, where she eased herself down to the board walkway. She unfastened the bungee cord and put it in her fanny pack, then dragged the heavy board back from the balcony to the scaffold. Before the police arrived she had just enough time to slide it into place where she had found it.

The flashing red and blue lights were gone, but Elle could hear the cars pull up at the front of the house. Doors opened and slammed, and there were metallic voices squawking from radios and heavy footsteps running up to the gate of the chain-link fence. Elle didn't have time to find an open window to climb inside the half-finished house. All she could do was lie down on her side with her arms straight, pull her body back toward the house so it was all on one ten-inch board, and stay still.

The beams of powerful flashlights swept the ground in front of the house, then moved along the sides, throwing shadows of the scaffolding onto the gray wall beside her. Now and then one of the beams would unexpectedly jump upward to shine in a window. Only a couple of times did Elle see a beam shine upward as far as the third level of the scaffold, and from ground level all it could do was shine on the underside of the board walkway.

She saw the flashlight beams moving along below her, flitting from side to side. Now and then one of them would switch off for a few seconds and then switch back on as though to fool someone who would think the police had gone away. At least two cops reached the rear of the building. They spent some time sneaking up on a tall pile of lumber, with guns drawn, but nobody was hiding there. Next they moved to the house and she heard them doing the predictable thing, which was to try the doors and the first-floor windows to be sure none of them was unlocked or broken.

There was more radio traffic, and then she heard two of the cops moving past the scaffold. When she could, she looked through the crack between the boards of her scaffold and saw the cops prowling around the house next door, checking its doors and windows too. She could see that they were not just going through the motions because they were here anyway. Somehow they had come to know that the house was either at risk or already being hit.

Time passed, and she had to let it pass. One of the best strategies for hide-and-seek was to outlast the opponent, to simply remain silent and motionless longer than he thought you would. She didn't like it much. It occurred to her that she also had a date tonight. She was supposed to go to dinner with a guy who wasn't exactly fascinating, but she believed in keeping her word and being fair to men who asked her out. She didn't want somebody with a legitimate grievance going around repeating it to every other guy and making her seem horrible. She had gone out with this one three times, so he would probably be madder if she stood him up now, because it would seem personal.

The police should have left by now, and she was beginning to get uneasy. She had never been arrested for anything, and the prospect of arrest terrified her. If she got caught with a set of bump keys, a big razor-sharp knife, a lockpick, a tension wrench, and what looked like half a million bucks in jewelry, she would be in prison until she was ninety.

And then one of the cops found a way in. She could see the beams of their flashlights inside the house next door. In a few minutes they'd be upstairs. That meant they'd be able to look out the window and see her up here on the scaffold.

Elle grasped the vertical pipe frame of the scaffold, held on loosely, and slid downward to the second level. She heard a radio voice again, and this time it seemed to be coming from two places at once. Then she heard footsteps, this time running, and she went down on her belly on the second level and froze. She saw the other two policemen running across the driveway to the house next door, the one she had robbed. She held on to the vertical support and slid to the ground.

As soon as her feet touched, she ran toward the street. She turned the corner of the house to the gate, lifted herself up, stepped on the chain and padlock, and slipped between the sides. Two cop cars were parked at angles so their snouts nearly touched at the gate, so she could barely get down without touching them. As she passed the open driver's-side door of one, she heard the sound of the car's engine, a quiet reassuring purr.

In an instant she sensed this was the way. It was as though she were on a circus platform and a trapeze was swinging through the air toward her. If she jumped for it and caught it, she could swing to the other side. If she waited, thought, and decided, the trapeze would swing away from her, and the next time it swung back it would be out of her reach and her jump would propel her into the empty air and death.

She slid onto the seat, shifted into reverse, grasped the steering wheel, and tugged the door toward her. She knew enough not to slam the door and enough not to drive past the house she had robbed. She swung the car around and gradually accelerated up the street. She turned the first corner, accelerated some more, and then made the next left. She parked the car at the curb near the third corner, turned it off, and took the keys. She ran around the corner to the street where she had left her own car. She had not wanted to drive right up to it and let the cop car's automatic plate reader record her license plate, or let whatever dashboard device it might have see her or her car. She got out and never looked back, just ran as fast as she could to her car.

As she drove, she noticed that she was breathing heavily. She wasn't winded, and she wasn't tired. As soon as she was a mile or so away, she began to shiver, and it lasted until she was home with her car in the garage and the doors locked. It took her over an hour before she felt calm enough to shower and dress for her date.

At dawn the next morning, Elle Stowell was out running again. She had been dumped last night, and the guy wasn't even her boyfriend. She had gone out with him three times — four if you included the breakup date. That part was astounding when she

23

thought about it. While she had still looked like a prospect to him, he'd acted so broke that she'd wanted to pay for herself, him, a limo for each of them, and some food for whatever starving relatives and pets he had at home. But on the night he dumped her, he bought her a fancy dinner. Was she supposed to go home and console herself with the thought that she had been let down and cast off, but at least she'd ingested four thousand calories doing it?

This one had been handsome but dense. She had spent three evenings listening for any indication that something was going on behind his eyes. Nothing ever peeked out. And his farewell speech was a variation on the theme that the problem wasn't her — meaning the shape of her body and the features of her face — but him. He just didn't feel he understood women.

It was interesting to her how often men said they didn't understand women. They were right that they didn't, but it wasn't because women were uncommunicative. Plenty of women she knew talked almost continuously. The problem was that men thought of themselves as being more similar to anything else on the planet — male horses or wildebeests or chipmunks — than to female human beings. Women were their opposite. To them, a thirty-two-year-old male physicist was more similar to a billy goat than to a thirty-two-year-old female physicist.

Not that Elle was thirty-two or a physicist. She was twenty-four and a burglar, a sneak thief. This wasn't a fact that she ever brought up with men, so it hadn't been a factor in her rejection, but it was an important part of her existence, since it was the part that paid the bills. So once again she was running. She was jogging along a beautiful road south of Sunset that wound around in Beverly Hills and offered the occasional view of the Los Angeles Basin, and her purpose wasn't to burn the calories from her valedictory dinner. She was casing houses along the route, looking for her next score.

There was esoteric knowledge involved in being a burglar — broad areas that took some thought and skill. There was choosing the house, entering the house, and finding the items that were worth taking. Elle Stowell was good at all three.

Elle was strong but small, so she couldn't carry a seven-foot television out of a house if she'd wanted to. It didn't matter because the real prizes were all small and dense — money, watches, jewelry, gold, guns, and collections — and usually they were to be found in or near the master bedroom suite. Some of the things she found in bedroom hiding places that fitted this description were revealing but not for her to take: secret cell phones for calling lovers, second sets of identification, bugout kits, or drugs.

Her small size helped her. She looked like a person who would be out running at dawn in a rich neighborhood, so she didn't worry people who saw her. There was a certain irony in this, because the same qualities made her a fearsome burglar. She could enter a house in dozens of ways that were impossible for a large man. She could easily crawl into a house through a dog door or take the glass slats out of a louvered window and slither inside. Both openings were common and neither was ever wired for an alarm.

Elle had seen practically everything that made homes vulnerable. Spare keys were hidden in or under pots, on top of lintels, inside hollow imitation stones, or hanging on small-headed nails on the sides of two-by-fours in garages or outbuildings. These were good places to look anyway, because if there was no key, there would still be tools that would get her into a house. She always looked to see where these buildings were and whether they were easy to enter.

She was also cautious. Before she committed herself she looked for a small, cheap car or two near the house, because these belonged to maids and nannies. Pickup trucks belonged to pool men and gardeners.

Elle knew that a burglar was a sorry, selfish thing to be, but she had gotten started at a time when she was too young to be on her own and had to eat. She had known even then that burglary deprived rich people of stuff their insurance companies would pay to replace. It also shook their confidence and made them feel violated. That was bad, but it also made the act a little bit sexual, which all the most tempting crimes were. A burglar saw everything they'd hidden and learned a great many of their secrets, and even when Elle didn't have time to accomplish that, they thought she had. They knew they had been exposed and, in a way, used for someone's pleasure.

Rich people felt the humiliation and loss more keenly than poor people did, because all those possessions and luxuries were dear to them, in some cases *were* them. Poor people had already been ripped off a thousand times and knew their possessions were crap. They had never invested anything useful in them, like their self-esteem or their souls. By adulthood the poor had been beaten into wisdom and detachment. Elle had known all about being poor by the time she was ten. Everything ever provided to her was cheap, worn, mismatched, and inferior. Even the name Elle had been a handicap.

She wasn't really sure why her mother named her Elle. She had once hoped it had been a naive feminist gesture, but suspected she was probably just named after the magazine or a person in a movie. When most people heard her name they asked her what the "L" stood for. Usually she just made something up — Lilith, Lorelei, Lamia.

Elle had spent her childhood in South Pasadena, in an old house that was teeming with cousins. Her grandmother had raised three daughters and then raised their children too. Her mother had been the middle one, the girl who had been universally recognized as the most beautiful of three beautiful girls, but also the stupidest. Elle's grandmother had admitted this freely in front of Elle. She had said, "Like a little china doll, and her head was just as hollow." Elle gathered over time that her mother had been in a car with a boyfriend when he had driven the car into a concrete viaduct. Nobody had ever told her whether the boyfriend was her father, which led her to believe he wasn't. No other candidates were ever mentioned to Elle.

Growing up in the big old house didn't take her as long as it took the others. She was out on her own at fourteen. Now and then she had brought back sums of money for her aunts and grandmother. For a time she had the notion that she would come back one day and live with the family again, bringing with her enough money to get the cousins educated. When concocting this plan she had assumed that everything would stay the same long enough for her to return before any big changes occurred, so they would happen right. They didn't.

Her grandmother died, and the aunts emptied the house and split up their nine children. Then the aunts went off with men, never for a second misleading anyone into thinking these would be permanent men; they were only the men for now. Men had never been members of the family. They were like the stepping-stones in the back garden, hard surfaces where you put one light foot while the other was already in motion toward the next.

Elle had started out thinking of her family's name, Stowell, as aristocratic. The old house was big, and the chimney had a metal "S" built into it. She was already fifteen and a novice burglar when she realized that the S-iron was common, not really the letter, but a support that masons used to strengthen the brick structure of a chimney. She also learned that the name Stowell was not a relic of faded grandeur, just a name her grandmother had assumed because she thought it sounded like a good one for an imaginary husband. It combined two historic New England names, Stowe and Lowell.

Elle had studied her profession. She had taken enough night classes in locksmithing, electronics, and other skills to wonder if the community colleges were mostly packed with studious thieves. She had recognized a few while she was there.

She had also learned what she could from other thieves she met when she was selling her prizes. An older man who called himself Shadrack taught her that carrying a gun was a bad idea. In California the sentence was worse for using a gun in the commission of a crime than for burglary. And besides, he said, when you carried one, it seemed the gun itself was trying to get you to use it. In her years working after that she had learned he was right. There had been a few times when she would certainly have shot somebody if she'd had a gun, but she had not.

As she ran she was feeling hopeful. She knew that Tuesday, Wednesday, and Thursday were the best times to fly out of LAX, so they were the best times to look for an empty house. The tickets were cheaper then than on Friday or Saturday, and Sunday was the day everybody's bosses wanted him to fly out on business, a way of getting a free day from an employee by placing him at some advantageous spot for the opening of business on Monday morning. This made Monday unpredictable, combining the passengers coming home from those Monday morning meetings and the vacationers who had decided to stay an extra day to avoid the late Sunday crowds. She avoided Monday altogether.

Morning was best because a person going to the East Coast had to go early in the morning or arrive too late in the evening to accomplish much other than paying for an extra night in an overpriced hotel. There was also the fact that strange things happened in the fall, winter, and spring in the parts of the country that had weather. When they happened, the whole airline system became increasingly backed up late in the day.

Everything was right this morning. Her outfit and exact way of carrying herself were calculated to convey the right impression at a glance. There was no point in staring at her, because that glance told a person everything. She had to run hard, because that was the universal way of the innumerable young women who ran in Los Angeles. They were serious year-round runners, and they ran as though they were in a race. And part of her disguise was driving the right car, so this morning she had parked a small rented Mercedes at the edge of the neighborhood.

Elle searched for the signs as she ran — people carrying suitcases to put into waiting limousines; houses where the morning newspaper landed on yesterday's edition, which still lay in the driveway; houses where the wrong lights were on at the wrong time of day.

She didn't stop right away at any house this morning. She picked out the most promising place and circled back later to make sure there was nobody at a window or standing outside one of the neighboring houses who might notice her.

At the house she picked she saw there was

a fresh sheaf of printed ads for local services stuck in the mail slot at the front door. The door was at least sixty feet from the front gate, where ads were commonly left. She saw the ads as a good sign. About a third of the people who delivered the ads were doorknob rattlers looking for an unlocked door so they could slip in and take something. She wasn't the only one who thought this owner wasn't at home.

The place she had picked was a large green house with a complicated arrangement of gables and peaks that featured a great deal of roof covered with composite shingles. It looked as though it had been inspired by a country house in England that was roughly the shape of a haystack. There were some eccentric details — tall, thick natural-wood doors under rounded arches, gardens hemmed by stucco walls with bougainvillea growing along the tops, old-fashioned windows that opened on hinges.

As she came up the driveway, she searched for her own way in and found it at the back. At the top of the slope of the overhanging second-floor roof there was an inch opening between a dormer window and the sill. Maybe that was supposed to air out the hot attic, or maybe somebody had neglected to shut it completely. Not only did it look like an easy way in for Elle, but it presented a possible shortcut to the second floor, where the master bedroom suite was almost certain to be. Best of all, the fact that it was partially open meant that there weren't contacts on the window and sill that connected to a live alarm circuit.

She wheeled the black garbage bin, which was heavier than the blue recycling one or the green one for trimmings, under the lowest edge of the awning over the patio, pulled herself onto the awning, crawled to the roof, stepped to the attic window, sliced two inches of the screen with her knife, unhooked it, and climbed inside.

The attic was dusty and hot even at dawn, and the floor consisted of two-by-fours with insulation laid between them. She tightrope-walked a two-by-four to an elaborate trapdoor with steps. She had seen these contraptions before. They included the trapdoor, the steps, and a weighted counterbalance that kept the steps from swinging down freely and hitting hard and loud, and made the steps easy to raise again. This system was a piece of good design and workmanship, so with a minimum of effort she made the steps sink quietly to the middle of the second-floor hallway and stay there while she descended.

She froze and listened for a full minute in case she had misinterpreted the signs of absence and someone was in the house. There was a difference between the sort of silence that meant a house was occupied but quiet and the sort that meant it was empty. When people were around, there were tiny hums from things that a person would turn off if he was leaving for weeks, and open interior doors expanded the space and absorbed echoes. This sounded like an empty building.

She began to look for the bedrooms. There was a length of hall behind her, another length ahead of her, and a turn to the left just off the landing of the swirling staircase from the foyer. The upstairs landing had a few white marble sculptures along the walls, but it was the paintings that distracted her.

They were eighteenth-century English portraits in the realistic grand style of Joshua Reynolds and his followers. All the subjects were male and unfamiliar to her except in type, but their painting was masterful. She didn't want to waste time on them, because she considered stealing art to be like volunteering for prison. There was no way to move fine art in the United States except famous paintings, and they were recognizable by definition.

But the paintings told her that the owner of the house had real money. Whether paintings like these had been bought or inherited didn't make much difference, but they made her eager to get past them and see what was in the master suite.

Since the master suite was sure to be the largest, and most likely to be near the rear of the house where the view would be gardens and not streets, she chose the left hallway. There was a skylight above the hallway that threw a dim, eerie light on the paintings hung along the walls. These were a departure from the ones on the landing. They were all women in French classical pastoral scenes. There were plump curly-headed blondes with blushing cheeks, small breasts, and buttocks like mares' consorting with lascivious cherubs and fauns, bathing in streams, or drying in the sun, their clothes cast aside on rocks or low limbs. Either the paintings were awful or the early morning light did not do them justice, but to Elle all that mattered was that they were expensive.

She reached the door at the end of the short hall. It was an odd door for a private residence. The door was about four feet wide and the hardware made it look like a hotel room. There was a large steel plate that was gilded to look like brass and a six-inch handle instead of a knob. She wondered if the door guarded something other than a bedroom.

She tried the handle and it moved without resistance. She pushed the door open and her muscles clenched. A woman who had not trained herself never to scream when startled might have screamed at that moment. What she saw on the California king bed in front of her was a strange tableau.

There were three people — a man and two women — all naked. They had been engaged in an act that involved the man kneeling behind one woman, who was straddling another woman lying faceup. All three had been shot in the forehead, had collapsed and died where they were, probably instantly, because otherwise they would be lying she was not sure how, but not like this. They looked as though they had all fallen at once in a pile.

At first she'd feared that they were all alive and about to shriek in horror and rage at her intrusion and maybe try to harm her. But then she'd seen that the glistening places on their bodies weren't healthy sweat; they were blood spatter and leakage.

Elle took a step backward toward the doorway behind her. She couldn't help keeping her eyes on the three people, gripped by a lingering fear that they weren't really dead and were about to leap off the bed to catch her if she looked away. But as she reached the doorway, she saw something she hadn't noticed at first. There was a camera.

It was set up on a tripod in the bedroom about ten feet from the bed, near the wall. Her eyes had not noticed it at first because it had been over there amid the background of paintings and furniture. Had these people been recording the event? And if the camera had been on during the threesome, wouldn't it still be running? She took one last step through the doorway and stopped. She was out of sight of the camera now. She had to think.

Maybe the camera hadn't even been turned on. If a camera was in plain sight, then everyone involved would have had to consent, at least tacitly, to being recorded. She stared at the three on the bed. The two women each had a big diamond ring and a plain band on the left hand. Would they have taken the chance that their husbands would see the recording? The man's left hand had no ring.

The blood had soaked into the bed from the three head wounds, and the red mist of the impacts had sprayed the three, the headboard of the bed, and the wall above it. The shooter must have come in the same way Elle had, since there was no other entrance, and fired the three shots so rapidly that the victims could not disengage. That could happen only if their terror at the first shot caused temporary paralysis in the other two who were still alive. She'd seen this happen to people in violent situations. They seemed to lose their ability to decide what their limbs should do, so their limbs did nothing.

There was a horrible smell to bloody death, a coppery smell and what seemed to be a scent of instant rotting too. It occurred to her that this might have happened a while ago. The blood on the white sheets was mostly bright red like paint, but it had gone thick and syrupy and dark where it pooled.

Elle felt shocked and horrified by this carnage. They had obviously been caught, earning somebody's rage. She supposed she would have thoughts later about the story of betrayal and selfishness that got them here, but not yet. Looking at them gave her a feeling of sadness and waste — three human beings who had been alive a while ago but weren't anymore. And they were beautiful specimens in full maturity: two females about thirty to thirty-five, and a male a bit older, forty-five at most.

The male was thin, with long sinewy arms and legs. His was the sort of body she thought of when somebody was said to look like a rock star. His hair wasn't at all like a rock star's. It was too short and expensively barbered. She had a feeling that this house was his and that he was not the man either of the women was married to.

She was aware that now was her only time to make a decision. One thing she knew was that it was terribly important not to be on whatever recording was in that camera. Whatever she was going to do had to be done now.

She still wore her latex gloves and baseball cap. She reached for the painting on the wall beside her, another fat, flushed eighteenth-century Frenchwoman at a spring. She lifted it in front of her and stepped into the room again, looking down at the floor all the way to the tripod where the camera was mounted. When she got behind the camera she set the painting down. She could see a tiny indicator light on the back that she assumed meant it was running. She unscrewed the knurled wheel at the bottom of the camera, aimed it away from her, turned the switch off, and put the camera in her fanny pack.

She picked up the painting and hung it back on the wall as she hurried to the hallway and the pull-down steps to the attic. She climbed up to the attic, tugged the steps up after her, and closed the trapdoor. She heel-and-toe-walked to the dormer, climbed out the window, stepped down the roof to its edge, lay down, and slid onto the awning. She moved to the edge, placed her feet above the lid of the black trash can, and dropped.

She remembered to wheel the trash can back to where she'd found it before she went out to the road to resume her run. Her rented Mercedes was some distance away, but her mind was fully occupied in going over everything that had happened. She felt guilty for stealing the camera. The police really should have it. She was withholding evidence that might help them solve the three murders, but she would have to think about that later.

When she reached her house in Van Nuys, she drove the rental car into the second space in her garage and closed the door so it couldn't be seen. She went inside, opened her laptop computer, and looked up the operating instructions for the camera. When she had read them and was sure she knew how to operate it and not endanger the recording, she started it.

2

Elle was not looking forward to watching whatever was on the camera's memory card. It wasn't that she was prudish or overly sensitive about what went on in bedrooms. She was between boyfriends at the moment, but she had not been completely companionless in the recent past. There had been an incident just two weeks ago.

Denny Wilkins, a gym rat she had met in a bar the previous week, had seen her leaving the same bar that night and asked if she'd like a drink.

"I just left a bar, Denny," she said. "You saw me come out. You don't know that means I've had all the drinks I want?"

"How about getting some food?" he said. "Drinking can make you hungry, and eating helps you sober up. And there are a couple of good late-night places I know."

"That's sweet, but I watch my weight, and not eating a fourth meal at night is an easy

43

way to keep weight down." What she'd said was true. Being a thief required a body that fitted in narrow places and was light enough to go over walls or climb trellises.

"Damn," he said. "What do I have to do to spend time with you tonight? Do you like movies?"

She said, "As a rule, if you want to take a woman out, you should call her a few days ahead and invite her. You're a good guy. I'd have a drink with you, or even dinner, which is a bigger commitment for both of us. Just give me a call sometime."

"I don't have your number."

"Would you like my number?"

"Sure. Yes, please."

She plucked the phone out of his pocket, maybe a bit too quickly and easily to hide the fact that she was a thief, and typed her name and number in his contact list, then put the phone back. "See? I'm not blowing you off. I'm just busy tonight."

"Doing what?"

"I've got to go pick up some stuff."

"Where?"

"At a guy's house."

"Can I come with you?"

She thought for a second. She had picked out the house a few days earlier on Google Street View. It was big and tempting. When she had cased it, she had decided the owner was away. Denny was nice. She had asked him the night when she'd met him if his blue eyes were tinted contacts, and he had replied that he'd never needed glasses. He was the perfect lookout. And he was in L.A. gym-rat shape, like all of those guys she saw running with no shirts on outside cross-training places. He could probably lift a piano.

She said, "If you want to, but it's going to be boring."

"It'll give us time to talk."

She clicked open the door to her passenger seat, he got in, and they drove off. He told her about his life before he'd come to L.A. — tales of a kind mother and catty sisters — and his life since he'd come west. That part was mostly "What is this strange place?" All of it she'd heard before from other newly arrived young men. She knew this one would do fine in time, so her sympathy wasn't strongly engaged. She listened for anything that might indicate he was interesting and actually caught several glimmers of potential. He read nonfiction books, he thought about them, and he was looking hard for an honest job. He was a bit lost and lonely for female company, but from her point of view that was not a bad thing.

She drove past the house, parked two hundred feet away, and told him to wait in the car. "If somebody comes and heads for the driveway or the door, text me."

"Okay."

"It doesn't matter who it is — male or female, alone or in a group."

"I understand."

Elle walked up the driveway and around to the back of the house, found a louvered window in the laundry room off the kitchen, bent the aluminum frame with her pocket-knife, and slid out six of the slats. She loved louvered windows.

Once she was inside, she only had to worry about stepping through an electric eye's beam on her way to the master bed-room suite. The house was one of the worst new designs. The interior of the first floor was as vast as a barn. It consisted of a marble floor that led a visitor toward the back of the house between open spaces. It reminded Elle of the giant furniture ware-houses that she'd visited, where one space would be furnished with a bar, some bar-stools, and a café table; the next with a couch, two easy chairs, and a fake television as though it were a living room; and the next with appliances and counters as though it were a kitchen, but with no walls between any of them. She hurried up the narrow stairs to the second floor.

In the master bedroom she found two big closets, but one held only things like golf clubs, tennis rackets, men's outer clothing, and shoes. There were no dressers.

In the second closet she found the main trove of male clothing. There was an island with a number of very shallow drawers. There was a lock like a desk lock on the top drawer, so she popped it open and found that the other drawers unlocked also. The top drawer held sunglasses — a selection of different brands, styles, and lens colors. The next drawer held condoms, lotions, and lubricants and a set of small vibrators. The third held seven pistols, with some ammunition and loaded magazines for them. There were three small .380s, two full-size variations on the M1911 .45 pistol, a .357 Magnum revolver, and an old-style .38 police special. Another drawer held a collection of men's watches, all very expensive. There was nothing belonging to a woman in the closet — no jewelry, clothes, or shoes.

Elle found a man's leather messenger bag hanging on a coat hook on the wall, so she filled it with watches and guns. She left the closet and prepared to explore the bedroom, but she felt her phone vibrate. She looked at the screen.

"Your friend is home."

She heard the sound of a Porsche engine gearing down and then silence. She began to run.

Over the years she had learned to retreat the way she had entered. It diminished the chance for surprises. She sprinted through the big house and found that the open-floor plan helped her increase her speed. When she reached the laundry room she stood on the dryer, gripped the frame of the louvered window, got both legs up and over, turned, and dropped to the pavement.

As soon as her feet hit, she saw the man jump from the back steps into her path. He held a pistol in his right hand and he was raising it as though to shoot her. She wondered whether she could reach into the messenger bag and pluck a gun out in time to change her fate, but her eye caught a quick movement behind the man, and there was Denny in the driveway too. Denny's left forearm hooked around under the man's chin and his right hand wrenched the pistol out of the man's grip and tossed it somewhere behind him into the shrubbery. The forearm tightened, and Denny's right hand grasped his wrist. After about ten seconds, Denny stepped backward and draped the man's limp body on the pavement.

Elle stepped close, looking down at the man. "Oh my god. Is he dead?"

"Of course not. I just choked him out. Hey, did you just come out of a window?"

"It's a long story. He's a close friend of my cousin, and I promised I'd pick up this stuff from him today at the latest, but I couldn't get here until night, and he must have gone out and then thought I was a prowler. The whole gun thing is really out of hand, don't you think? He could have killed me. I really don't want to talk to him right now. He's lucky I don't call the police on him."

She clutched Denny's arm and tugged him in the direction of the car, but it was like tugging a statue. Then he got the idea and went with her. She got in the car and started the engine. As soon as Denny's bottom touched the seat, she drove. Denny let the acceleration shut his door, found his seat belt, and buckled it.

"Are you sure he's alive?" she said.

"Yes."

"Where did you learn to do that?"

"I was on the wrestling team in college.

It's one of the things you're not allowed to do."

"I'm not surprised." She thought about what had just happened and about Denny. She said, "Where's your apartment?"

He told her, and she drove there. She hid the messenger bag in the car trunk in the wheel well, locked everything, and went inside with him and up the stairs.

Later, when she was telling her friend Sharon the story, this was where she stopped.

"What happened?" said Sharon.

"What do you think happened?" Elle said. "He knowingly faced an armed man and disabled him with his bare hands to save my life. None but the brave deserve the fair."

"You did him? Right then and there?"

"You're quarreling with the time and place?"

"No. The circumstances. I'm slut-shaming you."

"He is a clean, decent, attractive man who hit on me over a week earlier and had been bugging me to go out with him that evening. He deserved something for saving me. I knew what he wanted more than anything, so I made his wish come true, like the good fairy."

"The really good fairy," Sharon said. "So

now what?"

Elle sighed and shook her head. "When he was in the bathroom later I took my phone number off his phone."

"That's more like you. I'm surprised you slept with him, though."

"Let's just say it wasn't torture. And did I forget to tell you he saved my life? If my life weren't worth that much to me, then I wouldn't deserve to have it. Life is precious."

Elle watched the recording of the activities in the house where she had stolen the camera this morning, speeding through about twenty minutes focused on a series of paintings. There was a male voice that droned on about each one. The voice would say the name of the artist, the title of the painting, and the year and then add some anecdotal tidbit. There would be a pause for a still shot. Then the camera would be lifted on its tripod to the next painting and the process repeated.

This continued until there was a ringing sound, like a doorbell. The man appeared in the frame, lifted the camera on its tripod again, carried it with some dizzying moves to a place across the room. She could see him leaving the room, then hear his footsteps descending the stairs quickly. This was followed by a motionless shot of the empty master bedroom for about a half hour. The bed was neatly made, with hospital corners and blindingly clean white sheets and pillowcases. There was a tall wooden dresser that matched the bed and was about as wide. The paintings she had seen were all hanging on the wall on the far side of the bedroom, past the bed.

She had noticed that the paintings on the walls inside the bedroom were different from the ones in the hallway. These were mostly late nineteenth-century oils of sailboats under bright white clouds and blue skies, scudding along on the ocean off what looked like New England. They went well with the plain antique furniture in the room, particularly the unpadded straight-backed chairs along the wall below them.

Above them was a big old-fashioned Southern California window that opened on hinges and had white shutters. It looked out on a sunny garden with a stone wall covered by red, orange, and magenta bougainvillea vines. From Elle's perspective the planting was smart, because while bougainvilleas were revered for their radiant colors, burglars knew they had long, spiky thorns. Elle remembered that she'd seen an identical window on the other side of the room behind the camera and more paintings like the ones that had been recorded. Elle waited awhile, watching the unchanging recording, and then sped up the playback.

The two women entered the frame first. They were typical of the women in the richest parts of Los Angeles. They were exceptionally well cared for, with bodies that had been exercised and trained like racehorses but barely fed, faces that were born pretty and then given surgical shaping and smoothing and correction beginning in the girls' teens — noses had been straightened and narrowed, chins made tighter and more prominent, cheekbones sculptured. They were both too young for lifts and puffed lips and smoothed eyelids.

Their hair and makeup were terrific, a sign that people came to their houses every morning to do both. One woman had long dark brown hair that swung when she turned her head as though it had weight. The other had hair the color and texture of corn silk. Both wore it straight. They held themselves with their heads close, conferring as though they knew that they complemented each other — the blonde made blonder by the dark hair of her friend, and the brunette made to seem more vivid.

They stopped inside the door to glance back at the narrow hallway they'd just left, and there was a bit of giggling and whispering. "Beautiful skin," the dark one said. "But so much of it."

"She's a milkmaid," said the blonde. "All the butter must add up."

"Why would a milkmaid be naked?"

The blonde sang the line from *Lullaby of Broadway:* "The milkman's on his way."

The man arrived three steps behind. "Not a milkmaid, a shepherdess," he said. "It was a court fad, a costume for outdoor parties. The noble ladies would dress like peasant girls."

"This one isn't dressed like anyone," the brunette said. "You know, I think I saw this painting in France."

"Makes sense," said the man. "The de la Vierne family had lent it to museums for sixty or seventy years before I bought it. I overpaid because the story charmed me. The model was the wife of a prominent nobleman who neglected her while he was sending ships to French colonies to trade. The painting was shown at court briefly and improved her social life."

"Oh," said the blonde. "So at least she had a happy ending."

The man laughed. The brunette laughed

too and gave him a playful slap on the arm. "You love that, don't you?"

"I already admitted it. And collectors love a painting with a story that's a little bit naughty."

The blonde stepped ahead, trying to distract the man's attention from the other woman. "Oh, Nick," she said. "I just love these." She swept her arm across the space to indicate all the nautical paintings. She completed the circle, turning her body all the way around, completing her twirl.

Elle could see that her ploy had worked. Nick stepped close to her, took her hand, twirled her around a second time, and caught her by putting his hands on her thin waist like a ballet partner. With his height and grace he looked a bit like a dancer.

The brunette was walking along the opposite wall staring at the paintings. She stopped and said, "This isn't even American. This is a Turner. How the hell can you keep a Turner in your bedroom?"

"How can you not?"

"Don't be cute, Nick," she said. "You know what I mean. Cost. Risk. Insurance."

"There's virtually no risk," he said. "I don't invite collectors into my bedroom, so nobody knows these are here. A sane person would keep them in a vault."

"That explains why you don't," the brunette said.

"I was going to add that this house is like a vault. There's a super-elaborate alarm system that's monitored remotely. It comes with a squad of armed men, who will rush here at a moment's notice. And as I said, I don't tell people what's here."

"Very wise. But not as wise as putting the paintings in a vault."

"I swear I never bring anyone in here that I don't lust after."

The blonde sidestepped to place herself in front of Nick, smiling brightly. "Well, which one of us is it?"

"Both," he said.

"Really?" She looked skeptical.

"Well, look at you," he said. "You're like a perfect pair. You're heart-stoppingly beautiful opposites. You're best friends, close in almost every way. You could be close in every way. And of all the set we know socially, who would anyone rather fool around with than you?"

"Now that's a question," said the brunette. "But there's the little matter of husbands."

"Is that a problem to you?"

"We each have one," the blonde said.

"I sure won't tell them. And if you both want to play, neither will either of you. It'll be our secret forever."

The two women's heads moved together again and they whispered and then laughed.

Suddenly the brunette looked directly at the camera. "What's that?"

"It's a camera, sweetie," said Nick. "They're going to be part of a show at the gallery I'm planning for fall, and there's advertising, the catalog, the insurance, and so on. I was getting some shots when you arrived."

"Oh," she said, and when she turned around she saw that her friend was unbuttoning. She faced her friend and began to do the same, each of them staring into the other's eyes as though this were a contest to see who would lose her nerve first. Neither did.

What Elle saw next on the recording brought back a long-buried memory. When she was barely fourteen, she had a crush on a boy named Pete Flynn. He was in two of her classes, and he was lively and funny, with sharp dark brown eyes and black hair. In fact, he had the same body as this man Nick — long and thin, with muscles like cables instead of bumps. But he had a way of looking at a girl that not only hinted that he was thinking improper thoughts, but actually made her wonder what, specifically, they were and begin imagining possibilities. By January, when the kids all came back to school from vacation, Elle had thought about him and acquired a different attitude. She hadn't gained any sophistication, but she knew by then what she wanted. She wanted Pete Flynn all alone somewhere. It would have to be somewhere in his world, because "alone" wasn't something that existed in hers, which was crowded with aunts and cousins.

Elle was sure he would know the right place. Boys always seemed to know of places where they wouldn't be found. After another week she took up staring at him too. She thought she'd better try to get some education and learn what was going to be expected of her.

She went to her friend Becky Ransom's house. Becky was an only child, and she had a great desktop computer with a screen about twenty-five inches across and a super-high-speed Wi-Fi system to feed it. Her father worked at two jobs and saved most of the money for Becky's college fund. The computer figured into that somehow, as did Becky's mother's determination never to bother her when she might be studying or thinking.

Elle and Becky found many websites that

catered to their educational need. All they had to do was click on a box that said they were over eighteen and select from a list of titles that revealed very little to them. They spent a whole Saturday afternoon in Becky's room watching these presentations, one after another — about six hours without stopping. Since then Elle had always been convinced that the experience delayed the loss of her virginity by at least a year and a half, and when that finally happened, she was extremely wary of any move that Jimmy de Luca, her very nice boyfriend, made.

That Saturday afternoon of pornography with Becky was what this recording brought back to her. There was the same lack of real affection. They were performing. The three of them might just as well have been in an exercise class that emphasized repetitive motion. They were all adept at the parts they played, but there wasn't any joy, not even much sincere lust. The women were very conscious of how they looked, so they tended to pose. There was some female moaning, but it seemed to Elle that it was the kind a person did to tell the man it was time to bring things to a conclusion.

Nick had set himself a difficult task, and his strategy was to devote most of his attention to one woman for a few minutes and then the other, switching whenever he sensed it was time, like a person trying to start two fires and then keep them both burning. The result didn't seem to be very satisfying to the women, but she supposed he had been counting on them to keep each other from getting bored.

Things seemed to be building toward a culmination. Nick, who was paying attention to the blonde at the moment while she straddled the brunette, suddenly looked up. All he said was "Uh!" He seemed to see the gun and his expression changed to fear.

The man remained in the doorway instead of stepping forward into the room, but the women looked in that direction and saw him too. The brunette arched her neck and must have been seeing him upside down.

The blonde said, "How did you even know we were here?"

The brunette covered her eyes and pleaded, "Don't."

As the intruder's arm rose, Elle noted that he was wearing black. Was that a black leather jacket? His silencer was about eight inches long, and it wasn't homemade. The shots came quickly — one-two-three — and as the bullets hit first the man and then the blonde, they collapsed forward, pinning the brunette. The man shot her last, but the whole business took less than three seconds, and it didn't seem to be in order of preference. To Elle it seemed a matter of efficiency, aiming high, then lowering the aim to the middle and then the bottom.

He turned away from the bed without checking to be sure they were all dead. She saw a bit of black shoulder and nothing more. It was odd to Elle that he didn't seem to have noticed the camera on its tripod. He never really came into the room, so maybe he hadn't seen it. Or maybe he did not fear a recording, but Elle couldn't think of a reason he wouldn't.

The next phase of the recording involved a lot of time. Elle watched for a while to see if the man would come back, but he didn't. She sped up the playback. In quickened time, the unmoving tableau was shown in waning light and then darkness. There was a fixture in the garden that was on a light-sensitive switch, so at nightfall it turned on, and the unmoving figures were visible in the light coming in through the open window, their permanent stillness silhouetted on the bed. Dawn came again and the artificial light went out.

Elle stopped the playback and sent it forward at standard speed, then cautiously sped it up again. When she caught a glimpse of her own foot stepping into the doorway, she slowed to normal speed again.

So far, only the toes of her running shoes were visible in the doorway in profile. It crossed her mind that a diligent cop could identify the brand and ask the manufacturer for the names of places where those shoes were sold. But Elle had been working, and therefore everything on her was a costume. The shoes were high quality and expensive, but thousands of spoiled young women in Los Angeles had a pair like them, and she'd had hers for a year.

She caught an instant in which the bill of her baseball cap showed in the doorway, but not her face, and then nothing more for a while. And then a bizarre figure entered the room, a small human being who was carrying a painting over his or her head like a shield. The camera couldn't catch a face. The person moved close and the camera caught a hand reaching toward it. The image swept to the side and focused on a wall with other ship paintings on it. Then the screen went black.

3

She set the camera aside and read more about it on the website. The Sony Handycam AX33 4K flash memory camcorder was a nice piece of equipment for $800. It had a 128-gigabyte memory card, 18.9 megapixels "for gripping detail." It far exceeded HD resolution. She could attest to that. It had image stabilization. She could attest to that too. She was sure she had missed absolutely no gripping detail of the recording and that she could have identified any of the bodies from a randomly selected square inch of skin. She stared at the page for a long time, but she wasn't really thinking about the camera. She was thinking about what to do next.

If she was a good person she would take the camera to the police. If she was a bad person she would take the 128-gigabyte memory card out, destroy it, and sell the camera in another city with all of her other stolen goods. Elle was both good in intention and bad at carrying out good intentions, so she had to do some thinking.

She felt a sincere sympathy for the people who had been murdered. Nick was a self-serving, smug, predatory manipulator who had induced two women to do things he knew they would regret and probably would have regretted by the end of the day. But he was certainly better than the man who had stepped into his house and shot him in the face. And even though the two women had come to the house in the middle of the previous afternoon very much ready to betray their husbands — the very fancy and uncomfortable underthings they were both wearing when they'd arrived proved it — they seemed to have no intention of doing anyone any serious harm and probably had nothing to gain from it. They were obviously both rich already. The Prada Saffiano Cuir purse the blonde had carried was worth about $2,500, and her friend's Fendi Kan shoulder bag was around $3,500. The Omega Seamaster Aqua the blonde had on her wrist was around $12,000, and the Jaeger-LeCoultre Reverso Ultra Thin strapped to the brunette could be anywhere from $13,000 to $45,000 depending on extras.

64

Elle had studied the women's faces as they looked up and were shot. Neither of them had shown or said anything to prove to Elle that the shooter was either one's husband. The blonde had asked how he'd known they were here, which seemed to indicate that he was looking for both of them, not one. Elle had to apply the same test to the women as to the man. Were they worse than the man who had dropped by to shoot them in the face?

Elle decided that the police must receive the camera containing a recording of the murder. The recording would not include the footage of Elle Stowell showing up to burglarize the house. Since she was the last sight to appear on the memory card, all she had to do was erase herself.

She copied the recording from the memory card on to her laptop computer. Of course the computer wasn't hers in the legal sense, but she had it in her possession and used it frequently. She checked the copy for accuracy, visual clarity, and completeness. Then she transferred three copies to thumb drives. She hid one drive in a spot she considered safest — taped inside the hollow pole holding the set of heavy curtains in the living room. The others she put inside a jar of turmeric and returned the jar to the spice rack that slid like a drawer into the space beside the cupboard over the stove. She was a professional at finding valuables hidden in houses, so she was good at hiding them too. She needed to retain copies of the full version in case she was arrested and charged, to prove that she had arrived in the bedroom of the house many hours after the murders.

Next she returned her attention to the camera. She ran the recording back to the point where she'd arrived and erased everything after that. Now the tape looked to her as though it went along with all the fooling around from start to finish, a night of rigor mortis, and then a blank nothing. This was something she could feel comfortable placing in the hands of the police.

She looked at her watch, wiped the camera thoroughly, and put it into her fanny pack. This was a triple murder. The police might not find her DNA in the house, because she had worn latex gloves and hadn't hung around long after she'd arrived. She felt no guilt about removing the camera from its tripod, taking it home, and manipulating the recording, because she knew from the recording that the killer had never touched the camera. No evidence was lost.

Elle drove back to Beverly Hills. She had spent hours learning about the camera, playing the recording back, and editing. It was nearly nine A.M. already. But she had hope that the bodies had not yet been found, because there were still no police cars parked at the house. Nick didn't strike her as a person who punched a time clock. He had mentioned a show "in the gallery," and that business didn't usually take place early in the morning. If he wasn't at work by nine, people probably wouldn't get worried right away and investigate. The blond woman hadn't thought anybody had known where she and her friend were, so people probably wouldn't be looking for them at Nick's house.

She drove past the house and didn't see any cars in the driveway or the cobblestone turnaround beyond the hedges. She left her car up the road and around the bend, then approached the house as a jogger again.

She had come to suspect that on her earlier visit she had skillfully avoided setting off an alarm system that wasn't even engaged. Most people didn't turn their alarm systems on while they were awake at home, and she sensed that Nick was one of them. On the tape, he had run downstairs to let the two women in, but she hadn't heard any beeps from a control pad. And later the killer had apparently come in the door without setting anything off, even though Nick had claimed to have a sophisticated alarm system. And since then there had been nobody alive to turn the system on again. She would have seen or heard any such person on the recording.

As she ran toward the house she hoped that if any neighbors had been up and seen her run before, they would have gone out by now. This was a neighborhood where "out" would probably mean riding horses or playing golf or driving up or down the coast to do something social. If people saw her now, they wouldn't be able to add much information except to contradict the other reports of when the mystery girl liked to run.

She went to the back, climbed up on the roof, crawled into the attic as before, tiptoed to the trapdoor, opened it, and listened. When she'd done this before she'd thought of the silence as absence, emptiness. Now it was dead silence. She lowered the steps and climbed down. Then she walked to the bedroom. The bodies were still there, unmoved. She fitted the camera to the tripod and looked through the viewfinder to aim the camera at the bed. She adjusted the aim slightly upward so she could crawl back to the doorway without being filmed, tightened it there, and turned the camera on.

In spite of her recently acquired rationality, Elle was tempted to stop and look around. She knew that the women's bodies wore some very expensive jewelry, but the idea of taking it was disgusting to her. It was also a good way to get caught. She was far too intelligent to take any art, but she would at least like to see the rest of the swag that she was too smart to take. The dealer's markup on one of those paintings would translate into a lot of simple, unpretentious money. But she reminded herself that this was the scene of a triple murder. It involved rich and beautiful people having scandalous sex. And now, thanks to Elle, it once again featured a recording. The police would be all over this place, so the best thing to do was go without touching anything else.

She crawled out into the hallway, scampered up the steps, and pulled the steps up after her. The mechanism's counterweight made the steel arms fold as the steps settled back into their spot. As she reached for the ring to pull the trapdoor shut, she heard the front door open.

"Mr. Kavanagh?" So his last name was Kavanagh. "Mr. Kavanagh? Police officers." There was a pause while they listened for a response.

Elle waited until the cop shouted again before she closed the trapdoor so the cop's own voice would mask the sound. She remained still and listened. The cops walked around downstairs calling for a minute or two and then clomped upstairs.

They seemed to be making as much noise as they could, probably so the homeowner wouldn't mistake them for intruders. They sounded like five men instead of two. During their ascent she retreated to the open window where she had entered. If they got interested in the trapdoor above the hallway, all she could do was slip out again and run. She listened, poised.

The steps that led up to the attic were not far from the master bedroom, but if the cops were conferring down there, she wasn't able to hear them. This was a tricky moment. It would be dangerous to be here once cops discovered the bodies and called in to their station. Cops were like ants. They never went away after they'd found something, and this place was going to be infested with them for days. She heard their feet arrive on the second-floor landing. She had to move now. She slithered out the window and looked around her, but her view was blocked by the tall trees. She crawled to the peak of the roof and stared at the neighborhood.

She could see police vehicles racing toward the house from three directions. She had been here for seven minutes, but she had stayed too long.

She slid on her bottom along the shingles to the next lower level of the roof. Then she crawled to the edge, clutched the gutter with her fingers, swung her body off the roof, hung at arm's length, and dropped. She landed on the patio hard, but recovered quickly and walked to the back wall of the yard, hoisted herself up, and rolled over to the next yard.

Elle decided that jogging around the block to her car would look too much like running away, so she bent low and sneaked along the side of the house behind Kavanagh's and out along the hedge to the next street, then walked to her car, got in, and drove. She was out the other end of the block and up to Sunset before she saw any more police cars. They entered her intersection from the west just after she turned right to the east. She was hoping she had left in time to keep the police cars' automatic license plate readers from seeing hers and recording it.

It felt like only a couple of minutes before she was back at the car rental on Hollywood Way in Burbank turning in the little white

Mercedes. She walked a half mile and then called for a Lyft to take her to Van Nuys near her home. Her house was a simple white one-story ranch-style bungalow. What she loved most about it were the California oaks that shaded it and partially veiled it from view. She unlocked her front door, went inside, and pulled the shades. She had become increasingly wary about being seen or recorded from a distance. There were so many ways for the police to find a person. The Beverly Hills police were not much of a threat in the short term. There were only 250 of them — about the size of some family reunions. But the LAPD was like their big brother — ten thousand cops who always came when the Beverly Hills police called.

The LAPD had every kind of toy: armored vehicles, choppers with night vision and infrared scopes. They were also testing drones, and what could the test be but using them to catch people like her? They could access surveillance cameras on the freeways, or go full southern sheriff and send dogs to sniff for burglars on foot. Sometimes it seemed as though it were all aimed at her.

Elle took a long, hot shower. She wasn't exactly a competitive runner, but she had impersonated one for about three hours today. She could feel the strain, which she had compounded by climbing around, jumping from roofs, and crouching in an attic.

She dressed and turned on the television, which was a good model but only about three feet wide, because when she had been shopping in someone's bedroom for one she had not wanted anything big.

The local newspeople had picked up the story already, but none of them seemed to have learned any details. The police spokespeople weren't on camera answering any questions, so she kept the television on and glanced at it occasionally while she made plans for the evening. She was feeling frustrated. She had just expended a great deal of energy and taken considerable risks to steal from what turned out to be the home of Nick Kavanagh, but she had ended up not stealing anything except her own image on the memory card of a camera, which was not actually stealing. It was some other crime that was much worse.

Her recent efforts left her with the same dwindling money supply as before. She tried to operate most of the time on the cash she stole. This time she might have done pretty well. There had been the purses of two spoiled Beverly Hills wives and the cash stash of a man who apparently owned a serious gallery. Of course, she couldn't assume anything. Over the past couple of years she had noticed that fewer people carried much cash. People like those two women walked around with credit cards that would cover the cost of the average house, but only a hundred or two in cash. And lately the few big cash collections she'd seen in houses seemed to be there only temporarily, waiting to be smuggled offshore to further tax evasion schemes. She had no idea if Kavanagh had any cash, and because of the killings, she would probably never know.

Understanding her loss didn't rectify it. Tonight she felt like going to see some friends who spent time in a quiet bar in the northern end of Hollywood. Its name was Serendipity, but all the neon except the last four letters had burned out and never been replaced, so everyone called it the Pity. The name the bar had chosen for itself fitted the mood inside better anyway. She knew she should be working, but she felt like talking to someone.

She kept checking the television set, which was now showing endless, dizzying footage of the Kavanagh house from a circling news helicopter. There were about ten police cars, a few crime scene trucks, and a couple of coroner's vans. The newswoman kept saying that she didn't want to draw any conclusions, but the presence of coroner's vans and no ambulances did seem to be a bad sign. "No shit," Elle muttered.

She tried to get herself to think about practical matters. She had used up the part of the day when she preferred to work. Breaking into houses after dark was a good way to get shot, but she still needed money. She had stolen some valuable items but hadn't had time for a trip out of town to sell them. But a day ago she had spotted a couple of houses in Trousdale Estates that had multiple newspapers turning yellow in their driveways, and both had porch lights turned on during the daytime.

Elle didn't like selecting houses just because the owners were careless, but she also didn't like watching her supply of cash dwindle. She chose one of the two on an impulse without going back to look at them again. Driving past the same house twice was as suspicious as most things a burglar could do.

She took a nap that lasted for seven hours, woke up feeling stronger, and turned on the television again. In those seven hours someone had leaked the nature of the crime scene. The local news stations were all airing minute-by-minute updates, which teased salacious information, went to commercials, and came back to restate the lead-ins again without paying off on the sex. She could glean that the reporters knew that the three victims were found naked but weren't saying it yet, but they did say they were all shot in the master bedroom and that the women were both married.

When the local news shows were all over, Elle dressed for night work — a pair of black jeans, black leather running shoes, a black pullover, and an oversize denim jacket. She tucked her hair under a baseball cap. She put altered plates on her car before she opened the garage door to back out.

The drive took her south, away from her part of the San Fernando Valley toward Beverly Hills. As she drove, it occurred to her that since the local news reports were over, the news vans and the lights and cameras would already be gone from the Kavanagh house. She felt a strong curiosity about what would be going on there now. Would there still be a hundred cops walking around in white coveralls and masks, dissecting the place to its atoms? Did they guard places like that at night or just put tape across the doors? The cops had been in possession of this one for eight or ten hours by now.

As she drove south of Sunset she felt drawn to the Kavanagh house. As her car moved along the same roads she had traveled this morning, she kept reminding herself that going there tonight would be foolish. On the other side of the argument, she was driving her own gray Volvo now, not the rented white Mercedes she'd used in the morning.

In another couple of minutes she was approaching the house. There was no longer a huge crew of forensic people, there were no news vans parked on the road and no detectives in suits. There was a single black-and-white parked in the driveway, but there didn't seem to be anyone sitting in it. There was yellow tape strung along the edge of the property, and there seemed to be some kind of notice posted on the front door.

She moved past, diminishing her speed to study the place. She kept going until she was out of sight of the house, then turned around and headed for Trousdale Estates. As she drove toward the house she had picked out to rob, she made a series of resolutions. One was that, unless something unprecedented jumped into her hand, she wasn't interested in searching for anything but cash. There was such a thing as being too greedy and too impatient. She was not going to even enter the house unless she was sure it was safe.

She went along a winding road leading upward until she saw the chosen house. She went past, stopped, turned in the downhill direction to park, and then walked from there. The houses were all built on level spaces carved into the sides of high hills. Beyond some of them she could see reflections of the sky that had to be infinity pools.

When she reached the right house, she moved close enough to slip into its shadow and then waited, watched, and listened. The newspapers were still in the driveway. She moved to the garage door. There was an SUV in one of the two spaces, but the other space was empty. If they'd had only one car, some of the stuff the occupants had piled neatly along the walls would have begun to drift into the empty space — cardboard boxes, bikes, pool toys, or cases that probably held soft drinks would have taken it over. It was a scientific law of garages. There was another car, and the occupants had gone somewhere in it.

As she moved from there around the house, she verified that the place still looked as empty as it had a couple of days ago. She found a window that allowed her to check the control panel of the alarm system by the front door and verify that the alarm was turned on.

All good alarm systems worked by wiring the door and window frames to the floors or walls of the house. If the door or window moved, a magnetic connection broke and the alarm sounded. She decided the safest way in was the sliding glass door overlooking the pool. She opened her lock-blade knife to scrape the dried putty along the edge of the glass. Then she used the tip to pry the glass free of the frame. She let the glass lean outward to rest against a lawn chair, then stepped over the unmoved metal frame into the house.

Once she was in, she found that the electrical outlets all over the house had plug-in timers, which bolstered her confidence that the family was away.

Elle took her time searching the place, but she knew exactly what she was after, so the process was simpler than usual. Money was compact and foldable, so it could be hidden anywhere in a house, but it usually wasn't. Things that were valuable like money tended to be hidden in the bedroom. The money this time was in one of the purses hanging on a hook in the closet. It caught her eye because all the other purses with it were expensive brands and very pretty. This one was cheap and out of style. She realized that the woman had been afraid a burglar might steal one of the others for its intrinsic value, but this one was safe.

Elle was not looking for jewelry but found some. The jewelry was in a flat plastic box in a cabinet under the bathroom counter. There was an antique diamond ring, a ring with what seemed to be a real emerald, a diamond tennis bracelet, and a few pins of uncertain value. Tile cleaners and drain openers were sitting on top of the box, so it drew her eye. Since she hadn't used up much time yet, she also took off the lid of the toilet tank and found an extra envelope of hundred-dollar bills taped there. Encouraged, she went back to the closet to check the backs of drawers to look for more envelopes. She was forming a theory that the wife had gotten into the habit of raking off small sums from the household money in cash and hiding it. The other popular spaces Elle checked were clear.

She found no high-end equipment. The only gun she found was a Smith & Wesson K-frame .357 Magnum revolver like the ones that were popular around the 1960s. She didn't think the resale value would be great, but taking things she could sell made sense and leaving them made none. She swung out the cylinder and saw that the pistol was loaded, looked in the nightstand for the box of ammo and found it, then unloaded the weapon and saw that the box was now full. The pistol probably had never been fired.

The rest of the house yielded only some petty cash in a pot in the kitchen. The house was tasteful and expensively furnished, but Elle wasn't in the business of selling used Italian leather luggage, crystal vases, or grand pianos. She had come only for cash.

When she stepped out through the sliding door onto the covered patio where she had entered, she took the time to lift the glass back into the doorframe, lean the chair against it, and then run a couple of strips of duct tape over it to hold it in place. There was no reason to leave the house open and vulnerable to bugs and rodents.

She slowly drifted along the wall of the house and stopped amid a row of shrubs to watch and listen. She had not heard or seen anything, just felt a few hairs on the back of her neck stand up. Maybe it was a chill, just a slight swirl in the air currents, but maybe it was something else. The body was always sensing things, sending tiny alerts to the brain. She waited to see what had changed.

She waited a full minute before she heard the feet. At first she wasn't even sure that was what was making the soft crunching sounds. They were slow and seemed to come from somewhere near the back wall of the yard, but she didn't see anyone in that darker zone. She reached into her right jacket pocket, felt the revolver, and reached into the left and found the box of bullets. Maybe it had been a mistake to separate them. The footsteps sped up and then seemed to be coming from the road. Her ears lost the sound, but then a car started. She heard it move off slowly but could not see either the car or its lights.

Elle decided to stay away from the street. There were houses on both sides of the street, and the one she had robbed was on the side closest to the downslope. The backyard of each house occupied the outer edge — pools, tennis courts, and gardens that were built to end before steep precipices. She found a house three lots away where she could lower herself below the level of the house and walk through the brush of the hillside. Her car was parked a distance away, and she had to estimate how far she had come. When she was fairly sure she had traveled as far along the hillside below the road as she had to go, she began to look for a way back up.

Two houses later she nearly tripped over a plastic pipe and knelt to examine it. The pipe was an inch in diameter, like the polyvinyl chloride pipe for sprinkler systems, but this one was black and it was above-ground rather than buried. She looked up the steep incline toward the back of the house above and assumed it must come from there. She followed the pipe for a few feet and came to a sprinkler head, so this must be a sprinkler system. She kept going, finding a sprinkler head every few feet. There were a few places where someone had installed pipes that were horizontal to the main pipe, and those had sprinklers too.

As she studied the pipes she understood. This place was a natural spot for a brush fire. This part of town had been the estate of the oil-owning Doheny family a hundred years ago, so it had been here long enough to build up plenty of kindling. This home-owner had installed a sprinkler system, not to water the brush, but to save the hillside in an emergency. When she climbed the final steep section, she clutched the pipe and used it to haul herself up the slope to the level of the lawn above.

When she raised her head above the level

of the lawn she looked hard at the house, the shrubs, the fences. The owners were gone or asleep, but there were two fixtures on the sides of the house that she recognized as motion-sensor lights. If she got up and walked toward the street, she would set one or the other off and be in a spotlight.

She felt like cursing, but cursing was not silent. She had no real evidence that what she had heard at the first house had been people trying to surround and corner her. It could have been a couple walking their dog or wheeling a baby around to put it to sleep. And all her clever evasion had only brought her here, to a worse, more precarious spot.

Elle knew ways a person could turn off a motion sensor, but she didn't see any circuit breaker boxes and suspected the one she needed might be on the side of the house beneath a motion-sensor light. She decided the best way past the sensors was the crudest. She would try to pass far enough away from them, but if she failed, she would stay low and run. People in the hills would be used to coyotes, raccoons, skunks, and opossums walking by at night. If she set off a light the neighbors would probably take her for a passing animal. She just hoped the people in the car she'd heard earlier wouldn't be waiting somewhere nearby and see the light.

She moved along the right side of the house slowly, keeping her silhouette small. She studied the path ahead of her to choose her way off the lot. When she began to get close to the house she climbed the brick wall between it and the next house. She rolled over to drop onto the next lawn and found herself bathed in light.

She had triggered a motion sensor mounted on the next house. She ran for the street. A quick sprint took her to the front gate, and she jumped halfway up and scrambled over it. While she was climbing, she was far enough away so that the motion-triggered light went dark again. She dropped to the driveway and realized that she had misjudged her distance. She had gone far past the place where she had left her car. She ran along the descending road past about six big yards. She reached her car, got in, and started it. She left her headlights off in case somebody was looking out a window to see what had set off the light. As she came around the first curve, she met a black SUV parked on the other side of the street, facing her.

She switched on her lights and saw that there were people in the driver's seat and the passenger seat. She flashed past them without slowing. The roads were winding, so she was out of their sight in a second. But when she reached the next straight section, she looked in her mirror and saw the SUV coming down after her.

The only strategy that occurred to Elle was to speed up. She was a good driver, but at high speeds this area offered only sharp, unexpected turns and narrow shoulders that could serve as runways into empty air if she made an error. She tried to remember the exact features of the road ahead but couldn't form a picture that was complete enough to be useful. The night was dark and the roads were not well traveled late at night, so she was very aware of the headlights trailing her. Were the people in the SUV cops?

If it was a police car chasing her, then any second the lights and siren would come on, and since she wasn't going to pull over, a helicopter would arrive above her head shortly after that. She should never have driven past the Kavanagh house. They must have noticed a small woman driving by too slowly and followed her car to Trousdale Estates. While she had been taking her time looking for envelopes full of money in the house, they had been driving around until they spotted her parked car. All they had to do was wait until she emerged again. As she drove she reached into her fanny pack and took out the revolver. At some point they were going to catch her, and when they did, this thing would get her a very long prison sentence.

She pushed the button to open her window and felt the hot wind flapping her hair and slapping her face. She waited until she was on one of the worst curves, where there were no houses because the hillside fell away for what looked like a thousand feet, and then hurled the gun out the window. She followed it with the box of ammunition and closed the window.

She made it out to Beverly Glen, still driving as fast as she dared. She knew she was doing something that the cops expected suspects to do: drive toward the area where they lived. That was stupid, and the least she could expect of herself was to avoid being stupid. When the descending roads out of the hills landed her in Sherman Oaks, she didn't slow down. She flashed through the red light at the Casa de Cadillac showroom on Ventura Boulevard and onto the fork to Moorpark Street, heading east away from her house. She considered pulling into the parking lot at the Sherman Oaks library and hiding back there, but decided against it. If she was going to risk everything on one strategy, it wasn't going to be waiting to get caught.

Moorpark was long and straight from here, and she could nudge her car up to eighty, blowing past traffic signals until she came to the one at Coldwater Canyon Avenue, which was too big to ever be empty. She stopped there and waited for an opening, then kept going to the alley just before the corner of Moorpark and Laurel Canyon Boulevard. She turned right between the gas station and the big apartment building, passing fast beneath the balconies overlooking the alley. She made it to the end and turned right again, this time backtracking to Whitsett Avenue, where she turned left and sped up to the light at Ventura Boulevard. She went through it on green and drove fast up the next alley that ran behind the businesses on Ventura. The alley ended at Vantage Avenue, and she turned right, then left at Maxwellton Road. Just before she reached Laurel Canyon Boulevard she turned onto the last alley. This one ran between the houses on Laurel Canyon and the ones on Mound View Avenue. On both sides it was lined with high walls interrupted only by the closed doors of garages. She turned off her lights and drove.

About two blocks up the three-block alley

she reached the back edge of a construction site where a house was being built on Mound View Avenue. There was a chain-link fence in three sections, all chained together with green fabric over them. She stopped and ran from her car to the fence. When she got there, she found that the sections could be moved, and her lungs seemed to fill with air for the first time since the burglary. She half lifted the right-hand section of the fence. She walked the section out of her way, drove her car onto the site, and walked the section of fence across the opening again.

She backed her car behind a twenty-foot cinder block wall that had been left intact during construction and waited with her window rolled down so she could hear. It occurred to her that this was one of those times when if she'd had a gun she would have been in danger of using it. Throwing away the one she had stolen had taken away that decision, but now she wondered if she had made a mistake.

Elle had no plan, so she started to work on one. If the black SUV came all the way up this alley, she would leave her car where it was and run. Maybe she could find a route up over the hills that she could follow on foot. Her car was registered in a false name, and right now it had plates that she had stolen and altered with black electrical tape. She had wiped it down before driving it, as usual, and she was still wearing her surgical gloves. She heard cars rushing along on the other side of the houses on Laurel Canyon, but Mound View remained silent.

After about fifteen minutes, Elle stepped to the front of the construction site and looked up and down the street. It was empty. She returned to the temporary fence at the back of the lot, looked up and down the alley, and then walked the section of fence outward to create a passage so she could drive her car off the lot into the alley.

She got into her car and backed it up almost to the place where the new swimming pool was going to be, then pulled forward and into the alley. She kept her lights off and made a sharp turn to head for the end of the alley. She pulled to a stop after about twenty-five feet and then prepared to get out and move the section of fence back into place.

Her rearview mirror caught the black shape of a moving vehicle. It seemed to materialize behind her, its headlights off and coming fast. Elle stomped on her gas pedal, felt the tires spinning crazily and making her car fishtail on loose gravel, but then felt them dig in at a place where the pavement was bare and catapult the car forward.

The driver of the SUV must not have seen the green-veiled section of fence without his headlights, or not have read the sight correctly because he could see objects through the green fabric stretched over chain-link, but somehow the frame of steel pipe didn't seem to enter his consciousness. He hurtled into the fence section, the chain-link wrapping itself around the front of the SUV and the steel upper frame hitting his windshield.

As this happened Elle accelerated, trying to stay ahead of the encumbered vehicle that was coming up on her.

Since the three sections of fence were held together by padlocked chains, the SUV dragged the second and third sections out into the alley after it at high speed. The additional resistance increased the pressure of the first fence section against the windshield, and the frame popped the glass and pushed it inward into the front seat. One of the fence sections caught on the corner of a garage and held, and the SUV swerved into a cinder block wall and stopped.

Elle turned right at the end of the alley onto Laurel Terrace, a road that hooked along the foot of a steep hillside through the neighborhood and back across Ventura Boulevard. She kept going onto Whitsett again and sped north toward Van Nuys. She never stopped until she had driven her car into its garage at home. Then she closed the garage door and turned off the engine. She rested her forehead against her steering wheel and sat for a few seconds in the dark, feeling the sweat that had accumulated on her body.

She got out, walked across the few feet to her side door, and went inside. She took a bath and thought about what had nearly killed her tonight. She had given in to her curiosity and gone to look at Nick Kavanagh's house, the scene of the murders. Amateurs were curious. Pros were not.

4

When Elle awoke at midday she spent time at home cleaning, doing laundry, paying bills, washing her hair, repairing her nails, and counting the money she had stolen last night. The total was under a thousand dollars, which was not enough to have risked her life for but was enough to meet her needs for now. She removed the false license plates from her car and bought groceries. When she had put the supplies away she allowed herself time to sit at her laptop and look at the reports of the crime at the Kavanagh house.

The police still weren't releasing the names of the women but had not been able to hide the name of the man who owned the house, since house ownership was public information. As night approached, the anxiety she had been feeling changed to physical restlessness, so she decided to go out. She felt more comfortable going out early instead of following her custom of waiting until late in the evening. The later it was, the higher the ratio of cops to bar patrons, and right now police scared her more than anything else.

There were a few customers in the Pity when Elle arrived. The interior of the bar was a collection of remnants from its many dismal lives, all of which had ended in bankruptcy. There was a jukebox that had been made in the 1950s and was full of B sides of hits from the early 1960s. In the left corner high above the bar there were artifacts of a tiki-island motif, including a ukulele, a set of crossed torches, and a canoe paddle. There was a stuffed lake trout transported from some distant place, probably the Midwest, and time. The rest of the walls were dominated by small neon signs advertising obscure regional brands of beer, all of them extinct. Crossing the floor beneath the display, she spotted her friend Sharon, who locked eyes with her, gave a little wave, and then sat at a table. Already at the table were Ricki and Sal, women with names that sounded male but weren't. Elle was relieved to see them, because these three women were among the few people in the city who knew how she made a living, and she didn't feel like censoring everything she said tonight.

Elle wove through the people crowded around the bar to get to them. Her progress looked at times like some martial art that involved getting oneself out of the way of the random movements of large people — sharp, high elbows; big feet; full drinks clutched in thick, clumsy hands. She emerged at the end and slid herself onto the open seat. A good burglar was not only fast but also limber.

"Hey, L," said Ricki. "Where have you been? Did you leave town?"

"The opposite. I've been working."

Ricki nodded in sympathy. "Are you doing okay?"

Elle shrugged. "My guidance counselor was right. I should have been a princess, but I'm fine."

Ricki said, "You know, I've seen a couple of places this week that might interest you."

"Oh?"

"Yeah," Ricki said. "I've been to a couple of parties in giant top-floor apartments in big old buildings. You walk in without passing a guard and take any elevator to any floor. No vicious dogs, no crawling in ventilator shafts. Sound good?"

Elle shrugged. "Those lofts downtown are renovated for hipsters. They get to walk in

95

and out through a lobby that used to be a bank, but they don't have much to steal."

"The ones I mean are in those buildings along Wilshire in West L.A. The buildings are all white and old-fashioned. The apartments are big, and inside they look like somebody's grandma's house. I was at these two parties in places that take up the top floor or two of a whole building. You'd think you were in some sprawling old house, except that just when you forget you're not, you glance at one of these big windows that look out over the city and remember you're up in the air. They both had outdoor patios too."

"Sounds nice. Maybe I'll work harder and buy one."

Ricki said in a quiet voice, "Maybe you should just make a visit. The one I was in last night has an indoor pool."

"Pools are hard to steal. You have to sneak it out a glass at a time."

"I was talking about money. This guy has collections — a lot of glass cases with old things in them — jewels, silver stuff from some king's table, old pistols, and gold coins."

Sal said, "Does he have a patch over one eye and a parrot on his shoulder?"

"No. He's in financial services."

Elle said, "Did you by any chance get a look at the man's bedroom?"

"Of course," said Ricki. "I was going to tell you. The room is beautiful, although the decorations are a little obvious. He's one of those guys who have kind of a naughty side."

Sal said, "They all have kind of a naughty side."

"I mean artistically. In his suite he's got a whole collection of Japanese netsuke with nothing but couples carved in ivory doing just about anything you can think of. Some of them are eight hundred years old. That's what he said, anyway."

"That is a little obvious," said Elle.

"You want the address?"

"No thanks."

"Why not?"

"For one thing, if he had you in his bedroom, he's going to remember you. And he'll make the connections between you and his stuff, one of which is that you're both gone."

"Really?"

"Really. You're pretty memorable. And anyway, I'd get caught trying to sell things like that. Or whoever I sold it to would, and they'd trade me for a reduced charge. Serious artifacts are either worth millions or too risky to sell, depending on who you are.

I'm nobody."

Sal tapped Ricki's arm. Sal, who covered most of her expenses by going from party to party, had spotted a couple of men who looked promising, at least for buying them a nice dinner. Since Ricki was modeling, she never ate, but she still drank, so they excused themselves and got up to make the capture. Desiree the barmaid used the opportunity to swoop in to take Elle's order.

"A double single-malt Scotch with one ice cube," Elle said. "Thanks, Desiree."

As Desiree left, Sharon leaned closer and said quietly, "What's bothering you, L?"

She shrugged and looked around the room, scanning the crowd. "I had a kind of weird experience yesterday."

"Did you steal something that had a curse on it?"

"A curse is being a person who believes in curses."

"Do you believe in bad luck?"

"Only in the wrong-place-wrong-time sort of way."

"Did you have one of those?"

"I guess so," said Elle. "I was running low on money, so I picked out a house in Beverly Hills that had a lot of signs that nobody was home at the moment. I got in through an attic window and went straight to the master bedroom suite. The door was closed but not locked, just as you might expect when nobody's home. But when I opened it I saw this big California king bed. On it were three dead people, all naked, and all shot once in the forehead."

"Oh my god."

"I backed out, still staring in at them. They were in a pile, sort of, like they were doing it at the moment they got shot. That freaked me out, of course. And then I noticed that on one side of the room there was a camera on a tripod. In one second it occurred to me that this threesome was taped."

"That's the only reason I can think of to have a camera aimed at a bed."

"These people were dead. If they were being taped, they had not said, 'Cut,' and turned the camera off. It was probably still running, and if so, I was probably on it."

"Jesus. What did you do?"

"I took the camera."

"Very good," said Sharon. "So you're home free. You destroyed the tape."

"Not a tape. A memory card."

"Who cares? You destroyed it."

"Well, no."

"Why not?"

"I went home and watched the recording.

The camera had been running for at least twelve hours, maybe longer. It had been running since midafternoon or so the day before."

"On battery power?"

"No, it was plugged in. But when I read about the camera I realized it probably would have run that long on batteries anyway. It was running when the people came into the room. The man had been taking pictures of some paintings and doing commentary, and just moved the camera when the others arrived but didn't turn it off. It caught them talking and then flirting, and the sex, and the murder. A man walked in, shot all three in their foreheads, and left them where they were for the late afternoon, evening, and night."

"Just like that?"

"The guy didn't even cover them or move them, just turned and left. Then, many hours later, I came in and found them. When I came back in and turned off the camera and took it, the camera was recording me."

"So then you erased it."

"I made three copies of the recording and then erased the last part of the original. The part with me in it."

"Why keep copies? They prove you were there."

"Because they prove I was there twelve hours or so after the murder. It proves I didn't arrive when it was still possible to kill anybody. And how could I destroy the record of who had actually killed them? That was on the same recording. The police need it. So I returned, put the camera back on the tripod, and left."

"I still say why, why, why?" Sharon said. "You were there and got away."

"Because no matter what, this was a triple murder. The police probably spent all of yesterday taking fingerprints, DNA samples, hairs, and fibers from every square inch of this seven- or eight-thousand-square-foot Beverly Hills home. Last night I drove by the house to see if I could tell what they were doing, and a plain black SUV followed me from there. After I made a stop in Trousdale Estates, they chased me all the way to Studio City."

"How did you get away?"

"It's a long story, and it adds up to me not knowing exactly. They just kept their lights off and crashed in an alley. The point is that they must think I know more than I do."

"What else do you know?"

"Nothing! I know small details that the police know by now too. I know that the two women wore wedding rings, but neither was married to this guy. I know the killer walked to the doorway. He saw this orgy going on, raised a gun with a silencer attached, and shot the man first and then the two women without pausing. *Pop-pop-pop,* just like that. It was over in a couple of seconds. I don't know if the shooter was one of the women's husbands, or a hit man, or just a thief who panicked. I didn't really see him, I saw just the toe of a black shoe, a forearm, and a hand with a pistol in it that had a silencer."

"Does this killer know you were there?"

"I wasn't there until at least twelve hours after he left. A whole night passed with the bodies lying there before I arrived in the morning. How could he?"

"He might have come back in daylight to pretend to discover the bodies. I saw on TV that some killers do that. He could have seen you then."

"Sharon, give me a break," Elle said. "I don't even have a drink yet."

Desiree the barmaid was on her way from the end of the bar carrying about two gallons of drinks on a tray, and she arrived in time to put one of them in Elle's hand.

"Sorry, L. The bar is full of thirsty people tonight."

Elle reached into her pocket and put two twenty-dollar bills on Desiree's tray and said, "Next time you swing by here, bring me another?"

"Sure."

"You know," Sharon said, "maybe you and I should go on a little trip. You said you were light on money, but I can take care of the money and you can pay me back later."

"Thanks, Sharon," said Elle. "But I went out and got money last night, and I can get some more if I sell a few things. Where should we go?"

"I was thinking Australia. They speak English, sort of. It's hot and miserable this time of the year — no, I guess it's cold and miserable. And it has saltwater crocodiles, poisonous snakes and spiders, and enormous wildfires."

"It sounds lovely."

"Think about it. Who would follow you there?"

5

That night Elle went through two of her hiding places looking for guns. In the house she had a single-stack 9-mm Rohrbaugh R9 pistol and a .45 Glock. She also had a shotgun she kept loaded with double-aught buckshot and a .308 rifle with a scope that was zeroed at three hundred yards. Los Angeles was a crowded place without a clear view of anything three hundred yards distant — there would always be a building in the way — but if she ever needed that kind of weapon it would be a hard thing to get at a moment's notice.

Her other arsenal was in the trunk of an old car she kept parked in the backyard and consisted of firearms she had stolen but planned to sell. Right now she had an Ed Brown signature edition .45 pistol worth about $3,000 and a Les Baer custom 1911 worth $3,200. The pistols were distinctive and expensive, and the military-style semiautomatic rifles she'd taken were illegal to own in California but not very expensive anywhere else, so they were needlessly risky. She tended to put off selling them until she really needed the money or the space.

She moved the pistols she wanted to sell into the trunk of her gray Volvo sedan and covered them with a layer of plywood and a carpet. Then she went inside. She picked up the Rohrbaugh R9 pistol. It held only six rounds in the magazine and a seventh in the chamber, but they were 9-mm, and this model had a barrel just over three inches and an aftermarket laser sight. She checked the three loaded magazines. She had found the gun in the house of a man who had long guns in cabinets in his bedroom and a pistol in nearly every drawer. That was the way the gun market went. People had no guns, or they had two dozen stored and a dozen more around to guard the others.

She stood between the big full-length mirrors in her bedroom and tested the various ways to carry the little pistol. The best was a wide elastic band that went around her stomach and had a pouch-like pocket to hold the pistol and a spare magazine. If she wore a loose top, the gun was invisible. All she had to do was lift the shirt with one hand and pull out the gun with the other.

Elle liked the laser sight. It would not make up for her lack of target practice, but it might slow an attacker by persuading him that his own death wasn't an unlikely outcome of a gunfight. She didn't like ranges much, partly because the men who were there either resented her or flirted with her. She suspected that the reason for both was that she looked about the age of the babysitter at home who kept turning them down. She'd even spotted a couple of men who put their wedding rings in their pockets before coming over to chat. Not having a wedding ring didn't make them attractive.

She put away all the weapons she didn't intend to sell, locked every latch and bolt that she could lock, and went to sleep.

The sun woke her. She lay there on her back for a minute trying to detect any feelings of fear or foreboding. One of the problems with being a thief was the fear that she could wake up any morning to the sound of police officers banging on her door to arrest her. But once again there was nothing. It was just another morning. She got up, walked around to check the locks and the glass. She took a shower and put on some clothes before she went out for the newspaper.

Most people her age had stopped getting

physical newspapers, but Elle hadn't, because she liked to have the paper serve as a subtle sign to older, suspicious people that she was solid and permanent, not a young squatter using the house to hide a meth lab, ready to bolt after the first explosion.

She was less surprised by how much coverage there was about the triple murder than she was by how little information was in the paper about the actual crime. There were photographs of the house, the winding street, and the grounds. There was an article about Nick Kavanagh's life that had the sound of a pre-written obituary.

Kavanagh had gone to Stanford University. He had been a financial services person with four consecutive firms — first as a broker, then a wealth manager, then a vice president, and then a consultant — and then, presumably, a very rich retired person. He owned the Kavanagh Gallery, and he spent a lot of time socializing. The female victims were identified as though Kavanagh were the target and they were innocent bystanders. The blonde was Anne Satterthwaite Mannon, the wife of David Mannon, owner of the restaurants Bissou and Muzu. The brunette was Valerie McGee Teason, wife of Santo Teason, one of the innumerable directors in Hollywood that Elle had never heard of.

The three victims were described as members of an exclusive set that included a number of well-known people in Los Angeles, and a few of those people had expressed their shock.

Some of the details seemed to have been planted by the police to tamp down the scandal. The victims knew one another, just three arty friends talking art.

Elle wondered about the female victims. She was not in the habit of getting herself into exclusive relationships, let alone marriages, but it seemed odd that neither of the women's phones had rung in their purses during all the time that the purses had been in the bedroom — during the talk, the sex, the murders, and the hours of growing rigor mortis, the phones were silent. No woman except Elle ever left home without a phone, and Elle did so only when she was up to no good. The women had husbands, but nobody seemed to have been calling frantically to find out where his wife was. No kids needed to be picked up at some game or lesson. And their host, Nick, had not had his phone ring either. He was a socialite and he owned a serious business, but no friends or customers or employees called him.

She tried to remember whether she had

even seen a phone. She was pretty sure that when Nick had opened his belt — or the blonde, Anne Satterthwaite Mannon, had — the slacks, loose on his long, skinny legs, had slid to his ankles and there was an audible thump that she thought was a cell phone in a pocket hitting the floor. Why hadn't anybody called him? Of course all of them could have silenced their cell phones, but none of them had checked for messages.

Elle was sure the police had noticed all of these things and more by now, but they weren't likely to release their explanations. She wondered if they were withholding information to see if one of the two husbands knew too much. They always started with the husbands. Of course, nobody like the husbands of these women would sit through a police interrogation without a lawyer, and most of the time when a person of interest called a lawyer, he got demoted to a person of no interest until the police had something to scare him with, and he got to go home until then.

Elle read everything in the newspaper that had anything to do with the victims or their murder, but the lack of information only frustrated her. She was glad to see that there was nothing in the paper about the police chasing a suspicious gray car on the evening after the killing was discovered. But that didn't mean they had forgotten or that they weren't busy searching the city for her. And it didn't mean that the killer hadn't somehow found out about her, as Sharon had said, and started searching too.

She folded the paper to obscure the articles about the killing and left it in the kitchen while she prepared to go out. Today she was going to face an errand she had been putting off for months. If she and Sharon were going to leave town for a while, it would take more money than she had stolen from the house in Trousdale Estates. It was easy to steal something small but valuable in her hunting grounds — a diamond tennis bracelet, a pair of emerald earrings — and sell it to a wholesaler, who would resell it to a dealer far away. But she got at most 5 percent of fair market value and often found it difficult even to sell items over $5,000. The preference for the small and cheap was a problem, because now and then she got something valuable.

Right now, hidden in the battery compartment under the floor of her Volvo's trunk, she had a necklace made of thirty matched yellow diamonds in the two- to six-carat range. It was probably worth $200,000 to $300,000 even broken up, but if she got

$20,000 she'd be delighted. It would pay for a long vacation with Sharon. She also had the beautiful sapphire necklace she had taken from the same house. Her problem was that trying to sell things that were really valuable was dangerous. There was a price at which it made sense for a dealer to forgo any future deals with her by simply shooting her and taking the jewelry she was selling. This critical figure was not the same with all buyers, or even with the same buyer from month to month. There were buyers who would not have $20,000 on hand but would be eager to have the piece of jewelry. There were others who had plenty of money because they had done terrible things to get it and were not averse to doing more. Negotiating was all a matter of watching for tells and tics and listening for lies.

She had some cash now, but if she wanted to travel to a distant place and wait there until the murders had been solved, she would need much more. The money was essential to her safety. If she had enough, she could stop stealing for the next few months and avoid adding to her risks. The time had come when she had to sell some of the valuable items she had stolen. There simply was no other choice.

It took her five hours to drive all the way

to the door of Steinholm's in Las Vegas. There really was no fast and convenient way for a burglar to travel when selling. The airline could ship her luggage to the wrong airport or lose it entirely. One of the luggage bandits at the airport could choose it and whisk it off the carousel and out the door. At least with a car her fate was in her own hands, because there would be nobody to serve her or protect her belongings or be responsible for her safety. She kept the odds in her favor by taking the battery out of her phone before she left the house so nobody could use the phone to locate her and the merchandise.

Steinholm's was a windowless cinder block building that had an old, worn white sign along the top with foot-high letters saying BASIC DESIGNS, and a phone number. She knew that putting up a sign that said something like PRECIOUS STONES WHOLESALE was probably a recognized method of suicide, so she could only respect Steinholm for putting up a sign that meant "Nothing you want." Old Mr. Steinholm, that was. He had been a skilled diamond cutter and jewelry designer from Amsterdam. How he had ended up in this cinder block building on the outskirts of Las Vegas was unknown, but she suspected that when he'd bought it, the building had been nowhere near Las Vegas. The city had grown like cancer for all of those years and surrounded it, probably about the time when he died and his awful son took over.

At that point the legitimate parts of the business had been replaced by an expanded line of stolen gems that had been removed from their original settings and reset, which was about all Steinholm the Younger had the skill to do. He had also diversified into the purchase of other stolen goods, which led him seamlessly into gunrunning, drug sales, money laundering, and other pursuits. He was about fifty and had greasy blond hair pulled back into a ponytail and wrap-around sunglasses that he wore even at night in the perpetual twilight of his shop.

Elle rang the bell at the loading dock behind the building and waited. After about two minutes, during which she felt thoroughly studied through security cameras and sunglasses, she heard a couple of electronic door locks buzz and make a mechanical *click* before the door opened. A current of cold air-conditioned air drifted out and enveloped her. The man at the door was Steinholm. He said, "Can I help you?"

She said, "You've known me for about ten years, Steinholm."

He said, "Yeah, I know you, L. But the question is the same. Should I say, 'What do you want?'"

"No, I guess offering help is fine. I brought some stuff. Want to see it?"

He stepped back and held on to the door so she could step in, then peered out past her and turned his head in several directions to be sure nobody was following her in. She noted that his T-shirt was an antique that memorialized the Sex Pistols and was uniformly dirty all over. He closed and bolted the door and led her to a larger room.

This had been his father's workshop. There were workbenches and stools, magnifiers on stands, soldering irons, buffers and polishers, elaborate sets of very small tools, viselike contraptions. Elle knew that the authentic workshop was now just camouflage for the various real forms of commerce Steinholm had taken up after his father's death. She wondered why the old man hadn't taught his son his trade.

Steinholm sat on one side of a workbench and said, "Show me." He leaned his elbows on the bench.

Elle sat across the workbench from him and said, "I have these." She took a jewelry box out of her backpack and opened it up while she watched his face.

He was good at keeping his mouth, cheeks, and chin immobile, but his eyes shot to the diamonds and stayed there for a moment, then jerked up to her eyes and back. "How many?"

"Ten. For now," she said.

"What does that mean?"

"That I have more. And other pieces, of course."

He snorted to himself and then inhaled through his teeth. "They're part of a necklace, aren't they?"

"Could be."

"Of course they are. They're all color-matched yellow and in graduated sizes."

"Would you like to make an offer?"

"No. What else have you got?"

"Wait a minute," she said. "Why don't you want ten very high-grade diamonds?"

"The color. An insurance company somewhere has pictures of the necklace. The stones are distinctive, and yellow is not worth as much singly as white."

"Suit yourself," she said. "I've got six watches." She removed them from her backpack and laid them out in a row. "Cartier. Rolex. Breguet. Vacheron Constantin. And two women's Patek Philippes with diamonds." She watched his eyes again.

"I'll give you a thousand each."

115

"The Rolex alone is worth about fifteen. The Cartier is more. The others —"

"I didn't drive across the desert to your house. Six grand."

She sighed. "Okay. I'll take the six."

"I'll go get your money." He went into another room. The old man used to carry a wide range of diamonds of all sizes in the vault just at the corner of the workshop. She had no idea what Steinholm the Younger kept there. Probably it wasn't money, because he never went near it. When he came back he had a big wad of money in his left hand. He counted out the price — sixty hundred-dollar bills — onto the workbench in rows of ten.

She noticed that he had a bigger wad of money in his left jeans pocket. She avoided looking at it as she folded the six thousand into the inside pocket of her jacket. "Thank you," she said. "I'll see you again before too long." She slid off the tall stool and turned to go.

"Wait," Steinholm said, and she stopped and looked at him expectantly. He said, "Let me take another look at those yellow diamonds."

"Okay," she said. "I understand why you don't want them, though." She took the box out of her pack and set it on the table,

116

where he could see the stones. He took one out, examined it through his jeweler's glass, and replaced it, then another and another. Finally he set the last one back and said, "No, I don't think so."

"Okay."

"Are you going to sell them to somebody else?"

"I'm going to try," she said.

"I'll tell you what. I'll give you five hundred." He seemed to recalculate. "No, make that seven-fifty."

"Thanks," Elle said. "But I think I'll keep trying."

He gave a false smile that didn't hide his irritation. "You think I'm lying, or that you know better."

"Neither," she said. "I'm just betting that I can find somebody who doesn't know as much as you do." She picked up the box. "See you next time."

"A thousand."

"I was thinking more like ten." She had moved her right hand under the bottom of her shirt, and now it rested on her belt, an inch from the pistol.

"I have to get a discount," said Steinholm. "You know how this business works."

"Sure," she said.

His hand came up from under the worktable and set a pistol on the wooden surface; he kept his hand close to it.

"That makes me nervous," she said.

"It's there for our safety. I should have put it where I could reach it before. I'll tell you what. I'll take the diamonds on consignment now, and I'll give you the ten thousand in a month."

"Sorry," she said.

"Look, I'm trying to give you what you want."

"After a month."

"I want the diamonds. I just don't have the cash right now." He paused. "And I'm willing to take the rest of the necklace for ten thousand when you come back."

"No."

"Now you're starting to piss me off." He snatched up the pistol and fired a round at the concrete floor that ricocheted upward and threw concrete chips toward the far wall. He looked at her as though that had settled it and set the gun down.

She pulled her own pistol and fired it into the ceiling above their heads, then instantly brought it down, already aimed at his chest. "No sale." She glared at him as she backed all the way to the door, keeping the red dot of the laser sight on his chest. She felt for the knob without looking at it, opened the door, sidestepped out, ran to her car, and drove off.

6

Elle stopped a couple of miles away, took out the $6,000, and hid it in the well under the trunk with the car battery. Then she made a long circuit of the dark streets far from the Strip, looking behind her frequently before she proceeded to a trucking company warehouse near the train tracks on the east side of town.

The owner was a man named Stubbs who was well over eighty years old. He apparently had started with the long-haul trucking company and then had begun using the trucks to deliver things his clients didn't want the police to see. He had long been known for delivering large loads: bales of marijuana, hijacked cargoes, parts stripped from stolen cars, groups of fugitives. The smaller items were said to have come later — overproductions and counterfeit versions of prescription drugs, jewelry, and other items that thieves like Elle brought for sale.

She knew the trucking company opened in the early morning, but it had armed guards on duty all the time, and that made the parking lot a safe place to sleep. The lot was vast, well paved, and empty at this hour except for a long line of trucks and about ten cars parked where there would have been room for two hundred. She parked in the open, far from any other vehicle; locked the doors; and slept until nearly dawn, when men began arriving and moving trucks around in the lot. She knew that when they were ready to meet with her the loadmaster would send someone out to summon her.

This time it was a man with a white cowboy hat and boots. He leaned on the roof of her car and said, "Hello, miss. Do you have something to ship?"

"Yes," she said.

"Okay, come on inside."

She had the merchandise in her backpack, so she swung it over her shoulder and followed him to the door beside the loading dock. He took her to the loadmaster, who was just getting set up for the day in his office. He looked at her and nodded. "You know how this works. You show the estimator the goods."

"Right."

He opened his office's inner door, which

led to a succession of rooms without ceilings built on the warehouse floor, and called, "We need an estimate!" Then he left.

A man about sixty years old with a bald head and a paunch that hung over his belt emerged from one of the other rooms beyond, carrying a paper cup of coffee in one hand and a clipboard in the other. He set the coffee on the desk in front of Elle and went back to get another from an unseen pot. When he returned he sat down and waited.

They stared at each other for a few seconds while he sipped his coffee. She wondered if he knew she would never drink hers. It would be too easy to have put something like GHB or Rohypnol in the coffee. In two hours her backpack could be trucking its way to a dishonest jeweler in New Jersey, while she was unconscious on her way to a brothel in Mexico.

Finally the man said, "Whatever you'd like to say, I'm all ears."

"Oh. You were waiting for me to say it first. I get it. I have some stuff that I would like to sell."

"All right."

She reached into the backpack on her lap and brought out the box of yellow diamonds. "There are thirty of these, ranging

122

from about two to six carats."

The estimator reached into a drawer, took out a jeweler's loupe, and adjusted the desk lamp to throw a bright concentrated light on one spot. He examined the stones one by one, setting them on the desk in a perfect line, largest to smallest, so she could see he didn't switch or hide any. He announced, "Two hundred each. That's six thousand."

"Five hundred," Elle said.

"Four. That makes it twelve."

"All right, four," she said.

"Anything else?"

"Two high-end pistols. A Les Baer special 1911 and an Ed Brown signature."

"Can I see them?"

She took them out of her pack one at a time and set them on the desk. He examined the finish on each one with a magnifying glass, from handgrip to muzzle. He opened the chambers and looked into the barrels. "Very nice," he said. "Mint condition. Of course, they stand out. They're numbered limited editions."

"They sell for three thousand each in this condition."

"Yes, they do," the estimator said. "I'll give you three hundred each."

"Five."

He smiled. "You know they need delicate

handling. They're dangerous to even own. We'd have to ship them far away to do anything with them at all."

"Yes," she said. "But you will."

His smile returned. "All right. Four."

He made a note on his clipboard. "Twelve for the stones, eight hundred for the pistols." He took the pistols off the desk and put them in another drawer.

She decided it was time for the hard one. "I've got a very good sapphire in an old art deco platinum-and-diamond setting. I'll understand if you can't afford it."

"Show me."

She unbuttoned the neck of her shirt and lifted the necklace off over her head, watching the estimator's eyes. She set it on the counter so the big sapphire faced him.

She could see he appreciated it. He was nodding to himself, and his eyes never moved from it. He held the sapphire up so he could see it with the magnifying glass. She said, "It's not like some of the new ones that are pieced together with epoxy or something."

"I can see that," he said. He looked at her. "Is it a work of art?"

"No."

"Has it been in a museum or a major private collection?"

"It came from a house. The necklace was in the safe in a closet."

He seemed to know she wasn't lying. "We still might have to cut up the stone into normal-sized jewels — maybe eight. If it were my choice I'd set each of those with some of the platinum and diamonds. It costs money to make a stone presentable and sell it to anybody but a billionaire."

"I know," she said. "Do you want to make me an offer?"

"Five thousand."

"Did you say twenty-five?"

"You know the problems."

"I do. But you could turn a fifty-thousand-dollar stone into eight thirty-thousand-dollar stones. Reusing the platinum and diamonds makes them forty-thousand-dollar jewels, and anybody who owns a car dealership or a real estate brokerage can buy that as a Christmas present."

"True," he said. "But it means having to pay for the work on eight pieces and then having to make eight safe sales." He looked at his watch. "Last offer, and then I have to move on to some other business. Ten thousand."

Elle made a face, pursing her lips and looking upward. "Okay."

She watched the estimator make more

notations on his pad. He looked up. "Now, where were these things taken from?"

"All from Southern California: Huntington Park, San Marino, Bel-Air, Beverly Hills, Encino." She knew he was making a note that all of it should be transported across the country for sale. Nothing would go back to L.A.

He made other notes. "You know anything about that three-way in Beverly Hills a few days ago?"

She considered denying it, but then she'd have to listen to his version of it. "I couldn't help it. They have it on the news twenty-four-seven."

"I figured. It's right in the middle of your territory. I heard both women were married."

"I heard that too. That leaves two rich widowers. Maybe I'll marry one."

"Suit yourself. Just don't give him a reason to shoot you." He used his phone as a calculator. "Twelve thousand for the yellow diamonds. Eight hundred for the pistols. Ten thousand for the sapphire necklace. I make that twenty-two eight. That sound right?"

"Sounds right."

He opened a third drawer of the desk and took out two banded stacks of hundred-dollar bills. "Ten thousand, twenty thousand." He reached in again and came up with two thin-banded stacks of hundreds. "Twenty-two." He reached in for another thousand, tore the band, and counted, "One, two, three, four, five, six, seven, eight," and put the last two hundreds back and closed the drawer.

"Thank you," she said, and worked to put the various stacks into order and slip them into her backpack.

"Don't mention it."

Elle hung the backpack on her shoulder, turned, and walked out the door. She heard it lock behind her. Twenty-two eight was good. Added to the $6,000 from Steinholm for the watches, it was $28,800. The total was about what she had hoped, roughly 10 percent of retail. With what was left of the cash she'd stolen the other night, she had pushed disaster $30,000 away.

That would do what she wanted right now and keep her and Sharon out of town — maybe even out of the country — for a long time. If she could have stayed home it would have supported her for six months or more. Traveling with Sharon was expensive. Elle would try to keep the cost to $500 or $600 a day, but probably fail.

The money didn't matter much to either

of them except as a way of buying time, and Sharon was a good travel companion. She was beautiful, long-legged, shapely, brash, loud, and completely without inhibitions, so she made friends instantly. She had been a poker player for a number of years, so she was an astute judge of strangers, and had gotten used to staying awake for days at a time, or taking a twenty-minute nap and waking refreshed. It was not unusual for her to go on an adventure with little money, because she knew she could make more when she needed it. Men had paid for most things in her life, and when they didn't pay, she could still play poker and was not averse to finding temporary work or inventing it.

Elle judged that if they stayed out of Los Angeles for just a month, the police would probably have a favorite suspect in the murder case. And they would certainly have determined that the murderer was a male. The recording that Elle had placed where they could not fail to find it would eliminate her. If she could stay away for a second month, the police would probably have made an arrest. In any case, they would not be searching for a female burglar of small stature. She could come home safely.

By then the ecosystem would be restored and probably healed. New rich people and the ones who wanted to mate with them would have arrived to replace the ones who had gone, bringing new parasites and sycophants with them. Life would be tranquil again.

As Elle walked across the huge parking lot to the center, where she had parked, she noticed that there were now many more cars. The main workforce had arrived and begun the day shift, and trucks were lining up to be loaded and on their way to distant destinations.

There was a set of headlights that went on in the parking lot as she drove off. She wondered who would be driving out right now — a night watchman? She had been one of the first outsiders to do business this morning. Maybe the man had forgotten that he'd had the lights on when he'd parked at night, because he turned them off after a few seconds. The sky was now bright, so she could see that the car was a blue two shades lighter than most people liked. It was almost royal blue.

Elle looked ahead to see where she was going and then back to see if the blue car was going there too. What she saw worried her. It was a second car, this one white, that was coming out of the lot on the tail of the first.

The two cars appeared to have little in common. Their moving now was a bit odd. When she had come out of the building she had not seen anyone else walking toward his car and saw nobody sitting in one. Had they been hiding, keeping their heads down, or had they run out of the building to follow her?

The best way to follow a car was to use two or more cars. That method allowed one car to keep an eye on the prey while the other either dropped back out of sight or pulled far ahead and kept in touch by phone. Few people were alert enough or scared enough to make the connection between the two cars. She decided she was scared enough.

She got onto Interstate 15 and headed for Los Angeles. The driving was seldom a problem at this hour unless there was construction on the road, and today there was none. She tried slowing down and then speeding up. Both the white and the blue car slowed and then sped up. After a few minutes the white car dropped back until it was not visible in her rearview mirror. When she slowed again, the white car reappeared and the blue one sped ahead.

Elle wasn't sure what was going on. She began to regret that her route and direction were so predictable. She couldn't elude a follower by turning off at Jean or Mountain Pass or Baker. They were just rest stops along Interstate 15. In her favor was the fact that she was in some of the driest, most inhospitable land on the planet, but it had an enormous, fast, smooth highway across it, traversed at all hours by thousands of tourists, interstate trucks, and military transport vehicles. It was a rather public place to pull a woman over in daylight and do her some kind of harm.

She stepped on the gas pedal and pushed her speed as high as she could as she crossed into California at Primm. If the men in the blue car and the white car were cops who had followed her from California, now was going to be the time. She was in California again and she was giving them a reason to pull her over. They would come after her now or drop back. If they were just creeps trying to get her they wouldn't want to be pulled over by police at ninety . . . ninety-five . . . a hundred.

She was heading for Barstow, and as she saw the signs she slowed abruptly and took Exit 184 onto Main Street. She kept going until she reached a mechanic's shop and turned in between two cars parked in front. As she got out and walked to the open bay she began to feel the fierce heat of the sun on her back and neck. The temperature had risen rapidly since early morning. She glanced back up the road but didn't see either of the two cars. She stepped into the shade of the building.

A man with freckled skin and strawberry-blond hair and eyebrows stepped out holding a red shop rag in his hands. "Good morning," he said. His smile was boyish and hopeful.

Oh that, she thought. Men her age all seemed to be interested in every woman until she was proved undesirable or scary. Elle could see her arrival had raised his initial idea of the potential of the day. All business, she said, "I think somebody may have hidden a transponder in or under my car while I was parked overnight. Some creep in Las Vegas, you know?"

He nodded. "That happens sometimes. Are you being stalked?"

"I'm starting to think so. I would like to pay you to take a close look at the car. If you find something that doesn't belong there, please take it off."

"Sure. It's just that I have a couple of cars ahead of you."

"I'll give you five hundred dollars in cash. You can give each of the two owners a hundred-dollar discount for waiting and still keep three hundred. I don't know who this is, but there were people following me until a few minutes ago. I think I surprised them when I pulled off the highway and they went past, but if we wait long enough, they'll be back here."

"All right. Are the keys in it?"

"Yes."

He got in, started her car, and drove it into the empty bay. Then he got out and raised the car on the hydraulic lift. He unhooked a light that consisted of a single two-hundred-watt bulb in a caged reflector with a hook and then began to walk back and forth, staring up at the undercarriage.

Elle said, "Do you have a bathroom?"

"Yeah, right around the corner of the building. The key's on that ring on the wall by the doorway."

She found the key and went to the restroom. It had a mirror that somebody had etched with a diamond: KYLIE + NEIL. She assumed the scratcher was Kylie. She promised the universe that if somebody ever gave her a diamond ring she wouldn't use it to deface a public bathroom. Then she took out the folded hundred-dollar bills from her jeans and counted out five of them.

When she returned and hung up the key,

the mechanic was wiping his hands on the red rag again and the car was back on the ground. She asked, "Find anything?"

He said, "I found three of them," and pointed to the workbench. There were two plastic disks, one white and one blue, and a flat black rectangle with two wires protruding from it. He picked them up one by one. "These two are battery operated. They probably only transmit for a few hours. They have a magnet, so you just put them on any surface that's steel, like a door panel. The black one was connected to a circuit in the fuse box under the dashboard. If you close the cover it can't be seen, and it lasts until somebody finds it."

Elle handed him the $500. "Are you sure you got all of them?"

"Pretty sure," he said.

"How do we make sure they're not working now?"

"Simple," he said. He opened the two disks, removed the flat coin-like batteries, and threw them into the waste receptacle, and then lifted the hammer on his workbench and crushed the plastic disks and swept them into the trash too. He hammered the flat black transmitter, tugged the wires off, and dropped it into the trash with the others.

"Thanks," she said.

He looked at her, squinting slightly for the answer to come. "I don't suppose you'd like to go to breakfast before you take off?"

She smiled but shook her head. "I'm sorry. Maybe next trip."

"Yeah," he said. He pulled the car out of the garage and left it running with the driver's door open. "Good luck. Drive carefully."

She pulled back onto Main Street and then returned to I-15 North toward Las Vegas. She turned onto Route 58 and drove across the desert through Hinkley, Four Corners, Boron, and Mojave as though she were headed for Bakersfield, and then down the Antelope Valley Freeway into Santa Clarita. From there, it was a thirty-minute drive into the northern San Fernando Valley and down into her neighborhood in Van Nuys.

There had definitely been people after her, but who were they? Were they just guys from Stubbs's trucking warehouse watching her for a chance to steal back the purchase money from the last haul, or a couple of L.A. cops? It wouldn't be the first time L.A. police had followed drivers across the state line just to see what they were up to. What she was hoping most fervently was that it didn't have anything to do with the murders at the Kavanagh house.

She weighed possibilities. If the cops had become aware of Elle Stowell, they would certainly try to find her. They would begin showing people her photograph, probably the one on her driver's license. Since she'd never been arrested they wouldn't have another. Maybe somebody would say to the cop, "Yes, I know her. Her name is L," short for whatever Elle had told the person. Would any of them know her real last name? Very few. And none of them would know the false name she had used to buy her house in Van Nuys.

The car she was driving was a problem, no matter what. Somebody had seen her car the night after she'd found the three bodies and followed her. The followers had waited for her while she had tossed a house. She had led them on a chase to Studio City, where they'd gotten stuck in the alley. And her car was where somebody had just planted transponders in Las Vegas.

When she reached her house she opened the garage door with the remote control, drove into the garage, and closed it behind her. She walked around to the back of her car to retrieve the money she had hidden in the battery compartment under the trunk.

The sudden attention worried her. Somebody seemed to be stalking her.

It was time to get started on her long vacation.

7

Elle was exhausted, but she didn't sleep in her bed that night. She built an effigy woman out of a stuffed sweatshirt, a wig, and a plastic skull she'd bought for a Halloween party and arranged the sheets and pillows to make the effigy seem to be asleep. She went from room to room in her house placing things in particular positions so she would be able to tell later whether anyone had visited while she was away. She balanced hairs on the tops of doors as she shut them. She poured a little hill of baby powder on the palm of her hand and blew it into a film on the hardwood floor at the foot of each doorway.

She put everything she believed she would need — the money from her sales trip, the Rohrbaugh R9 and its spare loaded magazines, her three sets of identification, her passport, and her second phone — into a black shoulder bag, locked the doors and windows, and walked out the back door.

Elle left her car in her garage, walked to an office building on Ventura Boulevard full of doctors' offices, and used her phone to signal for a Lyft ride. Her driver, Kassim, was polite, and he was quiet. He took her to Wilshire Boulevard near Sharon's apartment building.

Sharon lived in a brownish brick building about three blocks east of the tall towers of Park La Brea. It was a place that appealed to young people who didn't mind paying too much rent so they could live in this central, relatively safe, and pleasant neighborhood.

She went to the door and pressed the button for Sharon's apartment a couple of times, but Sharon didn't spring into action to let her in. She dialed Sharon's phone number, but Sharon didn't answer. Elle left a message.

Elle went down the front steps and walked along the sidewalk, studying Sharon's building. The functional structures of modern buildings were largely the same, from the concrete-and-rebar foundations to the plumbing, heating, and cooling to the roof. A burglar didn't see a building the same way other people did. Every building had ways in and out that a thief could find and exploit. Nothing was impenetrable or invincible. These buildings weren't designed to be. She only had to look at a building closely and the barriers seemed to fall away.

If there was glass, Elle could remove, cut, or break it. Even if there were bars, some of them were too far apart to keep her out, and others had safety mechanisms intended to release them in case of fire that she could reach and a larger person couldn't. She could open most door locks with a bump key, she could pick a lock or a padlock in a minute or two, and she could jimmy most latches with a pocketknife. Many vents and air-conditioning systems on big buildings had air ducts that she could open and enter. And she knew that no opening that wasn't intended to accommodate a person was wired into an alarm system. She knew that roofs of large buildings often had hatches and openings that weren't well protected from a person who was limber enough to climb a fire escape or a drainpipe.

The apartments between Wilshire and Third Street were all within easy walking distance of the La Brea Tar Pits, the Page Museum, the Los Angeles County Museum of Art, Farmers Market, and rows of shops and restaurants, so there were usually plenty of people on foot during daylight, but in the evening most people were in cars, so she kept close to the lighted entrances of apartment buildings as she explored.

During her walk-around she enumerated practical ways into Sharon's building — the laundry room's badly fitted utility door, a balcony she could reach from the thick limb of a tree, a hall window left unlatched, an underground garage gate that didn't close fully — but then she saw something better, a group of five people, a carload, arriving at the curb near the front door. They were all in their twenties, three women and two men. One of the women punched the intercom button that Elle had tried, said something, and grasped the door handle. As the lock buzzed and she tugged the door open, Elle began to move.

She timed her arrival to coincide with the entry of the last two people, a man and a woman who had hung back two steps to end a conversation. Each one's eyes were on the other's. She slipped in, nearly touching the back of the man as she sidestepped in past the closing door. They were still talking and distracted, so nobody wondered about the woman who came in behind him.

While the others gathered to wait for the elevator Elle stepped to the stairwell and was gone. When she reached Sharon's door she already had the right bump key out and opened the door faster than Sharon could have with a key that had all the proper teeth.

She turned on the lights, took off her jacket, hung it up, turned the lights off again, and lay on the couch. She had come with the idea that the two of them would launch their trip from here. She had traveled with Sharon before, but not often, and never for any business reason. She was a burglar, and burglars who didn't work alone tended to get caught. The only human endeavors she could think of that worked better with a partner were riding a teeter-totter and sex. They would have to talk about risks and plan carefully before they left.

As she lay in the silence and darkness, her day caught up with her. Driving home from Las Vegas after half sleeping in her car had left her tired, so she allowed herself to sleep.

Hours later she heard footsteps in Sharon's stretch of hallway. She was alarmed for only a second, until her ear for interpreting movement in the dark told her the person's weight was closer to 120 than 240 and that the new arrival was alone.

Sharon swung the door open, flipped on the light switch, jumped, and gave a squeak that had probably been the start of a scream that she stifled when she recognized Elle. "It's you. You scared the hell out of me."

"I'm sorry," said Elle. "I called you, but you weren't answering. I hoped you'd get my message."

"What are you up to?"

"I seem to have picked up a couple of followers in Las Vegas, so I needed a safe place to sleep tonight. Nobody knows I'm here and I left my car at home, so we can sleep without worrying."

Sharon moved away from the door. "I wasn't worrying until you said that. If you'll give me a few hours to sleep, I'll pack when I get up and we can go right away."

"Good night."

They didn't see each other again until afternoon. When Sharon padded out into her living room barefoot and in pajamas, Elle was sitting at the kitchen table drinking coffee and reading news on her telephone. She smiled at Sharon, who frowned and held up a finger in a "wait" sign, found herself a cup, poured coffee into it, and sipped. Then she sat down and sipped it again. "Good morning."

Elle said, "Good morning. Have a nice evening?"

"Not really. I had a date with Andrew Horan. You know him, right?"

"Slightly. I see him around. I've never dated him, maybe because he never asked."

"He's a guy who keeps buying drinks every five minutes, so they line up like soldiers until you'd die if you tried to drink them. I told him to stop. He said, 'Alcohol makes you less inhibited.' I said, 'I'm not inhibited, I just don't like you enough to want to do anything with you.' I guess alcohol makes you more honest too."

"I guess," said Elle.

"So I guess I'd better get packed up to flee the city."

"We'd better think this through," Elle said.

"Any thoughts you can share?"

"I was thinking about the City and County of Los Angeles."

"What about it — or them?"

"I'm as much a part of the fauna of L.A. as the ants and the coyotes. I know more of it than anybody but some old man retired from the post office."

"You're right," said Sharon. "You're like every one of those things."

"What?"

"Pests and cranky old men."

"I'm serious. I have advantages here. I know my way around. I've been plundering the residential neighborhoods of this city for half my life. Being comfortable here

144

might have made me overconfident. We need a plan."

"Are you saying you're not quite ready to leave?"

"I don't know. There are ten million people in Los Angeles County. It's got more people than any of the forty-two least populous states. It's bigger than Sweden or Hungary or Austria or Switzerland."

"You carry that info around in your head?"

"No, I carry a phone around in my pocket. It helps to have facts when you want to know something."

"What are you saying?"

"Since I got up this morning I've admitted to myself that I'm in worse trouble than I had allowed myself to believe. I had been clinging to the concept that since I don't know anything and didn't do anything, nobody would track me down and hurt me. But some people already chased me from a house in Trousdale Estates and other people chased me home from Las Vegas."

"Those sound like two good reasons to leave town."

"I think they are," Elle said. "I think I've got to go. But I'm not sure it's a good idea for you to go with me. I don't want to drag you into danger. I can't do that to anybody, let alone my best friend."

"I'm not afraid," said Sharon. "We can do it carefully. We'll pick out a destination that's even safer than L.A. We'll get reservations for everything we do, pack smart, and make sure it's not too obvious that we're running away. Maybe we could fly out of another city."

"That sounds smart."

"Perfect," said Sharon. "We'll stick with Australia as the main destination, and we'll spend a day just thinking and planning how we're going to get there and where we'll go."

"A whole day?"

"Well, I was just thinking your new cautious attitude was better because I have a date with Peter, and I like Peter."

"When? Tonight?"

"I'm meeting him at the Pity when he's off work. We'll go in my car, and when he and I are ready to leave, you can drive my car back here and go to sleep. I'll be home later."

"Sharon, I wasn't kidding about my problem. I'm really starting to get worried about whatever's happening. Having people see you and me together could get you in trouble."

"Don't be ridiculous. If people are after you, they'll be looking for you in your car, not mine, which they've never seen. And they won't be looking in the Pity — one of a million bars in L.A., and not a nice one. New customers only come in if their cars break down and they want to use the phone."

"There isn't any phone. The booth is still there because it's a quaint relic."

"To use the bathrooms then," Sharon said. "Either way, we're perfectly safe. Newcomers to the Pity are rare, lost, and clueless."

8

That night when Elle arrived at the Pity with Sharon, there were already a few people she knew. Desiree, who served as barmaid only when things were busy, was tending bar.

She said, "L, I need to talk to you as soon as I get your drinks."

Elle ordered the drinks for herself and Sharon, and then Alan Grober appeared at Elle's elbow.

He said to Desiree, "I'll have a Corona."

Elle said, "You might as well put that on my tab too, Desiree."

Grober said, "Thank you, L." He leaned close to her to say it, something Elle didn't like much, because like everyone who did that, he towered over her so she had to look up. He said, "Does paying mean you like me?"

"No, it means I'm talking to somebody, and if I pay, you don't have to stick around to do it."

When he moved off down the bar, Desiree said quietly, "You know, L, I think some people have been looking for you the past couple of nights."

"What kind of people?"

"Two guys and a woman. Late thirties or early forties, but trying to give off a younger impression. All three tall and in shape. The men had hair that was like the same haircut twice — short but not shaved or anything. The woman's was dyed blond, cut just at the bottom of the neck, so it looked kind of mannish too."

"Why don't you just say cops?"

"I can't be sure. Cops are dressed like they bought four suits for one amazing low, low price in a closeout sale, or they slouch around in slob disguises. These weren't like either. They were neat and pressed, so it was like it was two guys on a date, but with one woman. And it's still the shoes that give cops away. She was wearing high heels."

"Interesting," said Elle. "They just came in and asked about me? Did they have a picture of me?"

"No. They asked and then went outside. They were watching the parking lot last night. I saw the woman shoot a few pictures with her phone out there."

"Of what?"

"The parking lot, about the angle of the license plates, but with special attention to small dark gray cars."

"And because of the gray cars, you think they were looking for me?"

"Not entirely. They were describing you to people and asking who fitted the description. They cornered me while I was tending bar. They were asking me, they said, because the woman they wanted to find looked small and young. They were sure I must have checked your ID before I served you anything. Did I happen to remember the name on your license?"

"That really does sound like cops, though. When were you going to tell me this?" Elle asked.

"After I got your drinks," Desiree said. "No sense in giving you unpleasant news before you've even had a drink."

"Very civilized," Elle said. "I should get out of here."

The door at the back opened and three young women filed in. They were attractive, black-haired, and slim. Their faces shared a similar triangular shape, and they all had the same light green cats' eyes. "Hey," said the first one. "L. There were some friends of yours in here asking about you last night.

Did they find you?"

"It turned out they wanted somebody else," Elle said. Elle had always had a good time with the Simmons sisters, but she never quite trusted them. She had seen them in another bar one night when a male friend they'd been flirting with passed out. They had gone through his wallet to get money for their next round of drinks. Elle was a thief, but she didn't steal from friends.

A moment later, Sharon's date Peter came in the front door, strode across the wooden floor to Sharon, and kissed her on the cheek before he looked at the others. "Hi, everybody." He was tall and thin with coal-black hair and a smile that was open and sincere.

Sharon and Elle smiled and said, "Hi," in a tone that to Elle sounded disturbingly similar, and Peter edged his way to the bar on Sharon's other side. Elle tipped her head close to Sharon's ear. "Time to give me your keys."

"Really?" said Sharon. "This early?"

"That was the deal. Peter will take you home."

"Absolutely," Peter said. "Not right away, though. I just got off work."

Sharon fished for the keys in her purse. She slipped them to Elle. "See you later. Don't wait up."

Elle slipped money to Desiree, patted Peter's arm, and kept going out the back door. She went out to the parking lot and got into Sharon's car. It occurred to her that if she and Sharon left in the next couple of days she didn't want to leave her fingerprints in the car, so she wore gloves while she drove back to Sharon's apartment. She parked Sharon's car in the underground garage and then went upstairs to watch movies on television. Elle hated crime stories because they seemed too much like work and hated horror because her livelihood depended on not being afraid of the dark, but she liked romantic comedies. After two A.M., when the bars in L.A. had closed, she decided that Sharon and Peter weren't coming to the apartment, so she felt justified in sleeping in Sharon's bed instead of on the couch.

She woke at nine in the morning and felt fear grip her as soon as her eyes opened. She lay still for a few minutes, listening for sounds that might have wakened her. After a time she convinced herself that there were none. The three people who had been searching for a small blond woman had made a lucky guess at a good place to search, but they had not found Elle. They had been looking for a gray car but had not found her gray car, because it hadn't been in the Pity's lot. The fact that she had missed them only by chance and good timing made her anxious. She kept telling herself that close calls didn't matter, but they did.

She made herself breakfast and it gave her time to think about what she had learned last night. The three people who had been searching for her were not exactly unexpected.

The three were almost certainly connected with some law enforcement agency, probably the LAPD. Most likely they had been launched on their search by her foolish visit to the Kavanagh house and her escape from the unmarked black police car afterward. Now she had to stay away from the three people and hope that they didn't find anyone to tell them who the woman they described was. She couldn't be confident about that.

Part of the problem with being a criminal was that eventually all of your normal friendships would dwindle until the only people you knew were also criminals. Criminals tended to be people who were selfish, greedy, and untrustworthy. That meant that few of them were above ratting out a friend to a police agency. They did it in exchange for getting minor charges dropped or major charges diminished. They even did it so the friend would be locked up and they could rob his apartment or seduce his girlfriend.

She had no satisfactory explanation for the two cars that had followed her from Las Vegas. Or really, she had several plausible explanations, with no reason to choose one over another. Maybe they had worked for Steinholm in Las Vegas. Maybe they were just freelance thieves who knew that anyone who left Stubbs's warehouse was carrying either valuables or cash. They might or might not have been connected with Stubbs's trucking company. They might even have been Los Angeles police doing unofficial surveillance across a state line because they thought she might know something they didn't about the triple murder.

Today Elle would just stay out of sight and try to avoid searchers by being in places that criminals and police had no reason to visit and seldom did. The L.A. County Museum of Art was within easy walking distance. She liked all museums, but particularly art museums. They were great institutions that welcomed everybody. They said to the public, "This is good for you, but you'll like it anyway, and you'll go home with most of the money you started with."

She loved the Wilshire area and soon began the walk from Sharon's. She crossed the park surrounding the Page Museum, which was full of the animal corpses from the redundantly named La Brea Tar Pits. They were not pits, really, until the paleontologists dug them out. They were more like wells. The lawn in the park was a treacherous place to walk, because now and then black tar would bubble up from underground and threaten a person's shoes.

The biggest pit was an oily pond right in front of the museum, and it had been decorated with a melodramatic sculpture of a mother mammoth caught in the tar reaching back with her trunk toward her horrified baby mammoth on the shore. It was a heartrending scene and a peculiar thing to install for the edification of the city's children, in Elle's opinion. The only motive she could discern was to assure kids that even though their lives were shit, life on this spot had never been any better, so they had no right to whine.

She made it to the front of the giant LACMA complex, took the shortcut beside the water feature that looked like a canal, and then went to the main building entrance. She spent ten minutes looking at brochures, paying for her ticket, and going to the ladies' room, but actually she was studying the people who entered after her to be sure none of them was a threat. Then she began to move through the galleries.

When she had come in she had paid for a ticket to a special exhibit of the works of Degas. She almost regretted having bought it and put it off for a few hours while she ranged the permanent collection. She didn't really like going to big exhibitions. The artist's name was always the attraction, which brought in hordes of people who felt they had to voice an observation about each painting, drawing, or sculpture, even if the comment was just "Dancers" or "Horses." She studied a view of the stage of l'Opéra from the front of the orchestra pit. Dark silhouetted heads and instruments crossed the foreground in front of the glowing stage. A woman and her companion edged up beside Elle, and the first woman said, "This one seems to be more about the band." True enough.

Elle walked back to Sharon's apartment at five. There was no sign of anyone watching the building, but she was very aware of the fact that a thousand people could be watching it from the thousand windows of the tall office buildings along Wilshire Boulevard. Each of them could be aiming at her a camera that was connected to a computer and be sending her image to a thousand colleagues. There could be a million people watching her walk along the sidewalk on this bright summer afternoon. It could just as easily be a billion.

9

Elle stepped to the front of Sharon's building, used Sharon's key to get into the lobby, and walked to the apartment door. Elle's profession made her habitually reluctant to make noises, and she realized as she approached that she was walking like a burglar, but she didn't feel like correcting it.

She came in, walked from room to room, and saw that Sharon had not returned. The bed was still as neat as a bunk in a military barracks, and the coffeepot had timed out, turned itself off, and gone to room temperature.

Elle was almost glad to beat Sharon to the apartment. Sharon didn't need to know that Elle had slept in her bed and taken the liberties she had — using her expensive bubble bath and her nail polish, for instance. She stepped out of the dress she was wearing and put on the jeans, T-shirt, and running shoes she'd left in her bag. The bag reminded her that she'd left most of her money and her gun in the apartment. The money was placed in several envelopes from Sharon's best stationery and hidden behind Sharon's television set in the wall rack. The gun and its magazines were duct-taped to the wall in the closet above the doorway, so a person had to step into the closet, turn around, and look up to find them.

Elle gathered everything she had brought with her, washed the dishes, took the sheets off Sharon's bed and washed them, dried them, and put them back on the bed. She wrote "hostess gift" on one of Sharon's envelopes and left a thousand dollars in it. Sharon was a very good friend, but she was also a person who went through a lot of money quickly and saw cash as a token of sincerity. The extra money might even help remind her about the trip.

Elle considered calling Sharon's cell number again, but since Sharon had obviously chosen to stay the night and day at Peter's, calling would have seemed unnecessarily intrusive.

She left the keys with the envelope on Sharon's desk, picked up her big shoulder bag, locked the door, and set off. She walked a mile or so before she stopped at the hotel across from the Beverly Center and stepped in front of the door to take a cab. She got a ride to her neighborhood in Van Nuys.

She had decided that this trip was a necessary precaution. She had been out of touch with most of her friends for a few days and had not yet even talked to Sharon for a day. She didn't want anybody stopping by and leaving a note stuck in her door, or to acquire a pileup of mail that wouldn't fit in the slot, or to risk any other problem. When she was working she had often seen the results of leaving a house alone for too long. She had even broken into one and found that the hardwood floors had all been destroyed because of a pipe leaking inside a wall for the duration of someone's vacation.

She approached her house from the back, used her neighbor's stepladder to climb over the fence because she didn't feel like doing it the hard way, and then went to her own back door. When she opened it she saw a long blond hair on the floor, definitely one of hers. She stood on a chair to look and be sure it was the one she had propped above the door. She climbed down and listened. She had been gone for about two days, and in that time someone had broken into her house. She didn't feel outraged or violated the way a lot of burglary victims did. To her it wasn't personal, and she had learned from childhood that it was unwise to allow oneself to get attached to belongings or to invest emotion in them.

She went to the doors where she had spread a thin film of baby powder and examined the spots. There were footprints. They were large — male for sure. She took pictures of them to preserve the sole pattern so she could go to shoe stores and find out the brand and style if she needed to. They had relatively deep treads, but not the kind that basketball sneakers had. They were less dramatic, and they had a heel. They seemed likely to belong to some kind of hiking shoe.

It was time to assess the damage. Her new laptop computer was gone. It wasn't a big loss, since she had stolen it too, but it was a disappointment. She hadn't even used it yet. The one she had been using was hidden in the trunk of her car under the floor. Any amount of hacking or reconstruction on either computer would yield only the passwords and personal life of its rightful owner, someone she didn't know. Elle had always been too wary to communicate with anyone via computer. All an expert could find were records of her online searches, which would look blameless and lead nowhere.

The rifle, the shotgun, and the Glock pistol were gone. That alarmed her for a moment. She had an impulse to report their theft, but she reminded herself that they'd already been reported when she'd stolen them the first time. Her iPad, her Kindle, and the cheap jewelry she owned had all been taken. The television set was gone.

She checked the hiding places where she had left the thumb drives containing the recordings from the triple murder. They were still where she had left them.

She decided that the burglary had just been what she deserved. It didn't seem to be threatening, and she was certain that the intruder hadn't been from the police. The police cheated sometimes, illegally entering a house to see what was inside that wasn't supposed to be there and then leaving to get a warrant to search for those exact items, but the wrong things were missing. The police wouldn't take things of value. They wanted only something incriminating, and the last thing they wanted was to take it away.

Elle and Sharon weren't ready to leave town yet, but the time had come for Elle to move out of her house for a while. She decided that to move out without seeming to was the best way. She picked enough outfits that she loved to nearly fill one suitcase and left the rest hanging in her bedroom closet. She took all the financial papers she had in the house. The pink slip of her car was hidden inside the car. The deed and mortgage papers for the house and the information about her bank accounts in different names were all in her safe-deposit boxes. She had to use a different bank for each of her accounts, not because she liked having money spread thin all over town, but because she could hardly have two names at the same bank. Keeping these things sorted was all part of being a thief. But she was determined to remove anything valuable or incriminating from the house.

Hours later, when she had finished her housecleaning, the place looked much neater than it had since she'd bought it. Getting out prompted a great deal of dusting and polishing to get rid of fingerprints, hair, and DNA and a number of large black plastic garbage bags for the things that she wanted removed. There was little of any monetary value left in the house besides the structure itself.

Elle loaded the garbage bags and the single suitcase containing the few remaining valuables into the gray car, locked the house, and drove around for the early morning hours depositing the garbage in dumpsters. She stopped at a big pharmacy and bought a disposable phone. She stopped at the post office where the lobby was open all the time, filled out a yellow card to have her mail held, and put it into the slot. Then she used her old phone to call the *Los Angeles Times* and have her newspaper canceled.

She was conscious all the time that chores like this were much easier when there was another person to help, but she didn't want to call anyone she knew. The ones still wide-awake at night were sure to be doing something more rewarding than this — financially, emotionally, sexually, or all three at once — and they would want the favor returned some night when it was least convenient. She was also sure that what she was doing was best kept to herself. The less that was known, by the fewest people possible, the safer she would be. She knew that it was time to get rid of her dark gray Volvo. She drove to the hill above the Universal Studios lot and the hotel at the top.

When she had checked into the hotel, she went up to her room and considered her next move. The gray car was valet-parked out of sight in the cavernous hotel garage. The police routinely cruised around at night checking hotels for cars that came up on their license plate scanners as wanted for some reason, but she was pretty sure they didn't do it often at hotels like this one. And now that she was registered, until noon a couple of days from now she would be just a name on a credit card.

Before she went to sleep she looked up the Blue Book value of her gray car online and posted the car for sale, cash only, for about $300 less than the fair rate. She was pleased to see that the discount brought the price just below $10,000. She was going into this liquidation patiently. She was not going to get rid of Elle Stowell or her false names Elizabeth Walker and Katherine Ashton. She was just going to stop inhabiting them for a while. She couldn't kill herself off and then expect to sell a car and buy plane tickets. Too many people stubbornly insisted on dealing with the living.

10

When she woke and turned on her phone, she found there were three potential buyers for her car already. She called and made a date with the first one, who had the voice of an elderly man. She agreed to drive the car to his house to show it. She had already removed the contraband from her trunk with her valuables, and she had the pink slip in her purse.

He lived in the western part of the San Fernando Valley, so the trip took about a half hour, with an extra twenty-minute stop to have the car washed. When she arrived she saw that his voice had given an accurate sense of his age. He was in his mid- to late sixties, with thick, wavy white hair that she judged must have served him well with the ladies over a lifetime. She handed him the keys and let him drive the car around in his section of the Valley for a while. He returned the car to his house, checked the oil, squeezed a couple of hoses, and ran his hand along a couple of the belts. She followed his eyes to figure out what else he was seeing under the hood but didn't succeed. He shut it and walked around the car, looking closely at the finish.

Finally he said, "It was a good model, and it's been driven with enough care to keep from bumping things. You changed the oil and filters when you were supposed to. The mileage is reasonable. Ninety-nine hundred, right?"

"Yes, sir," she said.

"All right. If we drive to my bank to pick up the cash, I can pay you and drop you off at your house."

"As long as you're not planning to rob the bank, it's a deal."

"Not today," he said. "Let's go."

They drove a few blocks to his bank and she waited in the car until he returned with a big manila envelope. He counted out the money on the car console, she signed the pink slip and the bill of sale, and then they drove to a neighborhood in Sherman Oaks that wasn't near her house but that she liked because it was shaded by jacaranda trees that shed purple petals on the streets and sidewalks. She shook his hand, got out of the car, and watched him drive away.

She knew he would wash, vacuum, and wax his new car even though she had just paid to have that done. He was that kind of man, and he was from a generation that did things that way. He would be ashamed to show the car to his friends and family until he had done his best with it. That would remove the small number of remaining atoms attributable to Elle Stowell, and that made her feel more confident.

The car had given her good service, but she was glad to be rid of it because it linked her to several recent unpleasant episodes. She was striving to keep her anxiety at bay while she waited for the danger to go away, and the best way to conquer her fear was to take any precaution she could that would make her hard to identify and hard to find once she and Sharon left town.

When her car was safely gone, Elle sent text messages to the two other bidders to let them know the car was sold. Then she summoned a Lyft car to take her to Burbank Airport. There she rented a new Audi, one of several small black cars in the rental lot that seemed identical except for the logos on their noses, trunks, and hubcaps — Audi, BMW, Volkswagen. Elle drove the car over the hill and down Fairfax to park on Sixth Street and then walked to Sharon's apartment.

This time she entered the building by the back door, rushing to hold it open while a harried-looking woman with a strand of hair in her eyes stepped out to take a pair of trash bags to the dumpster. When she was out, Elle slipped in and let the door close behind her.

Elle walked down the hallway toward Sharon's apartment. She fitted the right bump key into Sharon's door lock, turned it as far as she could, bumped her shoulder into the door, felt the pins jump, turned the key, and entered.

The horrible image of the bedroom in Nick Kavanagh's house filled her mind. She nearly gagged. It was the smell of bodies — of death. "Not Sharon," she whispered. "Please not Sharon." She wanted to run, but she forced herself to walk across the small entryway into the living room.

The apartment looked as it had after Elle had straightened up while she was waiting for Sharon to get ready to leave for the Pity two nights ago. Elle had picked everything up, pushed each piece of furniture into its proper place in the configuration, straightened the pile of fashion magazines on the table so the edges were all even. The framed posters and prints on the walls were level.

She glanced over the marble counter into the kitchen and saw nothing different there either. Nobody had cooked or made a snack or even brewed coffee. Each sight that Elle verified was as it should be failed to persuade her that everything really was as it should be.

She couldn't keep putting off the bedroom. She walked the rest of the way through the living room to the short hall that led to the bathroom — nothing there — and finally the bedroom.

Peter was lying on the floor facing away from the doorway as though he had been shot as he stepped into the bedroom and fallen dead. The bloody mess at the back of his head showed that the entry wound must be in his forehead. His legs were crossed at the ankle, which she had heard was a sign that he had been standing when he'd died. There was something about the shape and balance of the human body that made it turn a little when it collapsed.

The sight of Peter made her remember the efficient aim-and-fire of the killer's sound-suppressed pistol in Kavanagh's bedroom — *pop-pop-pop*. The suppressor had choked the report not to a hiss or a whisper, just to a quieter pop. She looked down again. It was hard to look at him. He had been so handsome, such a healthy young guy. Now the sight of him was awful.

This time the killer must have been waiting in the apartment for Sharon and Peter to arrive. When Peter had walked in, the killer must have shot him instantly. But what about Sharon? Where was she?

Elle stood still in the doorway, looking past Peter. Why wasn't Sharon's body here with Peter's? As she considered the question, she allowed herself to nurse a faint hope. Could Sharon have unlocked her apartment door and let Peter in, and then paused there to close and relock it? Could she have crossed the living room after Peter, followed him toward the bedroom, heard him shot, then turned and run?

The killer would have had to be in the bedroom slightly to the left of the door, or Peter would have seen him. Maybe the killer had heard the door open and close and expected only Sharon to come in. When the one who came in was Peter, not a thin and pretty young woman but a tall, athletic man, the killer might have been surprised. It took most people a second or two to overcome surprise. Could Sharon have dashed out the door and escaped? If she had seen her boyfriend shot, she would run. Even Elle would have run. It was a reflex.

Corrective facts lodged in Elle's mind and blocked her hopes. If Sharon had escaped she would have called the police, and they'd be here. If she had escaped she would have called Elle. She had not done either.

Elle stepped past Peter carefully, to stay out of the pool of blood that had seeped from his wound onto the floor. She saw that the closet door was half open. She stepped to it and found Sharon lying on the floor with a dress clutched to her, as though she had grabbed it and pulled it to her before the shot had entered her forehead.

Her face held the expression Elle had seen when Sharon was confused or puzzled. Maybe she had been wondering how she had come to be killed over something she didn't understand by a person she had never seen before.

Elle knelt down and felt tears filling her eyes. She knew she couldn't touch the body and that even her tears might contain DNA, so she wiped them away on her sleeve.

She whispered, "I'm so sorry, Sharon."

She stood and looked around her. The bed was still made. The room still looked pristine except for the closet and the wall above the doorway, where the bullet through Peter's head had thrown a red mist. She stepped past Peter into the living room.

172

This had to be the same shooter who had killed the three people in Beverly Hills. She had to get the police here as quickly as possible, so they could find out who he was. She looked around for a phone, but then stopped. She remembered the envelope she had left for Sharon. That couldn't stay here, because it had her fingerprints, and she had licked the flap. She looked on Sharon's desk where she had left it, but it wasn't there. She found the torn envelope in the wastebasket, so she picked it up and put it into her pocket. She was glad Sharon had found the money before she had died.

Then it occurred to her that the ten hundred-dollar bills had her prints on them too. She spotted Sharon's purse on the couch near the kitchen. She looked inside. Elle took Sharon's phone, because it held her name, number, and address in its contact list. Then she found the ten hundred-dollar bills and stuffed them into her pocket too.

She went back to the bedroom doorway. She said aloud, "I wish —" She had been about to say, "That it was me and not you," but that was just not true. Even dead, Sharon would know that it was crap. Elle was always talking about how much she loved life, and she meant it. Elle said, "That

I had never gotten you into this. I wish you were both alive and happy. I promise that I'll do what I can."

She moved across the living room to the door and then stopped. She had no way of knowing exactly how this had happened, but she was fairly sure that the only connection between the first three murder victims and Sharon and Peter was herself. And the most likely reason the killer would have come here was to kill her.

It occurred to her that if the killer had come because she had been staying here and instead killed the two people who saw him, he must know that neither was Elle. It was likely that he could have gone outside and been waiting to see if Elle arrived, and here she was.

She remembered that when she had come into the building it had been through the back way, which the killer may not even know was possible. If he was still here he'd be watching the front door. She left the apartment, went down the hall, and slipped out the way she had come in. She circled the dumpster to pass behind it, stood on it to go over the back fence, and then began to run. As she ran, she used Sharon's phone to call the police.

"Emergency. What is your emergency?"

She said, "I just found two people murdered at 91375 Wilshire Boulevard, Apartment Six. Both shot to death. Send some
cops quick."

"What is your name?"

Elle switched off the phone, took the battery and the SIM card out, and then
smashed the circuitry against the next lamp-
post. When she reached her car on Sixth
Street she got in and drove off. At the
corner near the Page Museum she turned
and came east along Wilshire to see if there
was anyone in a parked car watching the
entrance to Sharon's building. She saw no
one watching and no pedestrians near
enough to be suspects.

She was only a block past the building
when a black-and-white police car sped up
Wilshire to the front of Sharon's building
and stopped with its lights revolving and
blinking. She kept going until Robertson
and then turned north toward the Valley.

That night at six o'clock the local news
channels announced the murder of Sharon
Estleman and Peter Rowen in Sharon's
apartment. Elle already had her phone
plugged in to charge in preparation for the
call she planned. She had always liked
Sharon's parents, so she wanted to be one
of the first to speak to them.

She was on the phone with them for about an hour. Most of the time Sharon's father was on another phone line talking to other people: police, friends and relatives, Mount Sinai Cemetery, the medical examiner's office. He had always been that kind of father. He was used to being in charge and he believed that things got done because he was willing to arrange them or do them himself. But when they were both on the line with Elle, she told them how much she loved and respected their daughter.

She praised her for her wit, good nature, loyalty, and kindness. Then, as one of the last favors she could do for Sharon, she praised her for qualities that she hadn't possessed but that her parents had wanted her to have — her ambition and tireless work ethic, her religious devotion, and her wise practicality.

The Estlemans had known Elle since she was in junior high school with Sharon, but they had never known her family or suspected that she was a thief. Sharon had periodically given them false updates on what Elle was doing. For years she had told them Elle was a student at UCLA. After that Sharon had said Elle worked for a digital company that did programming for the government. That way Elle was protected by the Estlemans' lack of interest in computers and their respect for government secrecy.

Mr. Estleman said the police were going to free Sharon's body for burial only after a couple of days of intense forensic examination and an autopsy. He told her he'd call her when he knew when it would be.

Late that night Elle drove down the hill from the hotel to the Ralphs grocery store on Ventura and bought snacks and drinks, and then stayed in her room until she received the call from Mr. Estleman.

Elle had never done much mourning before. She had always thought she would have cried for her parents when they died, but by the time she had heard such people had ever existed, she had already lived five or six years. She had accepted that some people had no parents and that she was one of them. She also knew that living meant accepting conditions as they were. By the time her grandmother died she had already heard her referring to her own death as imminent for years, so Elle had gotten used to the idea before it happened.

But Sharon had been important to her. Elle had met her in junior high, but she didn't remember when they had begun to think of each other as friends rather than rivals or enemies. She had heard people say they were like sisters, but that meant nothing to Elle because she'd never had a sister.

Now Sharon had been killed because Elle had foolishly and selfishly guessed it would be safer for her if she slept at Sharon's place for a couple of nights before they left on their trip. She hadn't spent enough time thinking about whether her staying with Sharon was safe for Sharon. It hadn't been.

She had done the unthinkable — got her best friend murdered. Each time the thought came back it made her lose control again and lie on the bed sobbing for a while. This had been happening to her at intervals since she had found the bodies. Her guilt and sadness made her feel worthless and ashamed.

She allowed the attacks of crying to last until she left the hotel for the funeral, and then she stopped them. She was determined after that to exert her self-control every minute when another human being could see her, until this was over.

The funeral was at Mount Sinai, the large Jewish cemetery on the hillside overlooking the 134 Freeway and the City of Burbank beyond. Elle drove her rented black Audi to the gateway kiosk and then to the parking lot beside the mortuary chapel. Before she turned off her engine she scanned the gaggle of people moving toward the chapel. She saw several motorcycle officers who had escorted another funeral procession and now were a distance up the ascending access road chatting while they watched everyone coming or going.

They were traffic cops, not the kind of cop who might be watching for her, but they were all armed and could probably be trusted to protect people.

Up the hill there were two other funerals coming to their conclusions. The graveside part was the end, she knew. There were other family groups, most of them two or three people, visible at various places on the hill visiting graves.

The size of the crowd going into the chapel for Sharon's memorial service made Elle feel relieved. She was aware that having a well-attended funeral was worth exactly nothing, but she wanted Sharon's family to be comforted. She turned off her engine and got out.

On the way into the chapel, Elle stopped, hugged and kissed the Estlemans, and then slipped inside to search for another family. She spotted the Corbetts. They had lived in another of the big houses on Elle's street in South Pasadena when Elle and Sharon were growing up. Linda Corbett had been their age and had been one of a large group of neighborhood kids who knew one another and played together. The Corbetts had been the only faction as big as the Stowells. They were Mormons transplanted from Utah, and they were eight children strong, including four sisters who were small and blond.

Elle went up to Linda, and they hugged and exchanged air-kisses. She was introduced to Linda's husband, then moved along the line and kissed the other Corbett girls, meeting their husbands but ignoring their married names, which she never expected to remember. Then she moved back to where she'd started and asked Linda, "Is this seat taken?" then sat down. She had picked the Corbetts because she looked like a Corbett, and blending in would make her safer for the next two hours.

The mortuary provided a rabbi in residence to preside over the service so it moved along smoothly, but the Estlemans had brought the rabbi and cantor from their own temple, so the funeral was personal and warm, with stories about Sharon as a child, a student, a bat mitzvah, and a young woman.

During the service Elle occasionally looked to see if anyone new had come in, but she saw no one who worried her. She kept feeling the urge to communicate with Sharon in some way, but as she sat there she realized that this was what death meant. Nobody could do it. There was no Sharon now.

When the plain wooden coffin was wheeled out by the pallbearers, Elle paused with the Corbetts and exchanged platitudes for a few minutes so she could prolong her time of anonymity and distance from the center of things. Then she put on her oversize sunglasses and went to her rental car while the hearse was conveying Sharon's body up the hill to the grave.

Elle drove up the long paved driveway in the line with the rest of the cars, parked when they did, and walked the rest of the way. At the grave the rabbi spoke and then said more prayers in Hebrew. After Sharon's body was lowered into the grave, people lined up and waited their turns to lift the shovel and put their measure of dirt in to cover the coffin. Years ago, Sharon had told her this was done at Jewish funerals and that burying the body was the last favor the living could do for the dead.

When Elle's turn came, she speared the shovel into the mound of dirt, lifted it, and spun it over to release a full load of dirt onto the center of the casket. She handed the shovel to a middle-aged man in line behind her and walked off, following the others to the side road where they had all been directed to park. Los Angeles was full of small black cars, so as she walked she looked at each car to find her Audi. When she thought she had the right one she squeezed the electronic fob on her key to unlock the door, got in, and started it.

She leaned to the right and looked at her reflection in the rearview mirror to be sure her eye makeup hadn't run, and saw that a man in a dark suit was opening her car door beside her.

Instantly she slipped the car into reverse, stepped on the gas, and made the rear edge of the door ram the man over onto the pavement. As she threw the car into drive, he scrambled to get up and push something into the open doorway, but Elle grabbed the handle and yanked the door, aided by the forward momentum of the car. The door closed on his hand, and whatever he was holding dropped, hit the door's rocker panel, and fell outward to the pavement. Her car lurched ahead a dozen feet before she hit the brakes and it stopped.

In the mirror Elle could see that the object was a pistol. She threw the car into reverse again and backed up as fast as she could, trying to run over the man or the gun before he could get to it and pick it up. She was moving fast, so instead of trying to snatch the gun, he dived onto the grassy hillside as she flashed past him.

She stopped her reverse motion, but she saw that he was still close enough to get to the gun before she could in high heels. The steep slope also meant she couldn't drive up over the curb and hit him. She caught more movement in the corner of her eye and saw a large black vehicle high on the hillside. Men were hurrying to climb into it and drive down to where she was.

She stomped on the gas pedal, drove to the end of the cemetery road, and turned onto the main drive. She sped downhill past the entrance kiosk, turned left onto Forest Lawn Drive, and headed west. The black vehicle turned up the side road to pick the man up and lost any chance of catching her.

In a few minutes she was accelerating up another hill to the hotel above Universal Studios. She reached the level space in front of the hotel, where she gave the rental car to the valet parking attendants and watched it disappear underground. While they took possession of the car, she stared down the long incline to the entrance at Lankershim

Boulevard and across the street to the overpass that led to Ventura Boulevard. There were no pursuers and no big black vehicles. She forced her breathing to become calmer and quieter and felt her heartbeat slow down.

She wasn't quite sure what had just happened to her. She had expected that police detectives would be at Sharon's funeral to see who else was there, but she had not expected them to be interested in her. And that wasn't the way police officers arrested someone in a car. They liked to surround a car with a couple of theirs so it couldn't move, have one cop approach the driver's-side door, and have another stand at least ten feet behind the car on the right side in the driver's blind spot. She'd never heard of a cop just stepping up to a car, flinging the driver's-side door open without speaking, and sticking a gun inside.

She walked into the hotel and kept going, calming herself as she pretended to explore the building. The man she had just escaped was very likely Sharon's killer. He hadn't been trying to arrest her. He'd seemed to be trying to kill her.

When she returned to the room she had rented she saw that the maid had already cleaned it. She had left a tip on the counter just in case that happened, so she took it as a sign that she was beginning to return to her usual level of alertness. She had to do something that would calm her down and give her a chance to think.

She put on her running shoes and shorts and went down to the gym. It was late enough now so that most of the traveling businesspeople would be out making money. The evening exercisers were still hours away. When she got there the room was empty. She did some push-ups, then spent a few minutes each on a stationary bike, an elliptical trainer, and a treadmill. She exercised with weights for a few minutes, then did pull-ups on a bar, keeping her eyes on the window to the hallway. As a rule, women were not good at pull-ups, so she didn't want to be noticed doing her twenty.

Afterward she returned to her room, put on shorts and a tank top over a bathing suit, and went out to the pool, stopping first in the hotel store to buy new sunglasses, sunscreen, and a paperback book. She set aside the outer clothes and swam lengths until her muscles were so thoroughly ex-hausted that they relaxed because they couldn't contract anymore.

She lay on a chaise longue with her eyes closed and her oversize sunglasses on and felt the luxurious sensation of the sun warming her skin and the water evaporating into the warm, dry air. As soon as her skin dried she applied the sunscreen. It was not good for people in the theft business to get sunburned, particularly in Los Angeles, where the only people over seven who ever got sunburned were visitors from elsewhere.

She opened her book to read, hoping it would distract her thoughts from Sharon. She was still feeling upset by the attack at the cemetery, but she told herself this place was as safe as any. People hunting for a Los Angeles–based fugitive wouldn't be likely to hunt in a hotel beside a Los Angeles tourist destination. If they looked in hotels they would choose hotels in San Francisco or Las Vegas or resorts along the coast. And being in a bathing suit helped her disguise. People running from pursuers seldom hid in bathing suits. They made a person unprepared to fight or run.

One reason she was wearing one now was that she'd noticed while growing up that although bikinis showed a lot, they didn't give anything away about identity. All women's bathing suits were pretty much alike — two small pieces of cloth that covered only the parts of a woman that people needed to be protected from by law.

Wearing one by a pool said nothing about her identity or history except that she was young and female. That much could be observed about several similarly attired guests around the pool at this moment. And even to Elle's discerning eye, most young women's bodies were pretty much the same from a distance. Today she was glad to see there were a couple of them who looked better than she did — more eye-catching, at least.

She used the cover of her big dark sunglasses to focus her eyes an inch or two above the printed pages of her book every few minutes to scan the area. The fact that she was hiding didn't necessarily mean nobody would ever find her.

She spotted a young man on a nearby chaise watching her and noted that he was attractive, with a trim, muscular body and a boyish blond look. She went back to reading, then noticed him looking at her again. She gave him another chance to look at somebody or something else, and when he didn't, she said, "We don't know each other well enough for you to give me your undivided attention. Your divided attention would be enough."

"Oh, I'm sorry," he said. "I didn't mean to."

"That girl over there, the one with the black nylon suit and the big earrings? She's so pretty I may go try to pick her up myself."

He looked at the woman, this time surreptitiously. "I don't know. She's a little scary to me."

"Get used to it. That's how we are in L.A."

"You're from around here?"

"No," she said. "New York. But I visit L.A. often." Talking about herself wasn't the best way to avoid attention, so she grasped at the only diversion she had — him. "Where are you from?"

"Calgary."

"What are you doing here?"

"I guess I'm trying to get on a television show."

"Any one in particular?"

"At the moment it's called 'Untitled Hector Staples Project.' It's a pilot about modern cowboys in Canada. There were a couple of producers and other people up there and I got hired to show them around for a few days. Now they're paying my way to audition."

"Are you an actor?"

"I wasn't until now."

"Are you a cowboy?"

"Mostly when I was younger. The work is hard, and the pay is lousy. You're always hot

188

or cold or wet. But I got good with horses. Since then I've been a horse trainer."

He was good with more than just horses. Either he was the best confidence man of the thousands within a mile of the hotel, or he really was what he said. No woman could have this conversation with him and not picture him patiently and competently winning over one of those big, beautiful, powerful creatures, reassuring it and soothing it, getting it used to his touch and his soft, strong voice. She glanced at her watch, closed her book, stood, and put on her shorts.

He said, "You're going? I hope I didn't scare you off."

"I don't stampede easily," she said. "I just don't think any more sun right now would be a good thing." She stepped into her sandals. "Break a leg." She began to walk toward the glass doors.

She made nine steps across the hot concrete before she felt his presence behind her. She slowed down to let him catch up and turned her head. "What?"

"I don't want to give up, so I thought I'd get out of the sun too. Will you have a drink and a snack with me? It's teatime."

She stopped, looked up at him through the sunglasses, and squinted to see him better. "Teatime? That's a first. Mmmm . . . I don't think so."

"Why not?"

She took a deep breath and let it out in a sigh. "Turning you down doesn't mean anything bad about you. It can mean that your set of coordinates in the universe, or your trajectory, is just not right in relation to me at the moment. You show signs of being a first-rate human. You're attractive and well-spoken and decisive without being too sure of yourself. You must be kind and gentle or some horse would have kicked your brains out by now. But to me, today, you're a distraction. You kind of entered my space unexpectedly from an angle, and sharing time with you would require that I slow down and move a few paces off the track."

He looked down at her, his expression still open and friendly. She wondered if he was stupid.

"I understand," he said. "I didn't realize you were having a psychological emergency. You must be a strong and disciplined person to handle it so well that I missed it. I'm sorry. I hope you have a wonderful day."

"Okay," she said.

"Okay?"

"I'll have tea with you."

"Really? Good," he said.

"I want to change first, though, not sit in a wet bathing suit."

"Good idea. We can meet in the lobby in . . . how long?"

"Twenty minutes." She turned.

"Wait."

She turned back with her eyebrows raised.

He said, "You're not just getting rid of me, right?"

"Don't be clingy. I say what I mean." She walked toward the doors, which slid aside to admit her.

Elle went upstairs, took the bathing suit off in the shower, and rinsed the chlorine out of it, out of her hair, and off her skin. As she dressed, she thought. He was handsome and in some kind of post-athletic shape caused by working long, hard hours with — and on — big animals and doing heavy chores for years. And he was smart, which was probably why television producers had considered him a find. Or they hadn't and didn't exist except in the story he used to pick up women. She was aware that nearly all women except her would see the two possibilities as opposites, good and bad.

For her, such distinctions were not so unambiguous. If he really was just a nice Canadian cowboy about to fall into an acting career, that would be fine. But if he was a con man smart enough to fool her and attract her at the same time, he would be rarer and more interesting. For now, she thought, he wasn't asking much. He was attracted to her and wanted to spend an hour with her. She didn't see that as an offense.

And Elle had a criminal's tendency to examine every situation for the possible advantages it might yield for her. She was trying to stay out of sight and safe for the longest time possible. He was about to buy her a treat on a day when she hadn't eaten much, spend some time indoors with her away from the sight of enemies, and provide some human interaction that might help her morale.

Elle didn't believe in being late just to give a man a chance to think about what a prize she was. She put some makeup on in a practical, efficient three-minute application, went to the elevator, and descended.

He was waiting for her in an armchair positioned so he could see the elevator door slide open. He wore pressed pants, a polo shirt, and wingtip shoes. He looked so neat and put-together that he seemed to be a visitor from another era, not just another country. He strode toward her. When they met he was grinning.

She said, "I wasn't expecting the urban fashion model look."

"I thought this would be better than jeans and boots."

"You were right. Where are we drinking our tea?"

"Right over there." He pointed across the lobby at a short hallway ending in a door. "You said you'd had enough sun, so I thought we'd skip the patio."

In the restaurant they let the hostess take them to a table. It was near the glass wall, but in a shadow so they could look outside without glare. When the hostess had taken their order for tea, sandwiches, and pastries and left, he said, "Do you mind if I sit next to you instead of across?" and patted the place to his left. "Right here?"

"It's fine," she said. "But if anything touches my thigh besides my napkin you're a dead man."

"I'll keep that in mind," he said, and slid to the next chair.

"So," she said. "I'm Annie McDowell. Who are you?"

"Tim Marshall. I'm sorry I forgot my manners and didn't introduce myself first thing. I was in kind of a hurry to keep you from running off."

"You've said you were sorry three times

so far. Do you do that a lot?"

"Canadians do, I think. But while I'm here I'll try not to do anything that requires an apology."

"You're doing very well," she said. "So tell me about your new career. Are they asking you to do anything, or just to hang around and wait?"

"This morning I went to a meeting in an office in that building over there at the bottom of the hill."

"White or black?"

"White."

"That's good," she said. "It's the producers' building. The black one is for the suits."

"How do you know?"

"I worked there as a temp once, years ago. Both buildings."

"How long?"

"About two weeks each. There was a flu epidemic and I could type and spell. You might say I saved Hollywood."

"But you left. You didn't like the work?"

"It wasn't that. I got the flu, probably from a dirty keyboard, and not long after that I left L.A. to go back to New York."

"Oh."

She had actually done the job she described, but there had been no flu epidemic. She had been doing research. Clerical employees at big companies had access to private information. Nearly all of it was accessible from the computer at the desk of each person she replaced. She had no trouble finding passwords scribbled on pieces of paper in drawers.

She had compiled a list of the names and addresses of a large number of well-paid employees and contractual free agents who worked behind the camera and were not famous enough to need professional security teams at their homes. She also made lists of casts and crews working on movie and television projects that would be shooting overseas. Her information had remained useful for a few months, but projects ended and people moved on to others.

"I did learn a few things," she said. "You should make up your mind quickly if you want to do this. You won't get another shot at it when you're fifty and get tired of playing with your horses."

They talked for a time about his life in Canada and his possible new career. She liked him, so she encouraged him and gave him advice about living in Los Angeles. At no point did she ever forget that he might be a con man and not a cowboy, but she knew that her best strategy in either case was to appear to believe him. If he was a cowboy from Calgary he could use her help. If he was a con man he would know her advice was sound, and he would not have reason to guess she was anything but what she said she was.

When the check came she let him take it and noted the number of the room he put on the signature slip. When he closed the leather folder she said, "I'd better get going. Thank you very much for teatime."

He said, "Don't go so soon. I could talk to you all day."

"You could, but you shouldn't, and I shouldn't. Get up and move around." She focused on something across the restaurant. "That girl with the big earrings from the pool is looking your way. She sees you're with another woman, so she knows you're not violent or boring. And she changed the earrings."

"I'm not interested in her," he said.

"You will be when you get a closer look."

She didn't wait for an answer, just walked quickly to the elevator and rode it to the twelfth floor. After she was in her room she opened her laptop and tried looking up Tim Marshall on Google. There were dozens of Tim Marshalls, maybe hundreds. She spent some time scrolling down the list but didn't find one who was likely to be this one.

Either they didn't live in Canada or they were doctors or professors or businessmen. She knew it didn't mean anything — she wasn't on Google either.

She had spent enough time thinking about Tim Marshall. He had been a distraction for an hour or so and helped her to stop thinking about Sharon every second. But a man — probably the killer — had attacked her after Sharon's funeral today. She couldn't call the police, and she couldn't get help from anyone she knew. She was alone. If she was going to survive, she would have to find out who the enemy was. The evening had almost begun, and it was time to get moving.

Elle drove to Burbank Airport and exchanged her rented Audi for a silver Toyota Camry, because when she scanned the rental lot, the Camry seemed to be the most different from the black Audi her attacker had seen.

11

Elle drove her rental car to the street where the Pity was located, pulled to the curb a distance away, and sat there looking. The red neon sign above the door must have been brighter when all the letters still worked, but that had probably been before she was born. The surviving four letters illuminated only the few feet below the sign in a dim red glow. The city streetlamps nearby were old, dirty, and too far apart to light the sidewalks.

She looked at the cars in the parking lot, studied the people going into and coming out of the plain one-story stucco building, and then moved her gaze to the cars parked on the street like hers, away from the lot. She sat unmoving, trying to pick out anything unusual — people watching the place, or anything that might be a police vehicle. It was difficult, but eventually she was satisfied.

She got out and went through the parking lot to the back, where she was out of any overhead light and could see anyone sitting in a car watching for her. Judging from the number of cars in the lot, she decided there were more people than usual in the Pity tonight.

She went in the back door to the T-shaped corridor that led on one side to the kitchen and on the other to the restrooms. She was acutely aware of the positions and angles of the three security cameras in the Pity. The one in the hallway she was moving along now would retain only a view of the back of her head. She would stay away from the cash register at the end of the bar where the second camera was. The third one was aimed at the front door to catch people coming in, and it wouldn't see her face.

She saw Desiree tending bar again with Ron Gillespie, one of the relief bartenders who worked a couple of nights a week. She nodded at both of them before she went to the table where Ricki the model sat alone. "Are you waiting for somebody?"

"I'm always waiting for somebody, and it's usually a waste of time. Sit with me and you'll see."

"Okay." Elle pulled herself up onto the tall seat.

"I saw you at Sharon's funeral," said Ricki. "It was a truly shitty occasion."

"Yes, it was," said Elle. "I missed seeing you there. Or anywhere. How have you been?"

"You know my life, L," said Ricki. "I'm a huge success. I'm making plenty of money to eat, but I can't, because I won't be skinny anymore and I'll stop making so much money. I should be a character in Greek mythology."

"Isn't there a character like that?"

"No, I checked. The Greeks didn't think skinny was a good thing."

Elle went with the obvious. "You're looking great."

"I know." Ricki leaned on both elbows and rested her chin on her fists. "Did you ever connect with the three people who were looking for you?"

"What did they look like?"

"Two men in bad suits with bad haircuts. A blond woman about as tall as I am and thin, wearing tight black pants and a leather jacket, also tight. Not a good one. I hope I'm not insulting people you like."

"I don't know them. Did they talk to you?"

"No," said Ricki. "I'm not very friendly."

"If they approach you, please don't talk to them. I think they're cops."

"I do too," Ricki said.

"If you see them again will you tell me?"

"Sure. Watching people breaks up the time while I'm waiting for somebody." She tapped Elle's arm and stared across the room. "That's them."

Elle glanced in the direction of the front door and then slid off her tall seat. "Thanks, Ricki." She moved off without looking back and headed for the hallway. When she got there she went into the kitchen, edging past the cooks along the stainless steel tables to the door that led outside. It was propped open tonight because the kitchen was hot.

She was outside in a moment and trotted across the street and down the sidewalk under the trees to her Camry, got in, and put the key into the ignition, but didn't start the engine.

She was pretty sure that the three were making the rounds of the places where some informant had told them she would eventually appear. They would see she wasn't in the Pity and wait for a bit to see if she might show up, but when she didn't they'd move on to the next bar or club.

In fifteen minutes the three emerged from the front of the building and walked to a black Chevrolet Tahoe parked along the curb. Everything on the car that was usually chrome was black except for a border around the black grille and the inch-high TAHOE on the side. She started her engine and waited for them to get ahead and make the right turn onto Hollywood Boulevard.

The traffic everywhere was sluggish, and at times jammed. She could see that the crowds on the boulevard were still growing well after midnight. The men all seemed to be in black tonight. They wore dark pants with black jackets or T-shirts or pullovers, but the women tonight were wearing dresses, most of them light-colored and maybe too nice for the sweat and noise and press of the crowds. They made the men look like shadows passing among flowers.

The black Tahoe was doing just what Elle did, drifting in the right lane close to the sidewalk. Elle kept her passenger-side window open only three inches — just enough so she could hear the music, the yells from one person to another on the sidewalk, sometimes even make out a few words, but nobody could reach in and open the door. The club music sounded like a big machine that was pumping something through pipes beyond the open doorways. The noise didn't begin or end, it just continued, the pounding rhythmic bass notes loud enough to thump and rumble.

She kept her eyes flicking from the street to the black Tahoe and back, trying to keep noticing everything. She kept watching for the Tahoe to do what cop cars did, to pull in front of the red curb at the corner, or even up over it, and leave the car there with lights blinking while the cops investigated their suspect or witness or doughnut. That would have confirmed that they were cops. But they kept driving, which confirmed nothing.

She dropped two cars back and then let another car in ahead of her so that the people in the Tahoe wouldn't get interested in her. There were no floodlights on the Tahoe that she had seen; there was no sign of a computer or radio equipment, no extra hardware near the dashboard, no steel reinforcement on the front bumper.

She followed the Tahoe until it turned off Hollywood at Highland Avenue. She pulled out of line to go after it, but a nearby testosterone overproducer had seen the maneuver, tried to imitate it, and nearly hit her car. The driver leaned on his horn to punish her while she pulled the rest of the way out and moved off, but she had taken her eyes off the Tahoe and it was gone.

She turned right and sped up, weaving through the traffic and then straddling the double yellow line in the center for a block. At each intersection she glanced in both directions to scan for the Tahoe. She ran a red light at De Longpre Avenue, then tried it again at Fountain and narrowly missed a white pickup truck, but made it through and kept going.

The Tahoe was visible ahead of her now and just turning right. It kept going west until La Cienega Boulevard and then turned south again. The upper end of La Cienega was lined with restaurants that were mostly closing down at this hour, so the traffic was steady but not heavy. She pulled into the right lane behind a Mustang with black matte paint and dark tinted glass, but after a couple of blocks she realized the Mustang was too fast and was about to overtake the Tahoe. She watched it pull ahead and pass, and then she moved into the left lane to fall in behind a truck. She dropped back a few extra feet to watch the empty right lane and the empty left turn lane so the Tahoe couldn't make a turn without her noticing.

She was beginning to believe she knew the general area of their destination. La Cienega was the preferred route to Los Angeles International Airport when the San Diego Freeway wasn't moving. She let the Tahoe have more of a lead and kept watching for turns.

If the people in the Tahoe were police homicide detectives, why would they be going way down there? Kavanagh's house was up in Beverly Hills. Maybe the LAPD had been called in to help. There were also little pockets near Beverly Hills that were policed by the Sheriff's Department. Maybe these three were sheriff's detectives. Either way, they looked like cops and they acted like cops.

She drove past the zones of cheaper restaurants and windowless clubs, then the zones of car sales and repair, and then general manufacturing, and, finally, storage and shipping.

It was a surprise when the Tahoe turned to the right before the traffic sped up and got funneled into the approaches to the airport. The vehicle moved along the dark highway, then went into a driveway and up to a white, windowless single-story building about 150 feet long. It pulled around the back of the building out of sight.

Elle tapped her brake pedal, then admitted to herself that stopping would be insane, so she kept going, staring as she coasted past. Nothing was visible except pavement and white wall, but once she passed the building, her mirror reflected the headlights of the Tahoe as it parked at the end of a row of four identical Tahoes. That was all she saw before the next few buildings blocked her view.

If they were cops, they were a strange unit. They didn't have what she would have called a station. It was like a depot or a warehouse.

She allowed herself to follow the signs to the airport, around the oval, out to Sepulveda Boulevard, and up to the northbound entrance to the San Diego Freeway. She made good time all the way up to the San Fernando Valley and then along the 101 Freeway to her hotel.

12

Elle woke in the afternoon and lay in the darkness that was preserved behind the opaque curtains. She reviewed everything that had happened before she had slept. It was two before she was ready to drive to Burbank Airport and change rental cars again. This time she selected a Nissan Altima that was approximately the color of a year-old L.A. pavement — charcoal gray with a thin coating of dust. She drove back to the hotel, gave it to the valets to park, and went upstairs to begin her research.

The three detectives — if that was what they were — had given away their place of business. That was a small bit of progress. She supposed they might have been searching for her to charge her with some simple burglary she had committed and forgotten, but most likely they were trying to find out what she knew about the triple murder. So far she knew nothing but what she had seen on the recording. That was a problem.

She had devoted much of her energy to staying out of danger but had taken no real precautions, and her efforts had led the killer to Sharon. Elle's own stupid overconfidence would haunt her forever. It didn't make her feel better to suspect that one of her other friends or acquaintances had probably sold out both of them.

This afternoon she felt clearheaded. Sharon and Peter had not been killed for anything having to do with them. They were killed because Elle had stumbled on the murders in Beverly Hills. That meant Sharon's murder was not something that could be solved directly, because the motive and the killer were from the first murders. The best thing for Elle to do right now was not to run away and hide from the killer for a few months. It was to find out everything she could about the first killing, the murder of the three strangers, and make sure the killer got caught.

She had a laptop, but she didn't have a printer with her, or a drive, so she decided to see if she could use the hotel's equipment for the moment.

Elle went down to the hotel business center, where there were computers sitting idle in a quiet glass-walled room. She picked one and began to search for entries on the triple murder. She had read a bit about the three victims in the newspapers, so she decided to turn her attention to the two husbands. In her opinion they were the ones most likely to be feeling ill-used enough to shoot anybody. If they hadn't known the kind of thing their wives were up to, that wouldn't be true, but they were the place to start.

The husband of the blond woman, Anne Satterthwaite Mannon, came first. His name was David and he owned two restaurants that almost rhymed, Muzu and Bissou. She had read that before. To Elle one sounded like Japanese and one like French, but Google Translate said Bissou was a Maltese word but didn't offer to translate it, and Muzu was a word that didn't seem to mean anything in any language. Maybe they were both proper names. Or maybe they were worse, nicknames or pet names. They told her nothing except that whoever had named them was being cute. She had no proof, but she suspected it was Anne.

Elle maintained her patience. She had never had much affection for rich, spoiled people, and these were prime examples. But they had already paid the highest price for everything they'd ever done.

She clicked to open the web page for the restaurants. On the Bissou page there were photographs of a dining room with rough stone walls, a fireplace that was itself the size of a small room, and a polished bar that was long and glossy enough to skate on. The caption said the stone came from the walls of a ruined monastery in Greece. The furniture was heavily polished wood — also from southern Europe — and the menu was full of dishes from the Mediterranean.

There were pictures of Anne the blonde in a black dress with a décolletage that seemed to run nearly to her navel. There was a large silver cross hanging from a chain and resting over her sternum. Beside her was a man with curly dark hair wearing a tuxedo and smiling so his perfect teeth, white as a bathtub, were on full display. Surrounding the pair were people who seemed to be more friends than customers. Elle thought she recognized a couple of television actresses. The men all looked rich and a bit older.

She studied the husband, David, closely, enlarging his image. He was handsome and looked good-natured. She asked herself if this could be the man who had shot his wife and two friends. She studied his face, but looking at him told her nothing. Men got jealous, flew into rages, and killed their wives. He could be another. She had not seen the face of the man on the tape, and this was the first time she'd seen David Mannon.

Elle left the site and tried to Google Anne Mannon. She scrolled past all the entries about the murder, which seemed to be versions of the same story she had already read. There was a Facebook page about her. Anne Satterthwaite had been born in Middlebury, Connecticut, in 1983. She was a member of the Bryn Mawr Alumnae Association. She had graduated in 2005 with a major in art history.

Elle was pretty sure she smelled two kinds of money — the kind parents got from their parents and the kind that ambitious young men brought home. The parents were both professors of ancient languages at Wesleyan University. That meant there were at least two generations of very expensive educations with no potential for producing real money. That was a sign that the Satterthwaites had some already. But the restaurants came from the hardworking young man.

Two pictures caught Elle's eye — one of Anne at college age with very long blond hair and looking better than anyone else in the group shot, and the other of her at age thirty-four, looking the same except this time with a $600 haircut and some tasteful diamonds — no flashy settings, but big stones.

Then Elle fell into the rest of the cache of photographs — beautiful children, one male named Cole and one female named Phoebe. Elle's heart was torn. The two kids were left without a mother. Everyone had looked so happy — the wife, the husband, the kids.

Elle pulled herself back and tried to forestall any judgments for the moment. Right now she was gathering information, and she would limit herself to that. She felt sorry for the children. She had grown up knowing she was the daughter of a woman who could never be of any help because she had died in a stupid way. She pressed print and began to pluck the pages out of the tray.

"Hi. I figured you'd be here."

She spun her head to see the Canadian cowboy, Tim Marshall, a few feet behind her. "Hi, Tim." Her eyes shot to the side as her hand kept picking up pages. "What brings a thespian cowpoke like you into this workshop of global commerce?"

"I was looking for you, and you happened to be in a place with glass walls, so you weren't too hard to find."

"I wasn't expecting anybody to try."

"Are you going back to New York?"

"What makes you think that?"

"You were printing. Whenever I see people at hotel computers that's what they're doing — printing boarding passes."

"Not me," she said. "Just some work."

"Are you one of those people who don't like to talk about their work?"

"Yes. Some of it is confidential and all of it is boring." The printer stopped and she snatched the last three pages, slid them into her bag, pushed the door open, and held it. "You coming?"

"Sure."

He followed her out and along the corridor toward the elevator. Elle went past it to the stairs and began to descend.

"There's an elevator right here," he said.

"I know."

"Are you claustrophobic?" He followed her onto the steps.

She looked surprised. "You've seen me take the elevator to my room at least twice."

"To your room, sure. That's the twelfth floor. You didn't have much choice. It's too far to climb."

"How do you know that's my floor?"

"You were alone in the elevator when you went up to change yesterday. The lighted number above the elevator shows the floor."

She squinted. "Not all women like quite so much close attention."

"This is where we started," he said. "You telling me not to look at you."

"I think I just said you'd be happier if you spread your attention around. I still think that."

"Now that you've got your business done, would you do me a favor?"

"Probably not," she said. "What is it?"

"A little help and advice," he said. "They — the producers — sent a messenger over here this morning to deliver some sides. You know what those are?"

"A couple of pages of dialogue they give you to read so you can demonstrate your acting ability. I guess you're going to a casting session."

"I've never done this before. Would you help me go through my lines?"

"How?"

"You read the part of the other actor and tell me when I sound like an idiot or look terrible."

She noticed he'd found a pretty good way of manipulating a woman. There was nobody who would root for him like someone who had invested time and effort in him. She was busy, and she wasn't looking for male attention, but maybe the best way was to help him and then move on quickly.

"Where?"

He said, "I don't know. I didn't see anybody else in the business center, and it seemed to be soundproof."

"Okay. Let's get started."

They went back into the business center, found a small conference room with a table and eight chairs, and sat down.

Tim's sides consisted of a scene from what seemed to be a detective drama. She said, "I thought they wanted you for a reality show."

"They didn't say why," he said. "I figure there are about twenty actors who know how to act for every job, so I doubt they need me, but . . ." He shrugged.

She didn't want to tell him the truth, that there were closer to twenty thousand qualified actors for every job. "Maybe they just want to hear your speaking voice." She looked at the sheets. "You get the first line."

His eyes rose. "Mrs. McCutcheon, I'm very sorry about your loss."

"He was a good man," Elle read. "He always treated me right. We weren't rich, but that didn't matter to me."

"Do you have any idea who might have done this to him?"

"I can't imagine. Everybody loved Jonathan."

Tim said, "I heard that he had a fight downtown a couple of weeks ago with a man named Gerhardt. Did he say what the fight was about?"

The scene went on for two pages and ended with a revelation. Tim said, "The one person at the dinner with your husband who could have dropped the pistol into the milk pitcher was also the one who took the pitcher back into the kitchen — you."

If this was typical of the scripts, Elle wasn't optimistic about the longevity of the show. But the two pages had been typed according to the standard format she had seen during her brief time as a temp, so it seemed real enough.

They went over the lines again. "Too fast," she said. "Talk more slowly and evenly in the first part. You're a cop. All business, with just a hint that you're sympathetic and understand what she's going through." When he tried again she said, "You're looser now, but don't be too friendly with her."

After four tries, she said, "I think you've got it."

"Really?"

"Yes. If you want to do it one more time, I will. But you don't want to get stale."

He took back the sides. "Then thank you very much for your help. I'll thank you again from the stage the night they give me the best actor award."

"I'll be sure not to miss it," she said.

"Will you go to dinner with me?"

"I don't go out much on work nights," she said. "Too much to do."

"You can't make an exception?"

"I don't get paid to make exceptions," she said. "And I need to get paid. Sorry."

"Have you ever eaten at the restaurant at the Getty Museum?"

She felt startled. Was he a museum rat too? "I haven't been there in a few visits. I like it, but I'm tied up tonight. Thanks anyway. Have a good night." She went to the elevator and retreated to her room. She had waited long enough to go look at the homes of the victims. The police would be finished with their examination, and now it was her turn.

She had left the R9 pistol in the safe in her closet because she didn't want it lying around where the maids might see it. Now she took it out, checked the load, wiped it carefully to remove any prints, and put it and a spare magazine in the belly band. She selected the tools she would take with her from the kit she had in her suitcase. She chose only a few, and they were all light and compact: a pair of wire cutters and a length of thin, strong wire; her sharp, spring-assisted pocketknife; her ring of bump keys; a lockpick and a tension wrench; a lipstick-size touch-up can of auto spray paint. She inserted fresh batteries in her compact flashlight. She put everything in the fanny pack's zippered pockets so she could find the tools in the dark and they wouldn't jangle against one another if she ran. She packed three pairs of surgical gloves.

She looked out her twelfth-floor window at the night sky. She would not have to contend with a bright moon tonight. It was growing, but it was still a thin crescent like a fingernail clipping. She gazed down at the cars on the freeway to judge the level of traffic to expect on her drive. It wouldn't do to pull off a break-in and end up stalled in traffic. But the stream of cars was already beginning to thin out after the evening drive, and she wouldn't be leaving for hours.

She opened her computer and double-checked the addresses of the two houses. She looked at the satellite view of each of them, then the street views, and then expanded to parallel streets and cross streets looking for obstacles and opportunities. She kept pulling outward until her view encompassed many acres of the most expensive real estate in Southern California.

What she needed to do was determine whether it would be possible tonight to pay a visit to these neighborhoods without being photographed or arrested. After some study, she believed it would be possible if she didn't draw unusual attention to herself. Both neighborhoods seemed to have outlasted the sudden attention of the media, and the triple murder wasn't the sort of crime that anybody else had to fear. There wouldn't be police out watching for the next naked triple homicide.

Elle supposed that the police must be doing something to keep track of both husbands, but by now they were most likely working backward through phone and computer records, financial records, and interviews with friends and relatives. If anything was wired, bugged, or tracked, it would probably be the husband's cars.

She turned her attention to Santo Teason. She checked IMDB and the online ghosts of the trade papers to get an idea of his career as a director. He had a long résumé as a director of television episodes and films that sounded minor, most of them in Europe. But he also had made six American movies that she hadn't seen but were important enough to have Google entries of their own. He was supposedly signed to direct a feature remake of Robert Graves's *I, Claudius* in Rome sometime this year. How the demise of Valerie McGee Teason would affect that was not yet being discussed online, but she guessed he would be in Los Angeles most of the time for the moment. He had three kids who had lost their mother.

13

When it was after midnight, Elle dressed in dark work clothes, took the elevator to the second floor, and then took the stairs to the first. At the end of the hall she came to a doorway that led outside to the courtyard by the pool, then circled the hotel to the front of the building where the parking attendants were stationed. Her gray Altima was at her feet in two minutes, and she was on her way to Beverly Hills.

David Mannon seemed to be the best bet for her first visit. He was a chef who owned and ran two restaurants. A restaurant was the sort of business that required attention. If you didn't show up in person nearly every day you wouldn't have one anymore. There was no notice online that either restaurant was temporarily closed, and the reservation lines were still live. It had been over a week since the murders, so there was a good chance he wasn't still spending every night at home. Even if he was out, though, the two kids and whoever took care of them were likely to be there, so she would have to be cautious.

When she reached his address she drove past slowly. The house was behind an iron fence, set back on a lawn at the top of a slight rise. It had two stories, but the ceilings were high, so it seemed taller than that. There were no signs of police cars or other threats that she could see on the street. She parked a block away and walked back to the house.

She spent a few minutes studying and watching, trying to find a reason not to break in. She didn't detect one, so she pulled a ski mask over her head, climbed the ivied wall at the edge of the property, dropped to the lawn, and sneaked into the shrubbery close to the house. She crouched there studying the parts of the house that had been hidden before — the ground near the foundation and then the space up under the eaves, where she spotted the first security camera.

Elle came up on it with her back nearly touching the side of the house to keep the camera aimed outward away from her. She followed the insulated wire that ran from it to the next camera and the next, until she reached a small circuit box attached to the side of the building. She elected to disconnect the wire from the box rather than disconnecting the box from the power, because she didn't want to turn off all power to the place. Every alarm system she knew had a backup battery that sent an alarm signal if the AC power died. She stepped along the side of the house to the back, looking for more cameras and disconnecting them.

In a modern house belonging to a rich family there was no longer a way to be sure that the security cameras had all been disabled. Many systems had cameras in difficult-to-see places and even had some cameras in plain sight that were disguised to look like other things — light fixtures, doorbells, mailboxes. She carried a small can of automotive spray paint in case she needed to blind a camera lens.

She had noticed when she'd seen the house's image on Google Street View that along the side of the foundation there were small horizontal windows, partially obscured behind low plants. There must be a basement. Elle put her face close to one of the windows, shone her flashlight in to verify her impression, and saw a laundry room with two washers and two dryers. She moved along the foundation from window to window. Through the next one was a folding and ironing room. A few windows farther on was a workshop. It had shelves of tools, lightbulbs of various types, transparent boxes of screws, nails, fasteners, and hinges, and a workbench with a vise. There were cans of paint that had been opened and re-shut, and she was sure that if she made it upstairs she would see those colors again on walls up there.

She suspected that the owners probably never went down to the basement. A man with a couple of restaurants didn't have time to be a handyman too, and Anne Mannon had not struck Elle as much of a housewife. Judging from the photographs she seemed to have served the restaurants as a hostess.

She turned her flashlight to study the nearest window. Each basement window was about two and a half feet wide and about a foot and a half high. Each was locked by a latch consisting of a metal lever with a short hook on the fulcrum end that slid under a metal holder. She moved to a corner so she could shine her light through one window and examine the inner wall set perpendicular to it. There were no wires running over the concrete to the basement windows. That meant the windows weren't on the alarm system.

Elle moved from window to window trying to insert her knife's blade between the frame and the pane, or to find a window that had not been properly latched from inside. In the end she had to use a length of the bare steel wire she had brought.

She bent the wire into a curve and inserted the tip between the metal rim of the window and the frame. She fed the curved wire inside and pushed until it came back out past the catch. Then she rotated the wire into a loop over the catch, twisted the wire around itself several times to tighten it, and then gave it a sharp jerk to the right to pull the catch free. When she saw the handle come up, she inserted the blade of her knife and pulled the window outward.

She knew that the size and shape of the windows had been selected on the assumption that an intruder couldn't slither in. It was a tight fit even for Elle. She slid her feet in and lowered herself onto the workbench and then looked around her. For the moment she decided not to search for anything specific but to be alert for anything odd or out of place. Her general goal was to figure out whether David Mannon had killed his wife and her friends, and the evidence could be something she'd never anticipated.

She was pretty sure that the police had immediately searched both husbands' houses for the gun and the silencer. But there were other things that might turn up, and she might be better at finding them than the police had been. If she could find signs that David had been spying on his wife, or searching her computer or phone, or recording her calls, or hiring other people to follow, tape, or investigate her, then Elle would know that he had mistrusted her. Anything, in fact, that showed he'd been paying attention to her but not liking what he learned would make him a suspect.

Elle could see staircases at either end of the basement. She chose to climb the steps that were nearest to the rear of the house. They emerged in a hallway that was part of the kitchen complex. There was a walk-in pantry on one side and a set of six cupboards, each the size of a house door, on the other. She could see that the kitchen was large, about forty by twenty feet, with two eight-burner gas stoves, three big Sub-Zero refrigerators, two end-to-end islands separated only to produce a shortcut from one side to the other, and counters and sinks. Few restaurants anywhere had kitchens as well finished and equipped.

She opened a couple of the refrigerators to see if the kitchen was real or ornamental. The first one held champagne and white wines served chilled, so she wasn't sure. But the others held perishable food: chickens, steaks, cheeses, eggs, vegetables.

Elle's mental clock reminded her to move on. The dining room was about what she expected after the kitchen. There was a very long wooden table that looked as though it had been made from a plank cut from a giant tree. The chairs were the kind of design that artists rather than factories made, but she couldn't identify which one had made these. They were in a modern Italian style that involved buttery leather over a chrome skeleton. The wall on her left had a long window with open shades, and the wall on the right had what looked like a panoramic color photograph. She turned her flashlight on it to verify that it was a photorealist painting.

The painting was a family scene on a white beach with a vast expanse of blue sea and tame surf. David was visible off to the right, barefoot, wearing white shorts, an untucked and half-buttoned blue-and-white short-sleeved shirt, and a hat that looked like an inverted bucket. The two blond kids were in the foreground, but the central figure was their mother, a laughing blond Anne running toward the viewer wearing a small red bikini. It was this bit of bright color that somehow made the rest of the picture work.

Elle hurried on. The house was obviously cleaned and cared for by servants, and she hadn't either located them or determined that they weren't the live-in variety. She thought about the decor of the house. Usually it was the wife who had the biggest opinion, and Anne's taste was good. The house was full of things like the big beach mural that made the place more human and personal. Maybe the husband had commissioned the painting, but Elle had also noticed that if there had been a divorce it would have been possible to paint over one figure, the husband, without ruining the composition.

Superb photographs of the family were everywhere in the public areas of the house. Frames held the four Mannons on ski slopes, in sailboats, in antique speedboats with shiny varnished wood, on bikes in a redwood forest. Since the entire family was represented in each, Elle had to assume they had been staged and taken by a pro. Maybe the family had a talented photographer friend who always went with them on their vacations.

It seemed to Elle that everything in this house was too perfect, evidence of the family's conspiracy to create an unreal impression on a visitor. It was as though Anne had been trying to get the kids into a fancy private school and known that admission really amounted to letting the family in. Look at how loving and wholesome we are. Here's the doting, patient husband, and here are the smart, athletic, attractive kids. And everything about us says "money." But above all, look at Mom. Won't she be something buttonholing donors for the campus building fund?

If David had been the man with the pistol and the silencer, they were probably long gone. But if there was any evidence he wanted to keep close to him, it would be in the master suite, so Elle went upstairs.

She easily followed the flow of the house along the upstairs hallway past four nicely furnished but unoccupied bedroom-and-bath suites, and then the two bedroom suites of the kids, and then a playroom that had been updated and redone as a study room, and then an office. The kids were not in their rooms. She felt intense relief. David had taken them somewhere.

The door of the master suite was at the

end of the hall. She could tell that the study and office had been placed to provide soundproofing between the kids' areas and the parents' area. She knew that people who owned restaurants were up late and probably slept late.

Elle had still found no bedrooms that might belong to servants. If there were any, they must be in a wing off the kitchen that she had missed or in a detached building behind the house.

As she moved to the master suite Elle had doubts. David might be somewhere with his kids, but there was no guarantee that he hadn't left them with relatives and stayed here by himself. And David might be a decent man who had just lost both his wife and the illusions that had made him care about her, or he might be a serial killer who had murdered five people so far.

She knelt on the floor and crawled close to the door. She put her ear to the wooden surface but could not hear anything. She tried the knob and found that it turned. She pushed the door inward, staying low. She ventured to stand so she could see a bit in the dim light.

The huge bed was made; the room had been straightened and left with nothing out of place, and it was unoccupied. Elle checked the clock on the stand by the bed. It was 1:08 A.M. David could still be out at one of his restaurants, or he could have taken his kids somewhere to help them get past the first shock of their mother's death, away from strangers' prying questions. Either way, the best thing she could do was to begin exploring the master suite.

The first closet was full of men's suits and sport coats on shaped wooden hangers, pants with their creases knife-sharp, the dress shirts starched and pressed and the informal ones soft or silky. He had more shoes than any man she'd ever met, and everything in the drawers had been folded by experts and stored in stacks. She ran her hands along the bottoms and backs of all the drawers but found nothing. When she had done a good search she moved on to the next closet.

This was even bigger. This was Anne's closet. It appeared to have been gone over — looted, really. Every garment left was either new with tags still on it or encased in a dry cleaner's plastic bag. Nothing in the closet had been worn. There was a clothes hamper, but there was nothing in it. If Elle could have come right after the murders, maybe she would have seen something, but not now.

Elle returned to the husband's closet. His hamper had some dirty clothes in it. Anne's clothes seemed to have been wrapped as evidence and moved somewhere as part of the investigation. The cops were probably having them, her car, and her other belongings checked for DNA and hairs and fibers. It was a logical thing to do to establish any ongoing relationships, and it made Elle feel better that the police were trying. And they would not have done anything like that except as part of a general search of the house that would have turned up anything obvious, like a gun with a silencer. She had never heard of cops doing that to a whole wardrobe, but what did Elle know about cops? Her life had been free of arrests.

There were two master bathrooms. She searched David's bathroom and found only the usual things — soap, shampoo, shaving kit, deodorant, toothpaste, and electric toothbrush. Men seemed to be happiest when they owned nothing, and this was close. None of the things in Anne's bathroom would seem suspicious at first glance either: bottles of expensive perfume, scented lotions, hair products, soaps. The towels were fluffy and new, and the bathrobes were either thick like the towels or silky and clingy. The mirrors were floor to ceiling except over the sink. The medicine cabinet had not been stripped of prescription medicines, but the only ones that didn't have one of the kids' names were the birth control pills.

Elle searched the usual sorts of hiding places — vents with scratches on the screws because they'd been unscrewed and opened, the backs of cupboards, the toilet tank, and the spaces under shelves, sinks, cabinets, and drawers. She found nothing.

She opened a drawer at the bottom of the vanity and found spares: extra brushes for Anne's electric toothbrush, unopened mouthwash, toothpaste, tampons, a box of condoms that had been opened and from which a few of the individual packets had been removed. She turned on her flashlight. The label said CONTAINS NO LATEX. The expiration date was five years in the future.

Elle went back to the bedroom and looked in the nightstands on both sides. She opened every drawer and found no more condoms. She lay on the floor with her flashlight and looked under the bed. She had already searched both closets. There were no condoms anywhere else.

There was a noise. Elle judged it had come from the far end of the house where the kitchen was. She began to move. Her profession had taught her not to react the way other people did, which was to freeze and listen for the sound to be repeated to authenticate the noise, locate it, and interpret it. She was moving fast. There was no interpretation of the noise that would make staying where she was a wise idea. There was no need to waste time choosing directions either. There were stairways on both ends of the house, and she headed down the nearest one, off the bedroom hallway.

In a moment she was down the stairs to the basement. She had gone up the other stairway the first time, so when she arrived now she almost ran into the big pool table. She could just tell in the dim light that this area had been outfitted as a poolroom, with a set of cues in a frame on the wall above leather benches and a large light suspended above the table. The balls had been left out on the felt surface in the rack as though a game had been about to start. The cue ball was at the near end of the table, and as she ran past she snatched it up. Above her head she could hear heavy footsteps on the first floor. Someone seemed to be stalking through the house to find her.

She ducked into the maintenance room, climbed onto the workbench, and slithered out the window where she had entered. She pushed it shut, then moved out a few feet from the house. She reared back and threw the cue ball high above the roof, aiming it so that it would arc downward to hit just beyond the crest of the roof toward the back of the house.

As she began to sprint, she heard the heavy cue ball hit, bounce, and then roll down the shingle roof, making a thump each time it rolled from one shingle down to the next. From the front of the house it sounded a bit like someone running along the roof to the back of the house. The lawn in front of the house was suddenly lighter. She looked back and saw that the living room lights had come on. She could see a man going from room to room turning other lights on. He wore a pistol on his hip over a black jumpsuit-like uniform. In the two seconds that the glance lasted she saw him pull the pistol from the holster and turn away from her toward a window that gave him a view of the backyard.

In two more seconds she was on the street, sprinting to the Nissan Altima she'd left around the corner. In ten more seconds, she was inside it, pulling away.

14

On the way back to the hotel Elle contemplated her visit to the Mannon house. The house had been intended to appear welcoming, a place for bringing relatives and friends together and for showing off. The enormous, fancy kitchen was there to celebrate the husband's profession, but it was also designed to feed a crowd fancy food. The rest of the house was full of pictures of all four Mannons together. But the big one in the dining hall was the tip-off. The room was all about her. The whole house was all about her, really. The kitchen was a trophy, showing she had won the famous restaurateur.

The house was her taste and her eye and celebrated her physical beauty and personality. Anne was the inspiration and the beautiful object and the designer and the connoisseur.

One detail Elle wondered about was the

birth control. Either you were taking precautions or you weren't. A woman might use birth control pills or an IUD, or her husband might wear condoms. What raised questions in Elle's mind was that she'd found two forms of birth control.

Elle's casual inspection of Anne's bathroom had indicated that she was using birth control pills. So why had there been condoms in the bottom drawer of the vanity? The box had been opened and some had been removed. Elle had looked in the two most likely places to find the missing condoms. Usually if a couple used them, they were kept in the nightstand on the man's side of the bed. If the couple considered the topic a little more erotic, the condoms might be on her side of the bed and she would put one on him. But there had been none anywhere in the bedroom. They were only in the box in her bathroom cupboard, in the bottom drawer, way at the back, where nobody but Anne was likely to find them.

Elle stopped the car on a dark street off Beverly Glen, changed into clothes that were comfortable and unambiguously female, bundled the others and put them in the trunk, and drove into the hills toward the Valley.

Elle wondered if Anne's cheating might have been habitual. In the video Anne had been going through the motions — not overcome by passion or caught at some moment of extreme vulnerability. The three of them had approached the subject of sex as though they were coaxing one another into accepting a high-calorie dessert. If you'll do it I'll do it.

Elle took out her phone, typed "shelf life of condoms," and waited. There were four or five answers visible on the screen at once. The shelf life was five years for standard types and three years for the ones with spermicide. The box she had found in Anne's bathroom was recently purchased. She could conclude only that Anne kept a supply of condoms for occasions when the man she was having sex with wasn't her husband. It was to keep her from coming home with an STD.

The close call Elle had experienced at the Mannon house made her decide not to take the extra risk of visiting the home of Santo Teason tonight. Her best strategy was to avoid the risks that she was too tired to take and to stay alive long enough to figure out who had killed the five people who were dead so far.

The hotel valet took her Altima and she

went inside. When she had taken five steps she saw that Tim Marshall was across the lobby inside the bar. He was sitting in a padded chair beside a small table. What was he doing drinking in a hotel bar alone at this hour? She didn't want to know. She looked the other way and walked faster.

As Elle moved across the lobby toward the elevator he spotted her and emerged as though he'd been waiting for her to return. "Annie!" he called. The lobby was quiet, so she heard him clearly. He headed her off while she was still twenty feet from the elevator, so she couldn't pretend she hadn't seen him. She said, "Are you staking me out for some reason?"

"I wasn't actually watching for you," said Tim. "I just happened to see you. I was about to have a drink in the bar before I go up to bed. It occurred to me that if you were finished with your work you might like one too."

She looked at him and admitted to herself that she had let the acquaintance go on too long without deciding what he was — a confidence man, somebody she might be able to use, or a Canadian cowboy about to get famous. She said, "I'm done. The least I can do is buy a round of drinks. Come on."

She strode ahead of him into the nearly

empty bar, stepped to the bartender, and said, "What's your best single-malt Scotch?"

"We have Talisker, Oban, Lagavulin, Laphroaig, Glenlivet, Glenfiddich, Macallan —"

"Let's try the Talisker," she said. She looked at Tim, then back at the bartender. "We'll each have three fingers of it." She held up her small hand. "Your fingers, not mine."

The bartender poured the two glasses, and she set a credit card on the bar and carried both drinks to the table where Tim had been sitting. As she returned to the bar to get her card and sign the bill, she watched Tim in the big mirror. If he was a con man or some other kind of criminal he might not be above putting a drug in her drink. But when she returned he was still standing by the table far from the glasses, waiting to pull out her chair. "Sit down," she said.

He sat, and she sat down in the chair beside him. "You like to sit next to the girl, right?"

"Right." He lifted his glass. "To ladies whose hearts are in the Highlands." He took a sip.

"Do you like that?" she asked, as though it were a test.

"I do," he said. "When it's late at night

and you're with a pretty woman, a single malt is like having a second friend at the table who's older and wiser and will disappear when you want him to."

She laughed. "Ancient Scottish wisdom?"

"We drink Scotch in Canada too."

"Have you started to miss Canada yet?"

"Not as much as I would have expected," he said. "When you think about it, you realize what you miss about home isn't there anymore. It's your younger days. I've always lived near Calgary. My parents moved to Edmonton when my dad retired, and my sister is in Vancouver. I see them on Christmas and Thanksgiving."

She said, "Thanksgiving, huh?" She had him. *Con man.*

"Yeah, Thanksgiving," he said. "We have Thanksgiving. It's the second Monday of October. Look it up."

She took out her phone and thumb-typed "Thanksgiving in Canada." There it was. And they even served turkey and pumpkin pie. "Good for you," she said. She meant the opposite. *Canadian cowboy.*

He shrugged. "Anyway, I do miss my family, and I miss the work I do. But this hasn't been a hard time for me. I expect to be thinking about it occasionally for the rest of my life."

"Why?"

"Because something happened. There are doors. Sometimes you recognize a door at the time but don't know what's beyond. This time is like that. I know that whatever is there, it's not like the side I've seen so far."

"You mean you'll be a star?"

"Not necessarily. Maybe you and I will get married and always look back on this as the time when everything changed."

She took a sip of Scotch and rested her chin on her fists. "This is quite a quick escalation, isn't it?" she said. "So when is our big day?"

"I don't know," he said. "We'll have to talk it over."

"We could plan it for Canadian New Year's or Canadian Fourth of July."

"I'm not sure what you're getting at."

"Just a question that keeps coming up in my mind."

"What's the question?"

She took another sip of Scotch. "I would like to know whether you are who you've said you are. If you are, that's fine. If you aren't, that might be pretty good too. You might be somebody who's even more interesting to me." She had said it as plainly as she could. "If that's the case, all you have to do is take a swig of that Scotch to get the strength and then say it, and I won't ask any more questions."

"I'm just who I've told you I was," he said. "If I were going to lie about it, I'd make up something more appealing than a guy who cleans horseshit off his boots. I'd say I'm rich and famous in Canada, but people in the United States aren't familiar with my name yet. I'm the genius inventor of a robot that does everything that people don't want to do — dive to twenty-three thousand feet, clean furnaces while they're fired up, deice the wings of a plane while it's flying. There probably is somebody just like that, and neither of us knows his name."

"Okay," she said. "I'll have to believe you're Tim Marshall the horse trainer turned actor. It's all I've got to work with." She finished her drink and set it down. "Meanwhile I'm off for a night's sleep."

"Want to see my passport?"

She shook her head. "If you didn't have something to show me you wouldn't offer. Like most people, I wouldn't know a Canadian passport from a French prayer book." She patted his arm. "The difference is that I know I wouldn't. Sleep tight." She started for the doorway.

"Will you go out to dinner with me tomorrow night?" he said. "I'm asking you well in advance so you'll get your work out of the way, and I promise it will be really special."

"Call me tomorrow. But not before noon." She walked across the lobby to the elevator and disappeared.

15

The next day he called her room telephone during the early afternoon as she was laying out her chosen outfit for breaking into Santo Teason's house that night. She looked at her watch. It was 1:30, comfortably later than when she had told him he could call, but not yet approaching the cutoff for being too late to call a person for the same night. She had to pick it up. "Hello," she said.

He spoke with a relentless cheerfulness without identifying himself. "I called some of the television people to ask for recommendations, and I heard about a really great dinner place. It's all the way up in Santa Barbara, but it's supposed to have the best food."

"The Ballard Inn," she said. "If we made it to Santa Barbara, that would still be a very long drive."

"A different place. It's called Sous les Arbres. It's new, and it's in the hills about five miles north of Santa Barbara City Hall."

"I come to California a lot and I've never heard of it."

"I'm not surprised. It's new. My producer said it was terrific. I was lucky to get the reservation."

She hesitated. She was anxious to break into the Teason house tonight. The police didn't seem to be making any progress on finding out who the killer was, and Santo Teason was her last visible suspect. At another time she might have felt intrigued by Tim Marshall. He was handsome and unfailingly pleasant, and he liked her, but he could never be as important as finding the man who had killed five people including her best friend. Still, she could see there was a more practical way to view this situation. If someone was watching her and deciding if she was a threat, then going on a date might make her seem harmless and ordinary. Being out of sight for a few hours wouldn't hurt, and having dinner in Santa Barbara wouldn't keep her from paying a visit to the Teason house later that night.

Maybe Tim was bent on going far away so they could talk during the drive, and he would work up his nerve to tell her he was a con man and not a guileless cowboy. *All right,* she thought. *Last chance.* "What time do you want me in the lobby?"

"Six. We'll be there by eight."

"See you then."

She put the burglary clothes back into her suitcase and went to the closet for the good dress she had brought from home. She'd had it for a month but hadn't worn it yet. As soon as she had seen it on the rack in the store she had been determined to have it. Trying it on was mainly about size. She had known she was enduring the process of putting it on and looking in all the mirrors partly because she liked looking at it.

Later, while she dressed in front of the mirror in her hotel room, she nodded. The dress was perfect. Most of it was black fabric, but as anyone knew, black wasn't just black, an absence of light like the inside of a pocket. There were red blacks, blue blacks, brown blacks. This one was gray black, which went with the small triangle of trim along the high neckline. It was more mature and sophisticated than most of her clothes. That was probably because it wasn't a disguise. The way it hung on her acknowledged that she was shaped like a woman without making a point of it.

The black high heels would bring her about an inch above Tim Marshall's shoulder too — about as close to his eyes as she would ever be. But as she looked at her reflection, she decided to cut back a little bit. She wanted to look attractive and sexy, but she wasn't going to send her brain on vacation. Until the killer was caught, she might very well have to run for her life at any time. She stepped down from the high heels and into her black flats.

When she arrived in the lobby she saw him through the big glass doors, waiting outside on the loop. He was standing there in a very nice subtly patterned gray sport coat and light gray pants. He hadn't worn a necktie, but with his muscular frame he looked more natural without one.

The car wasn't the stupid oversize SUV she had feared he might rent. It was a Tesla Model S, dark gray with black leather upholstery. He opened her door for her, and when he closed it, she felt pleased. He had been thinking about what sort of ride she would like.

She said, "This is a surprise."

"Yes," he said. "I like to rent cars I haven't driven before. Only this isn't a rental. It's a test-drive."

"Okay. Do we have to be back in ten minutes?"

"No. I've got it until tomorrow afternoon. I agreed to write a review for a Canadian car magazine so they provided me with a loaner."

"Are you sure there's enough battery range to get us there and back?"

"They told me this one is officially charged to a hundred eighty-two miles, but the actual range is unofficially longer. If it's true, it will be in my review. If it's not true, we'll have to walk home."

She looked at the clear, open expression on his face as he drove the car forward. Maybe he was lying to sound smart. Or maybe he had conned somebody at Tesla too. That would be a promising development. "Does it bother your conscience?"

"Of course not. I'm really going to write it. Elon Musk is a Canadian citizen, and I guess the company wants to appeal to national pride."

"If you don't like it will you write a bad review?"

"Sure," he said. "I have no reason to lie. If you notice something wrong that they can fix, they'll do it, be grateful, and sell more cars."

"I guess that would be true," she said. Whether he told the truth was an important question, the one she had been asking in a hundred ways since she met him. It was really the only question, and he had been answering yes every time she found a new way, new words, a new context for it.

If he was really this Canadian cowboy whose rugged handsomeness, gentle personality, and strength of character had charmed a bunch of Hollywood producers into bringing him here, then she wasn't interested. But if he was a highly skilled con man, that was an attraction. It would allow her to tell him who she really was, and they could, paradoxically, have an honest relationship. He might even be able to help her find the killer. And if one of his cons was making himself into a woman's idea of a perfect guy, he would find making her happy pretty easy.

She spent most of her time looking out the window at the mountains to her right as he drove. There was something keeping her from feeling comfortable with him. Maybe it was simple timing. She was afraid for her life right now and feeling loss and guilt about Sharon. She couldn't feel sadness, shame, and fear and still be receptive to the overtures of a suitor. She was unattached and that was the way she had to be for now. She was resolved to be pleasant, but that was about all she could manage.

The restaurant was close to living up to its sudden renown. Their table actually was "Sous les Arbres." It was outdoors under some graceful locust trees and beside a rocky brook that had an audible trickle of running water, which made Elle suspect it had been plumbed like a fountain. It was too late in the summer for a natural stream to be full. She forgave the artifice because the food was so good. They stayed a long time. It was about eleven when they got into the car and Tim drove them back into Santa Barbara and swung along the ocean onto Cabrillo Boulevard.

Tim seemed excited to be so close to the ocean. He said, "I don't get to be this close to the Pacific except when I visit my sister in Vancouver. It's not the same up there. It's not tropical looking, with palm trees and stuff. I've been meaning to get to the ocean ever since I got invited to L.A."

"Santa Barbara is nice," she said. "It's also more accessible than most of the coast."

Tim said, "The beaches right here are beautiful."

"True. I've been here a few times in daylight, and it's always a treat."

He pointed to the west. "Have you ever explored to see what's up that way? I mean along the shore."

"The road moves off the coast for a ways, and then you go by the university, which is on a point, so the ocean is visible again.

And there are places where you get a glimpse of beach and a couple of parks with beach access. Then the road goes inland a bit as a shortcut to places like Lompoc. Not a great trip in the nighttime, if I remember correctly, but pretty other times."

He drove along Cabrillo Boulevard with the beach on one side and the lawns of hotels on the other. When he reached a parking lot on his right he pulled into it. She expected he was pulling off only to check his phone for directions to the freeway entrance to head back to Los Angeles, but he coasted into a space and stopped where they could see the ocean. They sat in silence. The moon was low, and its reflection had formed a silver strip on the surface that seemed to point toward them like a spotlight.

"Whenever I see something like this I wonder if I'll ever get to see it again," he said. "Would you go for a walk with me?"

"I'm not really dressed for it," she said.

"We can take our shoes off. I'll roll up my pants, and your dress, while extremely elegant, is short enough so it won't get wet."

She looked at him. More than once she had wished she knew the kind of guy who wanted to take her for a walk on a beach at night. She said, "Okay."

He got out of the car and took a few steps to sit on the hood and take his shoes and socks off.

She stayed in the passenger seat to take off her shoes. Then she gave her purse a quick look to remind herself whether she had anything she didn't want to leave in a car. She had makeup, a burner telephone with the battery out so it couldn't be traced, false identification in the name Annie McDowell. She noticed her folding knife. It reminded her that Tim didn't know or suspect the kind of trouble she had.

She palmed the flat, razor-sharp knife, slid her hand up her right leg, and used the belt clip on the handle of the knife to secure it to the waistband of her underpants at her right hip, then covered it with the skirt. She patted the skirt from the outside and then tested to make sure she could reach the knife quickly if something happened on the lonely, dark beach that Tim couldn't handle.

She clutched her purse and got out.

"I'll put your purse and shoes in the trunk with my shoes," he said.

They stepped off the asphalt lot to the sand and began to walk, listening to the breaking of the waves on the wet sand about two hundred feet from them. There was no sea breeze now, just a steady current of cool air, the exhalation of the ocean.

After a quarter mile or more holding hands as they strolled on the beach, they were far from the lights of the harbor. They passed the beach volleyball courts and then came under the giant mansion at the crest of the first cliff.

"That's quite a place," said Tim. "I wonder who lives there."

"I actually know," she said. "It belonged to an heiress named Huguette Clark. Her father owned copper mines. She died a few years ago in New York. I read about it in the New York papers and remembered seeing this place. Now I guess there are probably just guards and caretakers."

She knew much more about the building and the woman and her family. What she didn't say was that she had briefly considered breaking in to see if there was anything to steal that hadn't been taken out and locked up. But she learned that Miss Clark had not lived there in decades, so she abandoned the idea.

They came to a fence-like outcropping of rusted iron jutting about two feet above the sand, and she used this as an opportunity to free her hand from his to pass on the other side of the barrier. They continued along the beach. Above them on this stretch were more cliffs, at first part of the estate. Somewhere up beyond that, unseen, were railroad tracks.

He said, "This is nice. We could stay the night at one of the hotels along the beach back there and leave after breakfast tomorrow."

She patted his arm and said, as gently as she could, "I'm not saying that's never going to happen. But tonight isn't going to be the night."

He shrugged. "Just a thought."

As they walked farther the beach began to narrow. The night was calm but clear, and she could tell they were a distance from another human being. The beach was lighter than L.A. had been last night because the moon was waxing.

The moon on the surf made her remember a night when she was fourteen. She and her cousin Nathaniel, who was twelve, had taken a bus to the beach at San Pedro and waited until dark for a grunion run, when the small, silvery fish would wash ashore and mate, and the females would leave their eggs and return to the ocean.

She had read that the best nights were the second and third of a four-night run. The newspaper said the best hours predicted for that run were from 11:05 P.M. to 1:05 A.M.

She remembered it was May 5. They left home in the late afternoon with a pair of cloth bags made from pillowcases, saved their peanut butter sandwiches to eat as late as they could stand, and tried to stay awake. When the run began Elle awoke to the sounds of people running into the water, laughing and splashing, and saw the thousands of six- to eight-inch silvery fish flapping and curling and slithering in the surf.

She and Nathaniel filled their bags with fish and took the first bus back home when the buses started running in the morning. They nailed bottle caps to some old wooden laths and scaled the fish, gutted them, and fried them in the kitchen of the big old house. She and Nathaniel had brought enough to provide two meals for the whole household and for the family next door that occasionally had fed them when there had been no food in their house. May 5 was a warm memory for Elle. She remembered both of her aunts and her grandmother smiling and hugging her and Nathaniel, saying how proud they were. By August that year she was on her own and never lived at home again.

There was a movement she heard but didn't see. Tim's arm had lifted behind her. Was he making his move to hold her and kiss her? She waited for a second, then started to turn toward him, but his big hands flashed in her peripheral vision and something jerked her backward toward him. There was a cord tightening around her neck. It was impossibly tight, hurting and choking. Then he was lifting her off her feet. She was being hanged.

Elle knew she would lose consciousness in a few seconds. She reached to her hip and slid the knife off her waistband, flipped the blade open with her thumb, and brought it down to stab him, then jerked it out of his thigh, spun it, and brought it up beside her head to cut and slash his hands.

One of his hands let go of the cord to try to wrench the knife away, and that let her drop to her feet. She brought the knife around hard to slash at his midsection as she turned. She was much shorter than he was and in a fighting crouch, so the knife slashed his thigh a second time instead of reaching his belly, but she could tell it cut deep.

She launched herself away from him with eight fast, hard strides, but she could hear him coming after her. She turned and slashed at his hands and forearms when he reached out to clutch her, and he recoiled in pain. She could see she had cut through the gray sport coat and that the fabric was darkening. She saw that the spot where she had stabbed and slashed his thigh was darkening faster, and she wondered if she had nicked the femoral artery.

He put his head down and charged toward her, but she danced to the side, spun, and dashed toward the hard-packed wet sand close to the surf. She could hear the hissing sound of his feet kicking sand as he came after her, and she ran hard. She reached the firm, wet sand; veered to her left; and dashed along above the surf.

She knew the Biltmore hotel was around one of the bends ahead of her, up a rocky incline from the beach and across a narrow street. There would be people. If she could just stay ahead she might make it. Then she realized she no longer heard him behind her. She whirled to face him, bringing her left elbow around ahead of her and gripping the knife behind her body in her right hand to stab him.

He was at least forty feet behind her. He had stopped, had taken off his shirt, and was trying to tear it into strips. He had tightened his belt around his thigh in a tourniquet above the wound she'd made. "You hurt me. I'm bleeding bad."

"What did you think I'd do?" she said.

"Let you kill me?"

He didn't seem to hear her, as though her words had gone out over the ocean. Or maybe they didn't matter. "Help me. Get me to a hospital."

He seemed to be weakening, but he tore the shirt in two and tied one part of it around his left arm and the other around the right. His coat must have been discarded somewhere, and the white strips from his shirt were already darkening. She called, "Why are you trying to kill me?"

"I wasn't. You misunderstood."

"Bullshit."

He breathed deeply a few times. Then he began to run toward her again, moving fast on the hard sand.

She pushed off and ran away from him along the beach. She held her head up and dug in with her toes, sprinting for her life.

This time he appeared determined to catch her, and he seemed to be straining to accomplish it. But again she realized she no longer heard him, so she risked a quick glance over her shoulder. He had stopped. He sat on the sand and stayed there as though trying to catch his breath. He lay back on the sand and looked up at the sky. He called out to her, "Elle!"

She hadn't told him that was her name.

She had called herself Annie McDowell. "Tell me why you tried to kill me," she called. "Did someone hire you?"

He seemed not to hear her. With difficulty he got to his knees, then his feet. He took a hard look at her and then began to walk. He was heading back toward the lot where the Tesla was parked. His walk had become unsteady. The right leg of his pants was wet with blood from the thigh to the ankle now. The bandages on his arms were doing nothing to stanch the bleeding there.

She began to follow. "Was it one of the husbands? If you tell me I'll try to help you."

He didn't answer. His whole mind seemed to be taken up with the enormous task of walking back to the car. He kept to the hard, wet sand, but the slope into the surf was steep in some places and his steps would involuntarily bring him down toward the water, so he would have to correct his course. He had begun to stagger.

To his left was the surf and to his right were fifty-foot cliffs. He had seen nobody within a quarter mile of him but Elle Stowell, and he knew now he couldn't catch her or fool her into coming close to him. He didn't know that the Biltmore was only about a hundred yards around a curve or that he was walking away from it.

The next time he collapsed, he was on the wet sand at the edge of the ocean, with the waves washing in close to him. Elle sat down on the sand forty yards away and waited. In a few more minutes, she knew, she would be able to go to his inert body, pull the keys out of his pocket, and drive the Tesla back to Los Angeles.

16

Her heart was still pounding as she stood, looked down at his lifeless body, and turned to walk toward the car. The night now seemed bright from the moon, and the car parked alone on the lot seemed terribly obvious. She had recovered from the fight and the running, but she was still panting. She kept looking toward the crowded harbor, the end of State Street, the lights far down Cabrillo Boulevard. As she padded along barefoot she became aware of how disheveled she must look.

She recalled that when she had first fought back against the strangling, her knife had hit an artery, and she had felt the warm blood spray the backs of her calves. Now her bare legs were covered with a paste of sand and blood. She diverted her course back down to the ocean, went in up to her waist, ducked down into the next wave, and let the force of the water clean her. She ducked under the next wave, then stepped up onto the hard sand, took her new dress off, wrung the water from it, and slipped it on over her head. She wrung more water out of her hair and shook her head to straighten it.

At the car she opened the trunk and took out Tim's shoes and socks and left them on the pavement, put her purse and shoes in the passenger seat, put a floor mat on the driver's seat so she could sit on it, and then started the car. She turned on the heat and put the fan up to its most powerful setting, and then began to drive. She knew it was almost certain that Tim had not told her the truth about how he happened to have the car. But he had been lucky enough not to get arrested for car theft, so probably she would be too.

It took an hour and a half to reach Los Angeles, and by then her short, thin dress and her hair were dry. She parked the car on a street in a residential neighborhood in Pasadena and cleaned the interior and the handles with alcohol wipes from her purse. She took the Gold Line train to Union Station at five A.M., the Red Line subway to Universal City Station, and finally the shuttle up the hill to the hotel.

She went upstairs, took a shower, and laid

out her ambiguous-sex burglary clothes and baseball cap. The surveillance cameras would record her, but she hoped to be able to keep her face below the brim of her cap and her hair under the crown. The latex surgical gloves she had were flesh colored.

The wallet she'd taken from Tim's body held his hotel key card, and the room number that had been written on the little folder in pen, 402, had been crossed out and changed to 1212. Clearly he had at some point decided his room should be near hers. If she had discovered it earlier this evening she would have dismissed it as part of his strategy to sleep with her, but now she supposed it was a way to kill her more conveniently.

She folded her outfit and put it into her big purse, then dressed in shorts, a tank top, and sneakers and took the elevator downstairs to the gym. She stepped into the ladies' locker room, put on her burglary outfit, and stowed her gym clothes in her big bag. She lifted the plastic trash bag full of crumpled hand towels out of the trash can beside the sink, put her bag of clothes in the can, and then put the trash bag back on top of it.

Elle went across the hall from the locker room to the stairwell, climbed to the twelfth floor, found room 1212, and used the key card to enter. The closet held the clothes she had seen Tim Marshall wear, all hanging neatly. She opened his suitcase and found more clothes, but in a pocket on the outside of the suitcase was a second wallet. This one held cash and all the kinds of cards the other one had, in the name Paul Wolcott. She put the wallet in the back pocket of her jeans and kept searching.

She looked hard at anything that had entered the room with Tim, but she found nothing else that was revealing, no weapons, no second phone, and no papers on which he had written anything. When she had finished, she left the room, entered the stairwell, and descended the twelve floors to the gym. She retrieved her bag, put on her shorts and tank top, and went into the gym to lift weights, jog on the treadmill, and do a few pull-ups. Then she walked to the elevator, rode it to the twelfth floor, and went into her room. After she had showered again she slept.

At ten she was up, had packed, had cleaned the surfaces of the room with antiseptic wipes and then hand towels, and had placed a tip for the chambermaid on the desk. She called to have her car brought to the front of the building and stopped at the front desk to check out of the hotel.

The next part of the day she devoted to disrupting any continuity between herself and the young blond woman who might have been noticed with Tim Marshall over the past few days. She returned her car to the rental lot and went to another, where she picked out a silver Honda CR-V, a small SUV that had little about it to make it stand out from the many thousands of others on the streets.

She drove to the south simply because she had not hidden there before. She checked into a hotel in Marina del Rey at four P.M. and took a nap before a late dinner. She had the feeling that if she wasn't actively investigating, then nobody was. But she needed time to recover or she was going to make new mistakes. Whatever she had done to put herself in Tim Marshall's way had nearly been fatal.

He had fooled her into imagining that the stakes were much lower than they really were, and from that moment on, she had stopped really protecting herself. She was alive now only because of luck. He had chosen a time and place that he thought were ideal for killing her, but he had actually chosen perfectly for her. The night and the solitude and the sand had made her more dangerous. When she'd been a teen-ager, one of the older thieves she'd met had told her, "If you're going to knife somebody, don't let him see the knife." She had stabbed Tim at least twice before he had realized she wasn't just pounding her fist against him in a futile attempt to struggle. Once she had started the bleeding he might have still killed her, but he was not going to get through it easily.

She tried to figure out her next move. The Paul Wolcott identification could be the real set. It looked real, and it had the right flaws. The photograph on the California driver's license was not good. The real man had been much better looking than that. The Timothy James Marshall ID with the Al-berta license and the Calgary address looked as attractive as she remembered him. That was a big sign of a fake. A forger could take all the time and care he wanted to get a good picture on a fake license, but the California DMV's photographic computer was not there for pleasing the drivers. It clicked and you got what you got.

The Canadian ID said he lived at Marshall Ranch, 4304 Route 11, Red Deer, Alberta. When she checked, it turned out that there was such a town, in spite of the fact that it sounded like something he'd made up. Still, choosing it was as suspicious as making it up.

Paul Wolcott's license said his address was in Riverside. That didn't seem to be fake, because it didn't make her think anything in particular and didn't seem to be part of a story she'd heard him tell. It wasn't a credential.

She went to bed and the physical cost of the past two days made her sleep. Fighting with a man who was twice her size and in good condition had been a terrible strain. Every movement she'd made was at fighting speed and force. Every fifty-yard sprint to escape his reach was a dash for her life. And then as soon as she had abandoned the Tesla and caught the two trains and the shuttle bus, she'd had to run up and down staircases and perform a credible gym workout just to search his room while seemingly occupied with her own routines.

Elle slept over eight hours before the steady wash of the waves was joined by the voices of people on the beach shouting and laughing. There was one woman in particular whose voice was seldom silent for longer than the break between "woo" and "hoo."

Elle got up and went to the much smaller gym at her new hotel, did a short workout with weights, ran on the beach for about a half hour, and then swam just outside the surf line for another half hour before she came back, showered, and went to the breakfast bar overlooking the ocean.

When she returned to her room she went online and looked at the *Santa Barbara News-Press.*

Harbormaster Dale Kraniak reported that the body of a male Caucasian about thirty to forty years old was found this morning floating in the harbor. The man appeared to have been stabbed in at least two places and slashed several times on the arms and hands.

Santa Barbara Police spokesperson Sergeant Maureen Costa said, "At the moment we're acting on the theory that this is a homicide, possibly in connection with robbery. There was no wallet or key or ID in his pockets. It's possible that he was involved in an altercation aboard a boat, but his lungs contained no salt water, so he didn't drown. He was dead when he entered the water."

According to Coast Guard rescue officer Calvin Slocum, the victim's body had probably been in the water for several hours, and he could have drifted into the harbor from anywhere off the coast. The body was found afloat between two boats moored along the docks, where it had caught and remained.

Elle clicked on several other news sources, but it was as though the news had stopped at the Santa Barbara County line. Tim's death was a purely local story so far, an unknown stranger's body found among all of those oceangoing sailboats and cruisers tied to the cleats on the long parallel docks. Tim had been at the restaurant north of Santa Barbara with her, but unless the paper or the television stations showed a picture of his face, there wasn't much reason for a waiter to connect him with this story. She tried to remember being in the presence of anybody else, but she couldn't. They had driven straight to the restaurant and then to the beach. They hadn't even stopped at a gas station, because the Tesla didn't use gas. She had looked for security equipment at the restaurant but had detected no surveillance cameras trained on the outdoor area, which consisted only of tables in a sheltered garden. Any cameras would have been inside, where there were things to protect.

She was still puzzled and unsure about the entire experience. At the moment of the attack, she had not believed for the first fraction of a second that he could be trying to kill her. After that she had wondered if he was trying to make her pass out so he could rape her while she was unconscious, a crime she had read about a few times. And then she had realized he was trying too hard even for that and wondered if he had fallen into a crazy rage because she'd turned down his hotel invitation.

Minutes later, when he had called out her real name, all possibilities dissolved but one. He knew who she was and he had brought her there to kill her. But why was he doing that?

Killing her seemed to be pointless and irrational. She had been the one to find the camera in the triple murder, but she had turned it in already, and she'd seen nothing on the recording that the police hadn't, except her own image. What threat could she represent to anyone now?

She had thought about it many times since the morning she discovered the bodies and walked herself through everything she had seen. There was no clear picture of the killer with the silenced pistol. She could eliminate large groups — black men, Asian men, men who were very fat or tall or short — but she couldn't say, "This is the one." Tim Marshall had turned out to be a killer, but he

271

hadn't seemed to be the killer who had murdered the others. And he had not had a gun or silencer with him in the car or in his room.

She had not noticed any car near Kavanagh's house that looked suspicious on the morning of the discovery. And why would she have? The killing had taken place at least ten hours earlier. She had not seen anyone alive in or near Kavanagh's house until the police arrived during her second visit. She had not found anything in the house, other than the recording, that told her anything.

Somebody must have learned that a woman fitting her description and possessing a burglar's habits had been in the house before the police got there. That much had to be true. Otherwise the two men and one woman would not have been out asking people who she was and, later, where she was. But there could have been other people besides the three who had done the same.

Elle kept running through the possibilities. One was that they thought the girl burglar had come in, seen the bodies, and still had the single-mindedness to steal something from the house. It would have to be either valuable or incriminating to make the effort to find her worthwhile. Another was that they believed she had seen something that she had not — the killer, back to clean up the crime scene, couldn't find something he was expecting and believed she had it.

Maybe he thought she had seen him on her morning trip. No, she thought. Maybe she had. Maybe what he had done was this: killed the three the previous afternoon, gotten away unseen, spent an entire night sleeping or establishing an alibi, and then realized in the morning that there had been a camera running. If he then went back to the house and found the camera missing because she had taken it to her house to watch and copy, or if he arrived just as she was returning the camera to its tripod, what would he do? He would steal the camera himself. And then he would begin to hunt for her.

She thought back to the newspaper stories. After the first few days there had been references to the way the bodies had been found. Had there been any direct mention of a recording? She would have to go back and reread the articles and interviews, but she didn't think so. She had been assuming that the recording was in the hands of the cops. But what if the killer got there first and took it? He might have been in the house during her second trip. If he had been, he could have seen her. That was another thing she would have to find a way to investigate.

Right now she had something new to look into, and she might have only today to do it. She checked out of the hotel after packing and wiping down the room. Elle got into her rented Honda and drove south on Interstate 405 and then switched to 55, the Newport Freeway, and reached Interstate 91, the Riverside Freeway, heading east.

Elle had never attempted any burglaries in Riverside, San Bernardino, or Kern County, or any other inland areas, so she would have to be cautious. There were rich people in the inland cities, but she had not studied them, so she had never tried to rob them. There were probably heirs to the giant citrus farms that had once dominated the area between Pomona and Riverside, or to the mines full of unglamorous minerals that were in the deserts. There were also vast new car and truck dealerships, hotels and restaurants that must be making serious money, but inland was too alien for her to feel safe there. The politicians these people kept electing were permanently stalled in the nineteenth century and notoriously mean. There were more gun stores than the visible population would seem to be able to support.

She would never have considered going where she was going in any other circumstances. As of this morning, the police had not yet figured out who the victim found in Santa Barbara Harbor — her victim — was. They therefore had no idea where he had lived, so this was her time. She had to do it now, before they found out.

She had not known Tim Marshall when she had checked into the Universal Hilton. As she saw things now, he must have been searching hotels and watching for her to turn up. Apparently he was a hit man, and hit men worked in many different ways, but this way was not one that had occurred to her. Some of them worked for a commercial entrepreneur — a drug dealer, a car theft broker, a loan shark — and killed competitors and snitches. Others worked for some organized crime figure and killed people he considered his enemies. She knew there had been a few who had offered a murder service and got referrals through surface figures — lawyers, bartenders, bail bondsmen. It was possible this was what Tim Marshall had been. Maybe one of the husbands had wanted his wife killed, and knew somebody who knew somebody. Both the movie business and the restaurant business had in the past proved attractive to fringe characters.

When she'd met Tim she had been suspicious of him. He was so handsome, and the persona he had assumed was calculated to send the signals that made women interested. He was tall and strong, but extremely attentive and gentlemanly and sensitive to what a woman was thinking. He observed a woman and listened to what she said. And after that he provided proof that he had taken it seriously, absorbed it, and acted on it.

What she had suspected was that he was a confidence man who preyed on women. She assumed he wanted either her money or easy access to her body or both. Yes, definitely both, which had not only brought her a slight tingle of pride and erotic speculation, but also pushed more frightening things out of her consciousness. Even though she believed a killer was hunting her, the idea that the killer might be Tim never entered her mind.

And he had gotten her interested, just as he would have if he were either an actual handsome Canadian horse trainer or a handsome con man. She had been pretty thoroughly seduced, she admitted. In Santa Barbara she had refused to check into a hotel on the beach because she had a job to do. She had been planning to come back to Los Angeles that night to break into Santo Teason's house, and that was what she'd intended to do.

She had guessed wrong about him. He had been maneuvering her into a quiet, dark spot where he could murder her silently and put her body in the ocean. She had never suspected it. At the moment when he had slipped the cord over her head and pulled it tight, she had been turning toward him to be kissed.

He had misunderstood her too. He had no idea she had a razor-sharp knife under her short dress, specifically one she could pull out and open with one hand. He had taken her to a beach in the dark, but that meant he didn't see her movement or the knife until it had nicked his femoral artery. He hadn't even imagined there was anything a person half his size could do to resist him, let alone hurt him, so he hadn't tried hard enough to disable her.

She had been able to outrun him, partly because she was a habitual runner and he wasn't, but also because he was already weakening from loss of blood. When she slashed his hands and arms to keep him from grasping her, that opened new wounds and increased the blood flow. She had gotten into this predicament by stupidity and survived it by luck. She couldn't help remembering her grandmother shaking her head about Elle's mother. "She was so pretty, just like a little angel. But she was so stupid." So was her daughter, Elle thought. And she didn't even get the looks.

When Elle crossed into Riverside County she used the app on her cell phone to bring up the female voice that told her how to get to the address on Paul Wolcott's driver's license. She followed the directions until she heard, "In five hundred feet your destination will be on your right," and then turned off the app.

The place was an apartment complex from another era. The buildings were two stories with gray clapboards and bright white trim. The upper units each had a white wooden staircase at an end of the building, so there were only four apartments in each building.

Elle coasted slowly past the complex searching for security cameras. When she was sure she had perceived the pattern that determined their placement she drove on and parked at a restaurant some distance away on a larger, busier parallel street.

She had dinner, paid the check, used the restroom to change into her unisex night burglary clothes, walked out the door to the car, and pulled past the rear of the building. Elle knew that most security cameras were not good for picking up clear pictures in the dark and that the ones with night vision, though brighter, were full of flashes, bleeding images, and distortion, so she wanted to wait for full darkness before she went back to the apartment complex. She parked her car in a part of the mall that included a popular Mexican restaurant, a bar, and several larger stores and businesses to ensure that there would be plenty of foot traffic and then set off.

She walked to the apartment complex and studied it as she passed. She verified that the A and B apartments were on the ground and the C and D apartments were on the second floor. She found the correct building number and the D unit, went up the stairs, used the key from Tim Marshall's suitcase to get in, and quietly closed the door behind her.

She was in a living room with a couch, two matching easy chairs, a television set, and a wide, low coffee table. She made sure all the blinds were closed before she turned on her flashlight. On the table were copies of *Entertainment Weekly, Sports Illustrated,* a magazine called *Horseman,* and another called *Trainer.* There were also copies of *Canadian Living, Maclean's,* and *Westworld Alberta.* This was certainly the right place. Tim Marshall was Paul Wolcott.

She ventured into the kitchen, where things seemed mostly clean. She guessed that when he wasn't traveling he had made coffee in the morning, poured liquor in the evening, and eaten nearly all of his meals in nearby restaurants.

The bedroom was an unpleasant surprise. It had been closed up while Paul Wolcott had been in Los Angeles being Tim Marshall, and the room smelled like him. Her nose was able to distinguish a familiar scent contained in a deodorant and also a musky smell that she had not noticed consciously on him but was absolutely Tim Marshall. She traced the smell to a laundry basket by his closet that held a full load of dirty clothes. The smell made her feel his presence, and it scared and confused her. She spent a few seconds seeing him again on the beach in the moonlight calling out to her to come closer so he could kill her with his hands.

Elle shuddered and then banished the feeling. She was in his bedroom, the place where she knew the secrets would be. She began to find things. There was a .45 ACP

Smith & Wesson pistol and a box of fifty rounds for it. There was a .380 with three full magazines. She also found a .308 rifle with a scope. But she found no silencer, and neither pistol had any modification like a threaded barrel to accommodate one. If he'd owned anything like that he had it hidden somewhere else. She spent a half hour looking in more and more obscure places for secrets, checking the air vents, the stuffing in the couch and chairs, and the upper- and undersides of every drawer, cabinet, and cupboard, then trying to find hollowed-out appliances, loose boards, and packages in the refrigerator and the freezer.

She exhausted those possibilities and turned to the search for paper. She went through every bill, receipt, check register, account record. She would lay it out under the intense beam of the flashlight, take a shot of it with her phone, and set it aside. Then she would go for the next pile.

Paul Wolcott had earned some money at his trade. His checking account at Bank of America always had over $200,000 in it. The monthly statement made it clear that the money deposited was from something called the Wolcott Trust, or it was cash in irregular sums, all below $5,000. He made it look as though he were paying himself from

281

investments, with small but regular infu-
sions of cash from something — maybe
gambling. She couldn't tell if it was a system
to hide the payer or to explain how a man
who never worked stayed solvent.

She found stock and bond mutual funds
amounting to a few hundred thousand dollars. She took phone photographs of all the
reports and put them back. She stayed
about three hours in the apartment, always
wearing the hat and surgical gloves. She
knew that this was her final visit here,
because the police would find out who the
body in Santa Barbara was before very long.
But she found nothing like what she'd
hoped for. She had wanted to turn up
something that illuminated the unseen and
organized the chaotic, but she simply didn't.

Before she left, she looked around a final
time. She had not perfectly preserved the
order of Paul Wolcott's apartment, but the
place didn't look as though it had been
tossed. And Paul Wolcott would not be back
to detect the small differences in his arrangement.

She looked out every window to be sure
there was nobody waiting out there, exited
and locked the door, and went down the
stairs. The walk to the car was a bit farther
than Elle liked, but she hadn't dared to risk

having her rental car's license plates on a surveillance recording.

She had walked about a hundred yards from the apartment when she saw a black SUV approach from the other direction. She stepped to the corner of the nearest building and turned back to watch. Two doors opened and men got out. They were both tall and moved as though they were in good shape. The two men hurried up the stairs to Paul Wolcott's apartment. Another figure got out of the backseat and stepped to the driver's-side door. This one was lighter and thinner — a woman? The person opened the door and the dome light came on again. It was the tall blond woman, the one who had been with the two men searching the bars for Elle Stowell.

The woman backed the SUV up over the curb and almost to the bottom step of the stairs. The men stationed themselves on the stairs and began handing things down to the woman, who stood in the back door of the SUV and placed them inside the cargo bay formed by folding the backseats down.

Elle could tell they weren't trying to preserve the order or condition of the things they loaded. They were trying to remove everything. They had a roll of big black plastic trash bags, and that was how most of

Paul Wolcott's belongings arrived in the SUV. In about fifteen minutes the three climbed back into the SUV, drove gingerly down over the curb to the street, and turned toward the freeway entrance. She knew exactly where they were going. And she knew, once and for all, that they weren't cops.

17

On the way home Elle stopped at an all-night pharmacy and bought a fine-point indelible pen, a padded mailing envelope, and a sheet of stamps. All were packaged, so she didn't worry about fingerprints or DNA.

At five A.M. Elle reached her house in Van Nuys. She took all the precautions, looking for the wrong cars parked in the wrong places, any changes in the way she had left her window blinds and curtains, and any signs of a break-in. There seemed to be nothing that she hadn't seen before. She checked the electric meter to see if the wheel was turning at its usual glacial pace or if things were turned on that she hadn't left that way. When she was satisfied, she unlocked the door and stepped in.

The air had the satisfyingly stale smell she'd expected because the house had been kept shut for a while. She checked the places where she had left the baby powder, and there were no new footsteps until she came to the front door, where the floor had one big print. She examined the door and guessed that someone had come in with a key or picked the lock. She let her shoulder go limp to slide her bag off onto the table and went to the slide-in hidden spice rack in the kitchen. She opened the jar of turmeric, looked to see if the two thumb drives she'd hidden there were in it, took one out, closed the jar and put it back, and slid the spice rack out of sight.

She dropped the thumb drive into her purse, turned to take a look around, and walked. When she reached her bedroom she found the note on her pillow. It said, "Call me. Nathaniel."

Nathaniel was her cousin, one of the few relatives she still acknowledged and went to see voluntarily. She put the note into her pocket and went around to the various doors blowing new powder on the hardwood floors. She had given Nathaniel a key after she'd moved in because she didn't want to die someday and have nobody find her. Five in the morning was too early to call any number but 911, so she spent time attending to other business.

She put on her surgical gloves and took

out of her purse the thumb drive copy of the murder of Kavanagh, Mannon, and Teason. She wiped the drive for prints and turmeric, and then used her fine-point pen to write, "HOMICIDE: PLAY THIS," on a small piece of paper, which she taped around the drive. She put the drive into the envelope, wrote the address of the L.A. police headquarters, and put the stamps on the envelope.

She drove to the post office on Laurel Canyon Boulevard, dropped the small envelope into the interior slot, and left. The cameras certainly caught her, but they would record the dozens of others who mailed things this morning, and the cops would not know which one had mailed that envelope, who she was, or maybe, with her baseball cap, if she was male or female. She wasn't positive that the police didn't already have the tape of the murder, but now she was positive they would have it. She would know their lack of progress wouldn't be her fault.

Elle returned to her house. She had searched the online version of *Variety* and the *Hollywood Reporter* each morning. Today she found the item she had been waiting for: "New 'I, Claudius' Shoots in Rome on 23rd."

She glanced at her phone to verify that today was the sixteenth. Then she took off everything except the belly band that held her Rohrbaugh pistol and went to bed. She woke in the afternoon, put her hand on her pistol, walked around and verified that nobody had been in her house and nobody was outside waiting for her, and then relaxed. She did what she could to refresh and replenish herself for whatever the next stage of things was going to be.

She washed a load of laundry consisting of the contents of her suitcase, hid more money in the suitcase and the purse, charged her phones, cleaned her pistol, cleaned and polished her shoes, and spent some more time trying to learn what she could about Santo Teason from public sources. Next she used her phone and looked at photographs of Teason's house from the street and from the air, and studied the neighborhood for the best ways in and out.

At three thirty she judged that it was a decent hour to call Nathaniel. She punched his number into her cell phone. In a second she heard, "Elle?"

"Hi, Nathaniel. It's nice to know you haven't lost my key."

"Not me," he said. "You haven't been in

288

your house in at least a week, and it's clean. Is something wrong?"

"Just avoiding somebody. But you're the one who got in touch. What's the occasion?"

"Louisa wants to talk to you." Louisa was the name of his mother, one of her mother's two sisters who had lived in the big old house in South Pasadena while Elle was growing up. Elle had always thought that the way her aunt had Nathaniel call her Louisa was an excellent accommodation for them both. He got to seem older, a contemporary of his mother's, and she got to seem younger, a contemporary of her son's. Elle remembered the way they'd seemed when she was a teenager, Aunt Louisa with striking red hair hanging loose almost to her waist like a woman in a pre-Raphaelite painting — beautiful — and Nathaniel much taller and always serious looking, like a man.

"I'd like to talk to her too. Do you have a current number for her?"

"Not on the phone. She wants to see you. At the old house. Can you do it tonight at around ten?"

"I'll be there on the dot." There was a slight pause, and she knew they both wanted to hang up, so she did. She thought for a moment. She certainly didn't want Aunt

Louisa in this house when she couldn't be sure she wasn't going to have another visitor. And there was an odd attraction to going back to the old house now. She hadn't been there in ten years, and she felt a mild curiosity about it.

That night as she was driving she thought about Aunt Louisa. She had been so pretty, with her long red hair and fair complexion and green eyes. Whenever people said, as they did say often, that Elle's mother was the prettiest of the three sisters, Elle had looked at Aunt Louisa. How could anybody have been prettier than that?

The Stowell sisters had been kind to Elle, but even as a child she had felt a difference. They were passionately attached to their own children, her cousins. They babied and fawned over and slapped and screamed at them. To her the aunts were unfailingly kind, as they might be to the little girl who lived next door, but what she did could never make their hearts either swell or break. She didn't have to make up for their mistakes in life, surpass them at anything, or even love them.

At the end of that era, when her grandmother died, the sisters both went away with their current boyfriends, taking their children with them. Elle had been out on her own for a few weeks foraging for money to contribute to the household. The morning she returned to the house it was deserted. The big dining room table was still there, and all twelve matching chairs, and a few that weren't, and the sideboard with the mirrored back. The couches and overstuffed chairs in the living room were there. But as she walked through the house listening for human noises, she also noticed that certain things were gone: the carving knives in the butcher block and the radio in the kitchen, the television set in the living room, some framed photographs in the hallway and on the staircase.

The beds were still there, but the sheets were not. She remembered looking into the room where she had slept, and the sheets and pillow were gone even from her bed. That night she had tried sleeping there, using abandoned clothes from the closets as blankets and pillow. But at around two, right after the bars had closed, she heard men laughing and talking on the street outside, and then men's heavy, hard boot heels on the porch. She heard their voices until just before daylight.

When she came by the house a month later, hoping that some part of the family might have come back, she found broken windows and a tall chain-link fence around the property, and the green lawn had become a patch of weedy ground where people had begun to throw little bags of dog shit and the wrappers and Styrofoam from fast food.

A few months later Elle had found Nathaniel's half of the family by asking around at stores where Nathaniel and his brother had once bagged groceries or bought food and at houses where they had once done odd jobs.

Tonight when Elle pulled up a few dozen yards from the house, she was surprised. At some point, before the house could fall into a pile, somebody had taken an interest in it and done serious work on it. The yard was a bit smaller, and it had a high steel fence that looked as though it were made of spears planted vertically in the ground. The house itself looked almost exactly as it had looked when she was fourteen. It had two full floors of rooms, a porch that went around it all the way like an apron, and a low-ceilinged attic on top. The clapboards had been replaced, but they were the same dark green color, and the white trim was whiter than it had been in her lifetime. There were lights on in the upper floors, and the driveway, once two parallel strips of concrete, was now made of paving stones. The two cars parked on them were a Mercedes and a BMW.

She saw a car arrive ahead of her and Nathaniel swing his long legs out and walk toward her rented SUV. The passenger door opened and she recognized the slim silhouette of Aunt Louisa, who hurried ahead of Nathaniel, tugged open Elle's passenger door, and climbed in. She had always been startling, but now, when she must be fifty, she looked about thirty, her hair now dyed to maintain its color and the pale skin of her face preserved with a highly skilled application of makeup. Around her neck was a beautiful silk scarf, and her arms looked as slim and graceful as always under the long sleeves of her black pullover. Her appearance was both a revelation and a disguise — things shown and things hidden. Her bright green eyes were glaring at Elle in the dome light, kept on by the door she held half open. "You remind me so much of Ellen. Your mother. You look a lot like her."

Elle said, "I always heard I missed out on her looks, but I guess I'm not as stupid either. It's a fair trade."

"Stupid?" Louisa said. "She wasn't stupid."

"It's okay. It won't hurt my feelings. I

never even knew her, remember?"

"So where'd you get that idea?"

"I heard Grandma say it. Just about every time her name came up, Grandma would say, 'So pretty, just like a little doll.' Or a little angel. Or a little fairy. 'But so stupid.' "

Louisa's neck and shoulders seemed to relax, and she smiled. "She didn't mean stupid like not intelligent. She meant something else. You knew Mother for plenty of time before she died."

"Until I was fourteen."

"So you knew my mother was a crook. She stole from people. It would be hypocritical to criticize her now, because that was what kept us alive. Everything we had was stolen. Even the house." She pointed at it. "That's some job of gentrification, isn't it? That's part of why I wanted you to see it. The effect is kind of spooky, because it's the same place, but it's not."

"Yes," said Elle.

"The reason we had to get out so fast after my mother died was that the place turned out not to be hers. She had worked for an old lady that she knew was going to die. The lady didn't have any relatives that visited her or called or wrote. Mother took care of a lot of the things she needed, and one day the lady died. Mother arranged her funeral and got her buried, but kept coming to work each day. After a while she decided nobody was ever going to come. So one day when she came to work she brought her stuff — mostly her three daughters. She kept everything going until she died, and then somebody took a look at the address on her death certificate. The city took the house."

"I hadn't heard how the house came or how it went. But why did she always say my mother was stupid?"

Louisa sighed. "Because Ellen was amazingly beautiful. Nobody ever denied that. She was also cheerful and funny and quick. She could have been the biggest thief, the biggest trickster, in the country, and that was what our mother tried to raise her to be. She knew from experience that being a small-time thief is a lot of work, and danger, and disappointment. Sometimes you get caught and people hurt you. Being a big-time thief is the opposite. It's like being a queen. Men all want to give you things. They do your fighting for you, and if you fail or lose, they take the blame for you. She wanted that for Ellen. And she wanted that for herself, to have Ellen support us all in a way she had never been able to. Ellen wouldn't do it. She felt sorry for people.

That's what my mother meant by stupid."

"Did Grandma put pressure like that on you?"

Aunt Louisa slowly shook her head. "Didn't have to," she said. "She had three favorites — the smartest ones, she said." Louisa's expression was grave. "Herself. Me. And you."

Elle watched as tears blurred Louisa's face. She pretended to sneeze, looking away. Then she wiped her own eyes. "The air is dusty tonight."

Louisa said, "Well, I wanted to see you, and I'm glad I could. I'm moving soon."

"Where are you going?"

"North Carolina," she said. "I know some girls who have moved there and don't know how certain games are played. They need my help, which probably will mean someone older to give them permission to do things they know instinctively but haven't dared to try. I'll be out of Los Angeles for a while. I always felt bad that we all moved out of this place in a hurry and had to leave you behind. We didn't think of it that way, because you were already just like a grown woman, but it must have seemed different to you. I didn't want to do that again."

"Wow. North Carolina seems like a big change."

"Well, Mother did come from there, and she always said nobody south of the Mason-Dixon line had a brain bigger than a cat's. We should do fine."

Elle said, "I'll bet you could use some travel money to get there." She reached into her purse and produced an envelope she had just packed at home. It was thick and the bills inside were all hundreds. She put it in Aunt Louisa's hand.

"That's so sweet of you, honey," Louisa said. The envelope had already disappeared somewhere on her body, under a scarf or a sleeve or a waistband. Aunt Louisa's sensibility was too delicate to let her count the money in front of Elle or even look at it. She got out of the car, so Elle did too.

She hugged Elle, looked into her eyes once more, and then turned. "It was a treat to see you, honey," she said in Elle's general direction as she walked toward Nathaniel's car.

Nathaniel appeared from the darkness and gave Elle a hug, then took a step after Louisa.

Elle said, "Are you going too?"

He half turned. "I took some vacation time. I'll just get her settled down there and come back. See you." He trotted to catch up, but when he did, all there was to do was get in the driver's seat and drive his mother away.

18

Elle stared at the empty road where Nathaniel and Louisa had been, then took a deep breath and started her car. What she felt was a little bit like her feelings on the day when she had come back here to the empty house and known she'd be alone forever. Maybe if Louisa had asked her to go to North Carolina tonight she would have felt better, but she would never have gone. She had other things to do.

It was time for Elle to turn her attention to Santo Teason and try to figure out if he was the murderer. She would have to find a way into the Teason family home.

She spent most of her time over the next few days casing the house and observing the family. The house was in a wooded area on a road between two ridges above North Beverly Drive, with two houses above it, on the slope of the north ridge, and a lot that was still covered with brush and a few scraggly California oaks but would, within a year or so, be the site of a third house. Elle used a small grove sheltered by a rise in the land as an observation point. The weather was hot, so the shade of the grove was welcome during the day. She often stayed until late evening, because the house had very large sliding glass doors and some windows that gave big views, both outward and inward.

Teason and his children were visible in and around the house often during that time. There were two boys, aged around twelve and eight, and a girl about ten. The house held a lot of people. There was a nanny who seemed to work exclusively with the little girl. She drove her to lessons and parties and back. The boys had their own adult minder, a man who seemed to be assigned only to them. He drove them everywhere, threw footballs with them, spotted them on the trampoline and the monkey bars and when they lifted weights, and jogged with them. He was the lifeguard when they swam. From Elle's perspective, their lives outside school were like a gym class.

The Teasons — both Santo and the late Valerie — seemed to have delegated most of their children's needs to other people. Besides the two minders, there were tutors, music teachers, and others who came for some limited purpose. There was even a dance teacher. Elle saw her once teaching the little girl to dance to popular music the way the big girls did, and not necessarily the high school honor students. Another afternoon she was teaching the boys ball-room dancing, with the little girl's nanny as the second partner. Since the nanny and the dance instructor looked like actresses selected by friends of Santo's in the casting business, it occurred to Elle that before long the boys might have a hard time settling for girls of their own ages.

On the twenty-first of the month, Elle arrived before dawn to see the employees working to load two cars with suitcases. Elle drove to LAX and parked in the structure at the Tom Bradley International Terminal, then walked to a bench near the ticketing counters and sat down to wait. The cars pulled up after about a half hour, and the girl's minder, both drivers, and the boys' minder all worked to get the luggage loaded onto carts and into the building. Santo and the kids and the two minders all got in line at Alitalia, picked up boarding passes, and proceeded with their carry-on bags toward the security checkpoint.

Elle was feeling good about what she had

seen as she walked along the first-floor area toward the door to the crosswalk and her rental car. She had thought it unlikely that Santo Teason would bring the kids to Rome for his shoot. Most Hollywood parents would have left the kids in the house and trusted the people who were raising them anyway to amuse and supervise them during the few dead times between sleepaway camp and the start of school. Clearly this father was making an exception because their mother had died, but she liked Teason better for it anyway. For the next couple of months he would be strategizing in the evening and spending his days bullying and cajoling an army of actors, extras, and technical people into reliving a series of Roman crises that the Romans didn't handle very well the first time. Kids were going to be a responsibility and a distraction, but he seemed to be handling the whole thing as gracefully as possible.

Elle expelled the thought from her mind. She was planning to evaluate him and figure out whether he had murdered his wife. She was not going to be swayed by his kindness to his kids. Every monstrous wife-killer she'd ever seen in television documentaries was eager to get custody of his kids. And since she had learned the three people who had been looking for her were not cops, maybe they were connected with him. Maybe he was affable because he had them doing the ugly stuff.

Entry to the Teason house would not be much work. She had seen the nanny drive the German shepherd away from the house in her little Mini Cooper the previous afternoon. The nanny had put a dog bed and a couple of rubber chew toys into the cargo compartment and returned later without dog, bed, or toys. A mature male German shepherd was a big dog, so the doggie door would be the same. It would be closed while the family was gone, but the only potential intruder that couldn't figure out how to get in a closed dog door was a dog.

When Elle arrived she went straight to the kitchen door, slid her pocketknife under the hard plastic insert that closed the dog door, pushed it up out of its frame, and slithered in.

She sat on the kitchen floor near the door and did her usual careful look around for electric eye beams, cameras, and interior doors that might have alarm circuits activated. Each device had its own particular limitations. A trap circuit had to be installed on a door that wasn't used much — a door to a furnace room or storeroom or basement, or simply a prop door that opened onto a view of the insulation in the wall. She assumed that in a house with lots of glass there would be alarms that were triggered by the sound of glass breaking. But those were almost always mounted in a living room or dining room, where glass didn't often break. The public parts of the house and the entryways were also where the cameras would be. They were usually trained on doors and were seldom installed in the bedroom and bathroom areas or the hallways in between.

After a few minutes of cautious exploration she knew where every alarm feature was, and by studying the best approaches to the equipment she had been able to unscrew or disconnect or cover everything.

Now it was time to learn about the house. She tried to form a general impression at a glance. She began in the foyer with her back to the front door, as though she were just coming in. She could look through the foyer to a wide, tall curved entry arch. Beyond it was a back wall, really part of a passageway that ran from the private areas of the house on the left toward the dining room and living room on the right. On this wall there were movie posters, which were something she had expected.

For people in the movie business, posters were like the diplomas hanging in a doctor's office. They held not only the name of the movie but also the person's credits — what he'd done on the movie — and the credits of the people he had worked with. She looked from left to right and saw a line of identically framed movie posters hung at the same height, probably in chronological order. Any guest heading for the living room or dining room would relive Santo's career. The first two were in Portuguese, the next three in Italian, and the rest in English, all the titles familiar to people in Beverly Hills.

She moved closer and looked at some of them. Santo had an impressive career, she conceded. He was only in his early fifties, and he'd accomplished a lot. As she turned to move up the passageway toward the living room, she saw that where the passageway began to have two walls, the right wall, which faced away from the front door, had another set of posters.

They were posters of Valerie McGee, and the earliest ones seemed to be patterned after the covers of paperback books. In the first one, a very young Valerie was wearing a dress with one strap torn off and the skirt tattered at the hem and ripped upward to the hip on one side. She was held around her very thin waist by a man in a suit carrying what looked like an Ingram MAC-10 automatic weapon. Had she been a Bond girl? No. That wasn't any of the James Bonds Elle had ever seen. It was a low-end thriller, with the title *Forced Entry.*

There was another with Valerie dressed in a nun's habit, also torn in a way that indicated to Elle that in the movie Valerie's character wasn't really a nun. In the next poster Valerie wore a pair of cutoff jeans short enough to seem structurally unsound and carried a shotgun that was also sawed off short enough to defy practicality. This movie was called *South of Valdosta.* Then there was *Satan's Sorority,* with Valerie dressed as a cheerleader. Some of the posters had Valerie in the center, clearly the female lead, and others had her picture small and in a lineup of other women. In a few of the earliest ones, a monster was the lead character, and Valerie's name was buried among the credits.

Elle never stopped walking, because she didn't want to waste time. She moved on to the left, where she guessed the private areas of the house were. Just past the end of the open part of the passageway there was a staircase, so she climbed.

There were a couple of public rooms, one an office and another a sitting room, then the kids' rooms — an exercise room and a room with a mirror and a barre that was devoted to dance — and then three bedrooms for the children and two for adults, presumably the kids' caretakers. As usual in this part of the city, the master suite was a door at the end of the upper hallway and took up both sides of the wing. This was where Elle had been headed from the beginning.

The bedroom was large, with light gray walls and heavy, luxurious furniture — oversize bed, couches, easy chairs, and a chaise longue. The only pictures on the walls were big dreamy black-and-white photographs that seemed to be abstractions of natural objects, like earth features seen from above. These were soft curves that might have been sand dunes in a desert or magnified dollops of vanilla cream, but they weren't. They were pictures of the skin of Valerie McGee Teason's nude breast, back, and hip, taken from inches away and vastly enlarged. Valerie had been a lucky woman. Elle caught herself thinking it, and then, *But of course she wasn't.* But she had been. She just wasn't anymore.

Elle moved on, looking for anything that

she had not expected to see. The clothes in Valerie's closet had been treated like Anne's: the ones with price tags or cleaners' wrappers on them were left, but the ones she had worn were not there.

She went to work on the husband's closet. He was the one she had come here to investigate. She opened every built-in drawer and cabinet in the closet. She had only a faint hope of finding anything conclusive, but there were facts in her favor. The killer had used a silencer and pistol on the first three victims but had not thrown them away. He had used them a second time on Sharon and Peter in Sharon's apartment, almost a week later. If he had gotten away with using them on two occasions, why would he throw them away? He still had Elle to kill.

Elle found two pistols in a top drawer on the inner wall of the closet. One was a big one that looked like an antique out of a western movie — a long-barreled revolver with bone handles. There was engraving on it, so she used her flashlight to read it. "Santo Teason, *Montana Wild,* 2015." It was a keepsake, apparently given to him by somebody who had worked on the movie. It was not loaded, looked and smelled as though it had never been fired, and didn't appear to be accompanied by any bullets. The other pistol looked more recent, a Browning M1911 .45. This one was engraved "Santo Teason, *A Pair of Aces,* 2005." It was also not loaded — it had only the magazine that was in it and there were no bullets for that either — and there was no silencer. There seemed to have been somebody in the cast, crew, or executive suite who liked to buy these keepsakes. The wording was too similar to be a coincidence. They were gifts given at the end of production.

She found an accordion-style envelope that tied with a string. When she opened it and ran the flashlight over the papers inside she saw they were photocopies done on a computer printer. Each sheet was a copy of an unlined page of an artist's notebook. Teason had made drawings and charts of scenes and camera angles, sets that would need to be built, and locations to be selected and had written notes on everything pertaining to the production in Rome. There were also miscellaneous scribblings of all sorts, including notes on phone calls, appointments, and meetings.

The vast majority of these things seemed to be information about the topic he'd thought about the most — his working life.

Right now, and apparently for the past year or more, that was the adaptation of Robert Graves's book. He had almost certainly taken his notebooks with him to Rome. These were backup copies in case the originals were lost.

Elle thought for a few seconds. She was not in a position to read them now. Should she take them with her? That would be a terrible thing to do to him if he lost the originals, and he was probably an innocent man. But the notebooks had dates and times of calls and meetings, the places where the meetings were held, and any number of other things. She might be able to prove or disprove where he was at the time of the murders or other events she didn't know about yet.

She felt the phone in her pocket. She placed the pages in a neat pile, took a picture of the first one, set it facedown beside the pile, and took the next, the next, the next. It took her a long time to be sure that they were all taken, all framed, and all in focus. She kept at it until the pages were all duplicated, put the pile in order, and returned it to the envelope where she'd found it. Then she continued with the closet.

There was nothing remarkable about Santo Teason's clothes. He was rich and famous, so he owned some really good suits. He was also a free agent who worked as an independent contractor instead of an employee, so he had a lot of clothes that were less formal than the suits. He had jeans, summer blazers to go with them, soft leather shoes for wearing without socks, fancy walking shoes, sneakers, slippers, and sandals. He had loose pants with drawstrings. And he was foreign, so he could wear brighter colors than an American could, or wear T-shirts under sport coats without being considered affected. Nothing he owned made him seem guilty of murder.

She kept at the work, looking at everything methodically. She felt that she was learning and expanding her powers of investigation, but not fast enough. She had done several burglaries since the murders, but not with the intention of taking anything. Instead she had needed to study these people's lives. She was desperate.

She spent a half hour searching the master bathroom, which was huge, with the usual three-quarters of the space devoted to the wife's things. But everything seemed to blend at the edges, so the sharing seemed friendly. She searched the medicine cabinet and drawers. Valerie seemed to have had an IUD inserted. There was a reminder sticker on the inner side of the medicine cabinet door that said her next checkup with her ob-gyn was in April, and the sticker was a free one with the logo of an IUD company. She and Santo must have been healthy, because all the prescriptions were for passing illnesses — a dispenser for liquid topical antibiotic for pinkeye a year ago, a painkiller that was three years old and didn't seem to have been used, a decongestant, another expired antibiotic that was taken as pills. There was nothing revealing.

This would probably be her only chance in the Teason house, and she had to make the most of it. She now knew that Valerie had not been expected to pick the kids up at their activities or lessons on the day of her death. The direct care of the kids had not been in her job description, apparently, so something else had to be. People who didn't have to do chores or earn a living always did something with their time. Elle studied the master suite, searching for some kind of work space. There was plenty of space but nothing that seemed to be used for work. If there had been some kind of clothing that pertained to an activity — tennis outfits, golf shoes, gardening clothes — it had been taken out.

She went back down the hall to take

another look. She went past the kids' rooms, the caretakers' rooms, and stopped at the room that looked like an office. She had assumed that since it was at the end of the hall near the kids' rooms, it must have something to do with their studies. She realized she'd been wrong.

The room had one large wooden desk with an empty top surface. It was made of a dark exotic wood that had been polished like the finish of a car. There was a matching file cabinet with four drawers that had little silver frames for cards to be used as labels. They had all been typed and printed on card stock: LACMA, MOCA, LA PHIL, and BREMMER.

Elle opened the file drawer marked LACMA, which was the Los Angeles County Museum of Art. The files were very neat, with hanging file folders like those business offices used and little white tabs on the hangers — BOARD MEETING AGENDAS, BOARD MINUTES, VISITING SHOWS, FUNDRAISING LISTS. The MOCA drawer was for the Museum of Contemporary Art, and the files had similar headings referring to board meetings, board activities, and art exhibitions. The L.A. Philharmonic drawer was full of information about concerts at the Hollywood Bowl and the Disney Concert

Hall. There were seating charts for weekly series, more fund-raising lists, and numerous schedules.

Elle couldn't help thinking it might be worth having copies of those season ticket lists and seating charts for particular series. Having a list of the names and addresses of people who bought thousand-dollar tickets and would never be home on Thursday nights could be valuable to a burglar, and at some point Elle was going to have to return to her profession to earn a living.

She selected a few oversize sheets from the files, laid them open on the desk, and photographed them. While she was doing that she glanced at some of the minutes from board meetings and saw that Valerie was on the boards of both museums and the philharmonic.

Elle was reluctantly impressed with Valerie. She had been well past the time of life when she could make a living as the most vivid girl in a bad movie. Apparently during her twenties she had not gotten famous enough to compete for roles as a character actress in her thirties. But she had broad cultural interests and must have had genuine knowledge of art and music. The other board members of these organizations would not have put up with her if she hadn't, regardless of the size of the checks she wrote. Half the members of art museum boards seemed to be crusty old artists who were always offending each other and denouncing the people whose only qualification was money, unless it was billions.

Elle sensed that she was getting closer to understanding what the three victims had in common. They all seemed to have an interest in art and a background as art fanciers, but no trace of artistic talent. None of the houses had a studio or even an easel. It was art-loving as a study and maybe a form of greed.

Elle knelt on the floor to examine the bottom drawer of the filing cabinet. This was the one that said BREMMER. Elle had known what that name meant since she was a child, and this was not the first house she'd broken into with connections to it. The Bremmer School was an institution that had always struck Elle as comically alien to the spirit of Los Angeles. As the seal on the stationery pointed out, it was founded in 1883. It was a private school, originally for boys only, and patterned after the prep schools in the East, but it became coed in the 1940s by means of a takeover of l'École des Filles. Elle had pictured that event as a *Rape of the Sabine Women,* boys in short pants in the role of Romans, carrying off girls in saddle shoes, kilts, and sleeveless sweaters.

A school directory in the file drawer confirmed that all three of Valerie's kids were enrolled at the Bremmer School. She had apparently been a big deal there, because her name was listed as the contact person for a couple of parents' committees. Elle didn't have any personal experience with private schools and felt a vast distance from ones like the Bremmer School, which was unabashedly for the children of the rich.

Elle leafed through the directory some more and found that Valerie had been a trustee of the school but had served her term. But it was someone else who caught Elle's eye. She almost missed it because the other name was listed as just plain Anne Mannon. The newspaper had called her Anne Satterthwaite Mannon. Apparently her kids went to Bremmer too. Elle checked the directory again. Neither of the husbands was listed as belonging to the school's power structure. They were listed only beneath their children in the general alphabetical entries of families.

Elle got distracted reading the names of other families whose kids went to the school. There were actors — many in pairs

— local politicians, musicians, and people with surnames that were the brand names of anything from stores to clothes to banking and insurance empires. She took pictures of a few of the pages, because the addresses were included, and some very rich people were careful about disseminating that information. But by now she had more names and addresses of the rich than she could use in a lifetime.

She closed the drawer and moved back up to the LACMA drawer. She pulled some of the hanging files forward on their frames so she could get a look at the files nearer to the back, and then she felt something hard and familiar. She carefully drew it out and looked at it. Valerie had hidden a Glock 17 in the back of the top file drawer. Elle released the magazine and looked at it — loaded. She found a second magazine and a box of 9-mm bullets at the back of the drawer. This was not a prop or an antique or a souvenir. It didn't commemorate some movie she had worked on. It was real and fully functional, and had been cleaned and oiled not too long ago. But it wasn't the murder weapon either. She would have recognized the distinctive Glock shape if it had been on the recording. Also, it had no silencer or raised sights to see over one.

What she'd seen when she'd frozen the recording had looked more like a pistol based on the classic M1911 .45. And once again, all the bullets in the box, the gun, and the magazine added up to fifty.

This was an odd place for a gun, in Elle's opinion. Most people who had guns for protecting themselves and their families from intruders kept them somewhere near their beds. This one was far from Valerie's bed in an office she shared with nobody. If she was afraid of something, it was specific to her. Was she waiting for her husband to gather enough evidence on her to want to kill her? Did she think somebody else was after her who would come only for her and leave her husband and kids alone?

Elle got up and went to the office door. There was a lock like the ones on the other doors in the house, which were pretty good. But in here there was also a dead bolt. There had not been one of those on any of the other interior doors. Maybe it was because of the gun that she'd had the extra lock installed. But if she'd kept the filing cabinet locked, it would have kept the kids away from the gun even without a door lock. Maybe having two locks was just the best she could do to be a responsible mother.

Elle took a few pictures of the written arrangements for the past few art exhibitions at each of the museums and the next few, so she could search them for information about the major players later. She added the minutes of the past few board meetings and moved on.

She felt she had not given enough thought to searching for the murder weapon. The things she had always found true of defensive weapons were not the same for murder weapons. Most smart killers got rid of them right away. Those who didn't would not keep them where they slept or anyplace where the police might find them.

Elle had always preferred hiding objects that might get her convicted of a crime in places that were outside her dwelling but not hard to get to, so probably murderers did the same. She tended to keep such things in the trunk of the car parked in her yard. This protected them with a lock, gave her adequate space to disguise or hide them, and made them very easy to move in a hurry.

She was aware that lots of survivalists bought lengths of large-diameter polyvinyl chloride tubing, inserted assault rifles and full ammo magazines in them, capped them at both ends, and buried them in their yards. An arrangement like that could keep a gun fresh and new for the postapocalypse they longed for, even if it didn't happen for a while. A pipe would hide a pistol and silencer even better, but it would be terribly inconvenient to keep burying and digging up a weapon for a series of murders.

She went to the garage and looked at the two cars. One was a Bentley and one a big Mercedes. She looked around in the garage for the keys, but there were none in any of the hiding places she would have chosen.

Then it occurred to her that there had been articles recently about criminals who had a device that would activate the key fobs of car keys remotely, while they were sitting on a counter in a house, and open the car doors. She had been interested because the device sounded like something she might want sometime if the reports turned out to be true. The articles had said the best way to avoid this scheme was to keep car keys in the refrigerator to insulate them from the signal.

She went into the kitchen, opened the refrigerator, and found two sets of keys in an aluminum coffee thermos. She went to the door, unlocked the two cars, and popped their trunks. She searched both cars for special hiding places, suspicious contents, and guns. She found nothing, and the cars were not parked on top of any suspicious depressions in the concrete either. She returned the keys to their place in the refrigerator.

She climbed the stairs to the second floor and searched the female and male caretakers' rooms, but found nothing suspicious. She discovered that the access hatch to the attic was in the ceiling of the male caretaker's closet. It was reached by a ladder that was attached to one wall. It occurred to her that this might be the answer. The caretakers seemed to be so good at everything that maybe Teason hired one of them as the shooter.

Elle climbed up into the attic and used her flashlight to search. She walked to the end of the warm, cramped place, but found absolutely nothing except wiring and insulation. She climbed back down and closed the hatch.

The view of the yard outside the windows had gotten dim. She had now spent the whole day here, been in every room of the house, and probably found whatever she was going to find. There was no evidence to show that Santo Teason had done anything except marry a woman who cheated on him and also got herself killed. Elle prepared to leave, making sure as she went that everything was left as nearly as possible the way she had found it. She walked through the whole house again, looking closely at everything. She found she now had to use her flashlight to see.

She reached the kitchen, slithered out through the dog door, and slid the barrier back over it. The whole day had gone by, and it was dark outside. She moved quietly to the side of the house and began to make her way to the back fence, when she heard an engine. She sidestepped beyond the house to the back without stopping to look.

The headlights of the vehicle lit up the driveway and the garage door for a second and went out. The engine was still running, and she heard it coming up the driveway toward her. She retreated about sixty feet to hide behind the pool house and waited.

An older dark green tradesman's van moved up the driveway, then made a slow turn around the garage to the rear and stopped there. The engine went silent. After a few seconds she heard two doors shut, and after a few more seconds two young men walked around the garage to the driveway. They both wore knit caps pulled down over the tops of their ears. She had always thought that was a stupid style for young men in Los Angeles. Except for a month on either side of Christmas, a person living here had less chance of getting chilled than of getting sliced up by a sushi chef. She watched them and noticed they were swiveling their heads around, looking to either side and over their shoulders far too often. *Don't tell me,* she thought.

They both reached up and pulled the fronts of their knit caps down over their faces to reveal eye and mouth holes, which they tugged to fit over their features. Fucking burglars. She was enraged. She wasn't sure she could have explained why, but she didn't feel the need to fully understand it. She had virtually cleared Santo Teason of murder, and she had been extremely careful not to harm him or his innocent children with her visit. These two idiots would now smash their way in, break doors, and throw furniture around, looking for something valuable that she had carefully left undisturbed.

She remained hidden and waited until the two had made their way to the side door of the house, the big glass French door. One of them tried the knob, and the other took out a suction cup and a glass cutter. When he stuck the cup firmly to the glass beside the knob and scored the glass, she waited.

When he rapped loudly on it to break it, she could wait no longer.

19

Elle ran at the wall around the rear of the house, jumped to bring her right foot about halfway up the six-foot surface, grasped the top, and let her momentum carry her up so her hips reached the top. She turned and rolled over the top of the wall and dropped to the other side.

The Teason house alarm was a silent one, but she knew it was going off, sending a signal to an alarm monitoring company. In a minute the company would have armed men on their way to the place while they used whatever on-site monitoring system they had installed. They would at least know exactly what opening had been breached and probably be deciding whether they should also call the police to respond to the alarm.

They would start by trying to make sure it was a break-in. There was a fine for calling the cops to a false alarm, and it escalated for subsequent false alarms. Some security companies had the ability to conduct a remote visual search using the house's security cameras. It would let them see if an intruder was an armed robber or a raccoon. It could tell them if a sound of glass breaking had been caused by a clumsy thief or a minor seismic tremor.

She knew she should keep moving, get to her rented SUV, and go. But she was already clear of the house and behind an opaque wall. She was almost certainly safe for now, and she was curious to see what the security company would do. She told herself that by staying she was conducting an experiment that would tell her what her natural enemies, the security companies, would do when an alarm was tripped.

She didn't have to wait long. A black SUV with its lights off appeared at the front of the house, swung into the driveway, sped up the long paved surface to the garage door, veered to the right at the last second, and stopped. It was now between the house and the garage. It was blocking the van from driving out from behind the garage and speeding down the driveway. The only place the van could go now was right into the pool.

Three men in black coverall uniforms

jumped down from the SUV to the drive-way. All of them wore utility belts with holstered pistols, pepper spray canisters, Tasers, and handcuffs. As they ran to check the perimeter of the house, Elle heard something else and turned to see it.

A second black SUV with no lights on sped up and stopped in front of the house. Three more occupants in black coveralls got out and ran toward the front door.

Their gear and equipment seemed too serious and too uniform to belong to a security company. Maybe this was a special squad from the LAPD. The police used unmarked vehicles every day, but it seemed to Elle that every security company car she'd ever seen served as a billboard for advertising. It would always have the company name on its doors and trunk.

Elle moved along the wall a few feet and watched the team at the back of the house. A lead man used a key to unlock the kitchen door. He swung it open and the other two went in with guns drawn, one high and the other low.

She trotted along the outside of the wall beside the driveway until she was close to the side door where the two burglars had entered. The French door was open and she could see inside.

The three from the front and the three from the back had entered fast, and she watched as the two teams converged on the pair of burglars. All six had pistols drawn, and all had incredibly bright halogen flashlights shining on the two young burglars, so the light seemed to hit their heads from every direction at once. The burglars squinted, held their hands over their eyes, and tried in vain to turn their heads away from the glare.

The auras of the flashlights lit the room and confirmed what Elle had thought at first was a trick of her mind. The six security men all had silencers on the muzzles of their pistols. She sucked in a breath. This wasn't what the under-trained and underpaid rent-a-cops hired by security companies carried. The last she'd heard, silencers weren't even legal to own in California. Gun laws sometimes changed without her knowing it right away, but it was extremely unlikely that this change would have taken place in California.

She had been resisting the suspicion that had been growing as she watched. Not only did the silencers look the same as the one she had seen in the recording of the first murders, but the security company had the same model Tahoe SUVs as the team of people who had been searching for her in the bars.

The six black-suited team members had the two burglars lying on their bellies now, and next they were handcuffed and dragged out to the driveway. Two men held each burglar's arms, and there was one man behind with his gun drawn. When they reached the first SUV they pushed the prisoners onto the floor in the back of the vehicle and closed the doors. A driver and two men got in after them, backed down the driveway to the street, still with headlights off, and drove away.

Two of the remaining three went to work securing the French door at the side of the house and probably resetting the alarm system. The third walked up the driveway and around the garage. He was carrying a set of keys in his hand. After a few seconds she heard the engine of the two burglars' van start and watched the van backing around the garage to the driveway.

Elle ducked below the wall and moved away from the security men toward the back of the lot. She went over the back wall of the neighbor's house and ran to her rented vehicle. She knew that the most sensible thing to do now was to drive to her next hotel and make herself invisible as long as she could while she studied the pictures she had taken in the house.

But she didn't. The two SUVs seemed to her to have arrived too quickly. Maybe they had been following the van because it seemed likely that an old van prowling these streets didn't belong to a resident and could be carrying burglars. But she couldn't be sure that she had not unknowingly set off an alarm before they'd arrived. She could have been on a security monitor earlier or even all day. And the security teams' arrival had occurred just after she'd left the house. Maybe they had only been standing by waiting to stop her, and she had inadvertently substituted the other two for herself.

Elle was almost certain she knew where the SUVs were based. She had seen a fleet of them the night when she had trailed the blond woman and her two companions from the bar. They had been parked in a row behind the plain building near the airport.

Elle wanted to get away from this, to place herself as far as possible from these people, but she had an irresistible need to know what was going to happen. The two burglars were almost certainly just a pair of young idiots who had read that a rich and famous person was going to be away from home for a few months and had imagined that they were ready for the job of robbing his house.

She knew that she was probably being foolish. If those two had caught her in the house they would certainly have robbed her and might very well have killed her — or tried to kill her. It occurred to her that she was still wearing the Rohrbaugh R9 pistol in the belly band, but she had no desire to use it and no idea what she should do if she did.

Elle pulled onto the San Diego Freeway off Sunset and began to act on her risky urge. She was racing the two SUVs to the place she believed they had come from. She was over the speed limit and still accelerating, but she calmed herself and settled on a few miles per hour above it, in the range that wouldn't interest the police. She had an illegal gun on her and she had a great many incriminating pictures in the memory of her phone, and she couldn't risk losing them. Getting pulled over and arrested now would be a catastrophe.

Elle drove toward the airport exits on the freeway and then went past, backtracking on the Imperial and Pacific Coast Highways and turning north up La Tijera to La Cienega. She saw a green van moving toward her on La Cienega. As she passed she saw the black-suited driver and was sure this was the van the burglars had parked at the Teason house. It flashed past, and she went on for a quarter mile, then coasted to a near stop without touching her brakes, switched off her headlights, and made a U-turn before she switched them on again to follow it. They must be turning the van and the prisoners in to the police.

The van turned eastward. Elle wondered if there was a special police station down here that held impounded vehicles. It seemed to her that it would have made the most sense to turn in the prisoners and their vehicle at the Beverly Hills police station. She supposed that the LAPD might be handling these things because it had much more extensive facilities.

They drove for about twenty minutes. She followed at the greatest distance she could manage and still see the van. She saw the van pull to the right, and when she got closer she could see that it had entered a dark, empty field, but the glow of its headlights showed that the field had once been covered with buildings, like a factory or warehouse complex. There were concrete foundation pads, now fringed with weeds, and a couple of strips of asphalt pavement that must have been on-site roads or drive-ways.

Elle drove past the place without slowing, going on until she saw a derelict brick building on the next lot, pulled in beyond it, and parked. She began to walk back toward the field where the van had stopped.

She had made her way about sixty yards before a new set of headlights appeared on the deserted road, coming her way. She knew she wouldn't have time to run back, so she dropped to her belly and rolled downward into the ditch beside the road. The ditch was summer dry and choked with weeds, but it was deep enough to keep her hidden.

She lay there and waited as the headlights grew nearer and brighter. She was waiting with her face down for the vehicle to pass her so she could lift her head, but it never reached her. Instead it turned off the road onto the vacant lot and pulled up near the burglars' van. Elle looked at it and saw that it was one of the two black SUVs. The three occupants got out, and she could see them in the glow that spilled from the headlights onto the ground ahead of them.

They all wore black coveralls and black baseball caps. Their torsos had a square look, and she recognized it as the look that cops had when they wore body armor.

Elle took out her telephone, shaded the screen with her cap, and pressed the icon for the camera and then the option for video. She kept the screen covered so the light from it wouldn't cast a glow on her face and began recording what she could see. There was something odd going on. Had these security people been in league with the burglars and taken them here so their colleagues wouldn't turn them over to the police?

The SUV's motor was still running and the headlights were still on, shining on the weedy field and the concrete pads. She could see the dark figures in silhouette in front of the light. After about thirty seconds of talk, the three who had brought the black SUV opened the doors at the rear, leaned in, and dragged out the two burglars.

The security men lifted them to their feet, and Elle could see that their arms were immobile, still held behind them by handcuffs. What was happening?

One of the black-suited figures said something to the burglars and kicked one of them. The two began to run. Their wrists were still cuffed, but they were young and fast, and they had run from enemies at night before. They instantly separated, veering in both directions out of the cone of bright light thrown by the headlights, and became hard to see in the unlit places. Elle felt some hope. They were doing the right thing. A person running straight away from danger was almost as easy to hit as a stationary target. A person running off at an angle into the darkness was much harder to hit.

The black-suited figures raised their suppressed pistols and began to fire at them. The pistol reports were diminished but audible, and the muzzle flashes were reduced. The shooters didn't seem to hit anything. Maybe they were just trying to give the burglars the scare of their lives and leave them here in cuffs. She'd heard from other thieves that some of the security people at big store chains just beat up the thieves they caught so they'd be afraid to steal again. Prosecution cost money and didn't end losses.

But two of the black figures ran and jumped into the black SUV and then roared ahead. Elle kept filming with her phone's screen covered, but she had to be careful now that the SUV was in motion. If the SUV driver decided to double back or circle one of the runners, a turn of the wheel could bring Elle into the white glare of the headlights.

The SUV accelerated across the field and turned to the left, and the driver hit the high beam lights. Even from where she was, Elle could see the burglar who had run in that direction. He had covered a surprising distance in the dark with his hands behind his back, but the SUV ate up his lead in a few seconds, then sped beyond him and circled to hem him in. It seemed to amuse the driver to roll along beside the struggling man, sidling closer and closer to him.

He stopped running. Elle was too far away to see his facial expression as he turned back toward the road, but his posture was slumped, almost limp, as he slowly began to walk.

The security man who had been driving the burglars' van was a bit slower and more tentative, but he caught up with the other burglar. The boy had to dive to the side to keep from being run down, and before he could get up again the two in the van got out and punched and kicked him a few times. When they raised him to his feet he began to run again. He had made it close to the end of the field. Until now the field had looked as though it might go on for some distance — maybe to a place where he could hide.

It didn't. There was a fence, a chain-link

barrier with three strands of barbed wire at the top. The wire was irrelevant, because the young man had his wrists handcuffed behind him. He couldn't climb anything higher than his waist. He threw himself to the ground and tried to slither under the fence where there was a little slack between two posts, but there wasn't enough room.

The two black-suited figures dragged him to his feet and back to the van. When they rejoined the black SUV, they threw him out onto the ground with his partner. They were rougher now, as though the two burglars had cheated by not letting their captors shoot them as they ran.

The two security men from the van raised their pistols and shot them both in the head. Then the other two security men took off the handcuffs and returned them to their belts.

They turned off the van's engine and its headlights, and then all four security men climbed into the black SUV. They turned off the SUV's lights and drove, bumping over the rough spots and then gliding onto the abandoned road to the street.

Elle remained facedown and never moved or lifted her head until they had reached the road and driven on for a distance. She knew that the driver would use his mirrors to glance back at the field. When she had given him time to do that, she put away her phone, stood up, and began to head the other way. As soon as she was on solid pavement she ran hard toward her rental car.

20

She got into her car, started it, and connected the battery charger to her phone. She was sure the battery must be low by now. Then she too kept her headlights off, drove to the street, and turned to follow the black SUV. She straddled the painted line in the center of the street so she wouldn't angle off into the drainage ditch.

She stifled an impulse to go check on the two burglars. She had seen them both shot in the head and then had seen the black-suited killers check them closely while they retrieved the handcuffs from their wrists. These were not people who would have hesitated to fire again if there had been any remnant of life.

The most useful thing she could do now was to make certain that these killers were who she thought they were. There had to be certainty. So far the only thing she could be certain about was that she had seen two more people caught and murdered.

Or maybe that wasn't all that had happened. Maybe the security people had been aware of her presence in the house for some time. Maybe the two burglars had been terribly unlucky and shown up just as the security people had been about to arrive and take Elle out here to kill her. Certainly they hadn't driven from down near the airport to Beverly Hills in ten minutes. It was possible they had been out patrolling the houses of their richest customers when Elle had triggered an alarm.

She turned on her lights when she reached the first intersection. It was late now, so the roads were more sparsely traveled. When she saw the stoplight she could also see that the nearest approaching cars were about a quarter mile off. It crossed her mind that the odds of one of them being a police car were higher than they would have been when the roads were crowded, but she accelerated anyway.

If the next car to reach the intersection turned out to be a cop car, she couldn't just give up as soon as she saw lights and heard a siren. She would make him chase her.

If she was going to be caught, what she could do was lead the cops on enough of a chase so there would be plenty of them and maybe a helicopter, and then drive to the building where all the black SUVs parked. The last video she'd taken showed them murdering the two burglars. She didn't know if the faces of the killers were visible on the video, but their cars, outfits, and equipment had been distinctive.

She kept glancing at her mirrors, but there were no police cars. Fate wasn't going to give her the chance to sacrifice herself to make up for Sharon. She was going to have to decide what to do and then take action without anybody pushing her into it. That was the hardest for her. She was good at reacting quickly to threats. She could think clearly and run, hide, or even fight. But to her, as a healthy, athletic twenty-four-year-old, seeing a problem and throwing her life at it seemed nearly impossible. The only thing that had brought her this far had been her guilt about Sharon. She had no idea if that could carry her much further.

Twenty minutes later the black SUV was approaching the place where Elle had expected it to go. It turned into the driveway at the low white building near the airport.

She was coming up on the building now. She saw that there were eight SUVs in the lot behind it. The front doors of one of the vehicles opened and the dome light came on. As the driver slid off the seat, he took off his black baseball cap, and Elle saw the blond hair freed from its confinement and realized this was a woman. As Elle watched, the woman ran her hand through her hair, disarranging it and making it stand up to cool her head.

Elle's car reached the driveway in front of the building and went past. She held the two people walking toward the back of the building in her rearview mirror before she lost sight of them.

She glanced back again and saw a second black SUV make the left turn into the driveway and head around the building. That had to be the men who had stayed to secure the door and reset the alarm. She supposed that her shocked and emotional state had made her drive faster than either of the SUVs. The killers seemed much calmer and more controlled than she felt. And they didn't seem to have trouble remembering that they wouldn't get bothered by the police if they obeyed the traffic laws.

Elle kept going, never letting her foot touch the brake pedal. She couldn't let the bright red brake lights come on and draw attention to her car. She coasted into a turn toward the airport parking lots on Aviation

Way. She reached Lot C, took a ticket from the machine, waited for the barrier to rise, and entered. She parked and patiently sent all of her photographs and videos to each of her internet addresses and then to her Iron Mountain account. Then she looked at the clock on her phone screen to see if she had enough time left before dawn.

The walk was longer than she had expected. She always had tried to get to and from the airport as fast as possible, and most of the surrounding land was flat, ugly, and dirty. She was able to stay a bit back from the road along this stretch, because it was mostly parking lots on one side and dying businesses on the other. She didn't want to get caught in somebody's headlights and look like an easy victim, so she hurried.

She trotted part of the way because she was impatient with the distance and frightened of people. She couldn't think of anybody she would like to meet out here right now, so she tried to stay out of any light, no matter how faint. Then the building was in her view, and she slowed down but stayed away from lights while she studied it.

When Elle Stowell looked at a building it was a special kind of look, a burglar's look. If an ordinary person studied this building he would see a wide rectangle about one and a half stories high, with no windows or doors in front. It sat on a concrete pad with a paved parking lot in back that had painted spaces for two rows of twelve vehicles. The nearest spaces were now taken up by ten identical black SUVs. A person might think that a flat-roofed building with no windows was just about impregnable, so it probably had been built to protect merchandise. And this one was close to a major airport, so it had probably been put here for shipping and receiving. He might even note that the outer walls were stucco, which was the most durable, cheapest, and lowest-maintenance covering.

Elle saw those things, but she saw more. A four-sided building was actually a six-sided structure, because the roof and the underside were penetrable surfaces too. The impervious building had to have ventilators to keep the air circulating. It was in Southern California, where a windowless building with no air-conditioning was an oven. A building couldn't serve as a business without bathrooms, which meant there were water pipes going in and sewer pipes going out. The place had electricity, which required insulated lines running from the nearest step-down transformer to the building and then inside.

A building intended to store goods of any kind would have originally had big doors, like garage doors, so the merchandise could be brought in and out on pallets by forklifts. They would be in the back of the building, and if not, then they had been decommissioned, taken out, and maybe boarded over and covered with stucco. They could be another way in.

She stayed back to study the roof. She couldn't see all of it yet, but she knew that many commercial buildings had some source of natural lighting that kept electricity costs down — skylights, usually. A skylight with a rectangular frame and a translucent plastic bubble was cheap. If it wasn't nailed down it could be lifted.

Warehouses almost all had concrete floors. Many of them had drains built into the floor so they could be cleaned with a hose, and some of the drains were not pipes but channels covered with fitted steel plates. But she was not making decisions about the place yet. She was just looking.

If a building was too hard to break into there were other ways. Often the easiest was to take advantage of common failings of human beings — carelessness, laziness, inattention, and impatience. Burglars sometimes came and went unseen because nobody had secured a door, fixed a latch, or gotten up and checked to see what had made a sound. Burglars had gotten into warehouses by climbing into loads that were to be driven inside.

She took pictures of the building from three sides with her phone, and then she went to the fence that separated the building's parking lot from the open land that lay between it and the margins, runways, and taxiways of the airport. She had to walk almost a hundred yards before she found a place where the fence was vulnerable. There was a hole that had been dug under the fence, apparently by a dog, and filled in. She was able to loosen the dirt and expand the hole with her knife and her hands until she could slip under.

Once she was on the weedy ground she was able to walk back to the area behind the stucco building. She stopped and lay down, looking at every feature she could see. Right now there were ten identical black SUVs, but only three private cars parked farther from the building. The killers she'd seen arriving must have gone home.

There was only one set of double doors. They were made of glass, and they allowed her to see the general structure of the place. She could see a small open space like a waiting room and, beyond it, a long corridor with doors on both sides. She could see she had been wrong about the big garage doors. The present double glass doors had taken the place of a single large door. If there had ever been others, they must have been along the windowless surface that faced the road. She took pictures, turned and withdrew back to the hole where she had slithered through, and walked to Lot C. Now she knew what they were and where they would be. She would have to figure out what to do.

21

She drove from Lot C to Century Boulevard and looked at the hotels. She picked one with a sign that said guests could park cars in its indoor lot during their plane trips. She didn't know whether anyone in the black SUVs had seen her rental car, but there was no reason to multiply the risks with every decision.

Elle went inside the hotel. The man and woman who were at the desk for this desolate shift didn't appear to notice the way she was dressed or how tired and rumpled she was. They had obviously learned that it wasn't possible to tell by appearance whether a reasonably pleasant-looking young woman in Los Angeles was a criminal or a rock star, so they treated her like a hybrid of both, neither friendly nor unfriendly, scandalized nor impressed. She was a person standing upright and holding a credit card. That was all she had to be.

They sent her to the fourteenth floor, which Elle knew was always the thirteenth mislabeled for the people whose idea of the borderline between reality and nonsense was flexible. She wasn't one of them, so she just hoped it would be quiet so she could recover.

The shower was good and the bed was good, so she was unconscious very soon. In spite of a continuous slow-moving set of nightmares, she stayed asleep. The dreams had been getting bloodier and grislier since the deaths of the three art lovers, and the deaths of the two young burglars now made them even worse. All through the night she was cleaning up blood. Every dream person shifted the responsibility for hiding bodies and cleaning the pools of blood to her. They were her corpses to manage. After a long night of this labor she awoke in the afternoon and went downstairs to the restaurant for breakfast.

While she ate she wandered the world on the screen of her phone. She found a site that said it would forward whatever she wanted to the recipient of her choice anonymously, through a site in Moldova. She paid and then tested it by sending one of her own sites a "Happy Mother's Day" message. She paid again and transferred the movie she had made of the deaths of the two young burglars to the Los Angeles police. She chose a fifteen-day delay for its forwarding. If she couldn't do anything to the killers within that time, she would probably be dead. The address she used was the homicide division office downtown. The detectives would recognize what they were seeing, and maybe the movie would help them with the various interlocking murders, including Elle's own.

When she had finished breakfast she went to the front desk and extended her reservation for another week. Then she drove to an enormous hardware and building supply store.

As she drove, she thought about why the murders of three strangers had taken over her life. It was because of the ones after that, the killing of her friend Sharon and her almost-boyfriend Peter in Sharon's apartment. She knew nothing about the motive for the first killings, but she knew about that one. The killer had come for Elle, and when he didn't find her, he killed the ones he found.

These people had no feeling, no sense of how precious life was. Her experience of growing up was simply trying to be alive — helping to find enough so everybody in the house got to eat, and then remembering not to eat everything up before there was something in the house to replace it. She had learned to be quiet and unmoving when the person at the door or walking past was a threat. And she remembered practicing her social skills, smiling and giving the expected answer whenever a school official asked about her or her family — the answer of happiness, health, and conformity. When she was sick she hid it so no meddling adult would turn her over for medical care that her grandmother couldn't pay for. That would have been a disaster, because there was no sin as bad as not having any money.

She got good at spotting other people like her. When one of them was held up to scrutiny, trying to make the lies brief and reassuring the way she did, their eyes would meet and she would try to convey with a nod that they were the same and that she understood. Sometimes it felt like being a member of an alien species that looked like people but weren't. They had to pretend to be like everyone else or they'd be unmasked. It was all just so they could be left alone and allowed to live.

Elle had never learned to assume everything was going to be all right, because most of the time it wasn't. Sharon had grown up differently, and she'd had a right to think that if she did nothing to harm anyone else, nothing would happen to her. It probably would have been true, but now she was dead because Elle had brought the trouble to her.

Elle pulled her car into a space at the giant hardware store and pushed a big orange shopping cart ahead of her. The place was organized just like a supermarket, with signs at the ends of aisles with numbers on them and categories like "Lumber and Carpentry," "Plumbing," "Lighting and Electric," "Ventilation and Filters."

Elle went through the store picking out equipment: a battery-operated variable-speed electric drill, a portable welding outfit with small oxygen and acetylene tanks, short hoses, and a protective face mask. The emphasis was on miniaturization and light weight. Everything was going to be used once and then discarded. She also picked up a can of flat black spray paint, one of white spray paint, and a piece of sheet metal two feet wide and four feet long. She bought titanium bits, hacksaw blades, and a few other compact hand tools.

When she was back in her car she drove to the Valley and stopped at the Unseen Eye, a store that sold security and spy gear. There were nanny cams, bugs, pinhole cameras, and a variety of other gadgets. Some of them were designed to be installed by electricians, but other items were meant to get the curious amateur hooked on eavesdropping, spying, and the darker uses of technology. She happened to notice a display of transponders for attachment to cars, and it included models exactly like those she'd had removed from her car on the way home from Las Vegas. She was startled by the fact that their familiarity gave her a sensation that was almost like pleasure.

She went straight to the displays of items that were in the glass cases along the counter, where bits of technology were presented on velvet-lined surfaces, like jewelry. This was a business that was about size, and the smallest devices were the best and most expensive. Some were disguised — computer drives, cameras, recorders, or microphones in the barrels of recognizable brand-name pens, watches, compacts, sunglasses, car key fobs. There were miniaturized devices intended to be attached to or hidden inside clothes, purses, luggage, or virtually any product a person could buy.

She picked out several devices she thought would be useful where she was going and then doubled her order before she paid and drove back to her hotel near the airport.

She spent a few hours testing, planning, and then sleeping to prepare for her night's work.

When midnight had passed and there were fewer people out on the roads, Elle drove from her hotel to the area northeast of the airport where the security company's building was. She was pleased to see that the night was dark and the air around her was a thick fog, as it sometimes was near the airport. To her the planes parked near the terminals looked half hidden in banks of glowing mist, but the lights that sometimes were reflected downward off low clouds to illuminate the world were not visible. She parked beyond a building that looked similar to the one where she was going, put on her backpack, and picked up her metal sheet.

She had made some modifications. Her sheet metal rectangle had been spray-painted black on one side and white on the other, and cut into it was a slot that looked like the opening of a letterbox. Her gear was all neatly arranged in her backpack. Being precise about packing things was something she had learned about working in the dark.

She walked along smoothly and easily until she was in sight of the building, and she kept up her pace as she studied the structure. She had inferred on the first night when she had seen the building that at least eight of the twelve black SUVs were always parked in the lot at night. Most residential burglars tried to arrive during the day, when the owners of houses were away at work. It was burglars of commercial properties who arrived at night. This company must have had mostly residential clients, because the black SUVs were in the lot again, but only three private cars.

Also, she had noticed on her first visit that the front and sides of the building had no windows or doors. What this meant to her tonight was that nobody was casually gazing out a window and noticing her. The only door was the big one at the rear of the building facing the edge of the airport. When she reached the nearest corner of the building she sat and craned her neck, looking for the places where the cameras along the eaves of the building were aimed. She took off her pack, reached in, and took out a spray can of furniture stain. She stepped around behind a camera at the corner above her, leaned her sheet metal rectangle against the wall of the building, and stepped up into the slot she had cut, using it as a ladder. She sprayed the bulb-like housing and stepped down.

The stain would not be opaque, so if

355

someone inside glanced at a monitor, he would still see squares for all the cameras, but one would be too dim and blurry for him to make out anything in its feed. Her experience of human beings told her nobody sitting through a graveyard shift guarding a stucco building against nothing was going to go outside with a ladder and clean the lens right now. Whatever the malfunction was, it would wait until daylight, when it would be other people's problem. Let them fix it or call a repairman.

She waited for a few minutes until she was sure nobody had noticed her and then went to work. She had chosen this side of the building because it was where the vertical vent pipes on the roof all occurred. Vertical vent pipes meant kitchens or bathrooms. They were necessary to allow air in so the water ran quickly down the drains. Usually a vent consisted of a simple pipe in the wall behind a sink.

She started at a spot with one drain vent, which made her hope for a kitchen. Kitchens, even small ones, had cabinets and counters along at least one wall. She found a round metal cover — a trap arrangement that hung down and covered a fan when it wasn't spinning and opened outward when the fan was running. She leaned her metal sheet against the outer wall, stepped into the slot, held up the cover, and looked inside. As she had guessed, the vent was under a hood above a stove. She studied the room, paying close attention to where the stove and sink were, and even closer attention to where the cabinets were. She could see that the kitchen was fairly long and across the hall from another room. The end to her left was not near anything but the small waiting area near the main door.

She crawled to the best spot along the outer wall, where she could not be seen by a camera, and used her knife to learn about the building. The outer layer was stucco that had been smeared over a layer of chicken wire that held it in place. She cut those layers away with wire cutters. Underneath them she found what she had suspected might be here. The inner layer was a sheet of corrugated steel bolted to a frame. The building had been constructed a long time ago, possibly even during World War II, when thousands of airplanes had been made in factories near the airport and shipped, along with every other possible commodity, to the Pacific theater. It had probably been erected in haste like a Quonset hut, because the corrugated steel had a coat of old olive paint that had chipped and rusted a bit before the stucco had been added.

She had chosen to bring an acetylene torch because it was the quickest and quietest way to get though a steel barrier. It took a few minutes to take out and assemble the welding kit — connecting the valves and regulators to the tanks and the hoses to the torch — and put on the safety goggles. Next she leaned the sheet metal against the pack to form a shield and hide the light and sparks she was about to produce. She turned on the tanks, clicked the spark striker, and then adjusted the flame to a small, steady triangle and cut the first line in the corrugated steel. She cut a square about two feet on a side, pulled it out with pliers, and then waited for it to cool while she dismantled and stowed the welding torch and tanks and selected the equipment she would need next.

She went back to the vent on the side wall to look into the kitchen again. There was no sign that anyone had heard or smelled anything. She used the drill on slow speed to make a line of holes in the thin synthetic wood backing of the cabinet and then a hacksaw blade to connect the holes.

When the piece of corrugated steel was cool enough to touch she leaned into the hole she'd cut it from, turned on her small flashlight, and examined the inside of the cupboard. There was plenty of room for her, so she crawled in. The only parts of the space under the counter that were crowded were about twelve feet away under the double sink. The two U-shaped drainpipes, garbage disposal, boxes and bottles of dish detergent, cans of cleanser, packages of sponges, rolls of paper towels, and other things had all been stored there, where they were used. Closer to Elle, the only obstacles were in the five inches of space above her head taken up by drawers for silverware and utensils. This was not a kitchen that was used much for cooking.

She used her flashlight sparingly, cupping the lens in her gloved hand so there was just enough light for her to see where the electrical outlets along the wall were. Before she did anything else, she sat still for a long count of a hundred and listened. There was no sound of another human being, so she slowly pushed one of the cabinet doors open an eighth of an inch.

The room was still deserted. It was furnished with three tables and a dozen chairs; a refrigerator, stove, and microwave oven; and a couple of coffeemakers. Through the open doorway to the hall she could see on the wall a whiteboard with a handwritten schedule. Beside it was a closed office door labeled EDWARD RANSOM. That had to be the name of the boss.

She still heard no activity in the building. She pulled the cabinet door shut and reached outside the building to bring in the electronic devices she had bought. She began with a small, flat, white square-shaped device designed to transmit sound signals to a remote computer. When she plugged it in, it looked like nothing, a barely visible object that might have been placed in a socket by the management to prevent the overloading of circuits. She plugged two pinhole cameras into other outlets, taped their thin insulated wires to the upper side of the divider between two drawers, and aimed them into the kitchen through holes she drilled under the edge of the counter.

She waited about a half hour before her next foray outside the cabinet. She stood on a chair from the kitchen and placed two more pinhole cameras in the main hallway ceiling tiles — one aimed at an office at the end of the hall, one aimed inside an empty office that included a big desk. She placed a fifth in the short L-shaped space leading into what looked like the radio dispatch center. She placed four in the suspended acoustic tile ceiling that ran the length of the hall, wherever she could find a socket that served a fan or a light. That left her with one more, and she saw no good place for it so she put it in her pocket and made her way back into the kitchen cabinet under the counter.

She cleaned up the sawdust from the drilling, then lay down in the space under the counter and took a last look at everything she'd done.

Using plug-in devices meant they were never going to lose power and range as they reached the end of a battery's life. They could be permanent if she wanted to leave them, and she certainly had no desire to come back here to retrieve them.

She crawled outside the building onto the lawn, replaced the fake wood backing and the corrugated steel sheet to plug the hole she had cut, duct-taped them there, and then spray-painted the surface with white paint she had rough-guess-matched with the color of the building.

She shouldered her backpack, picked up her sheet metal barrier, and headed through the field of view of the blinded security camera. She stopped to preserve the metal sheet in case she needed it again by shoving it under the dumpster beside a building a hundred yards away.

Elle's hotel on Century Boulevard was easily within a mile of the security company's building. The range of the audio bugs and the pinhole cameras was guaranteed to be three miles, and when she tested them, she found that all the signals came in strong. She had all of them recording to her laptop computer.

After speeding up the replay on each site to run through what she had recorded, she could see that this was going to be a long and frustrating way to learn anything. The late-night shift consisted of a man about sixty years old who had craggy features like a sculpture carved from wood, a plump Hispanic woman in a tan uniform who occupied the dispatch room, and a black man who spent most of his time in the office with the older man. They both seemed to be doing bookkeeping, because they were reading small sheets filled out by hand, hitting the number keys along the tops of their computer keyboards, and occasionally printing out the results.

The two men chatted only when they both happened to end a unit of work around the same time. The woman appeared only when she walked across the open door on the way to or from the bathroom or kitchen. Then they would all greet one another, but nobody would stop to talk about murdering anybody.

Elle would let her devices transmit to her receiver site for the next day and night and see what they caught. Meanwhile, she got ready to return to the Kavanagh house.

22

It was morning, and being at the Kavanagh house again brought back every feeling of the first morning she had come here. The fact that Elle was able to enter the building by exactly the same route meant to her that the police had never learned that she had been here and searched inside. She felt a little disappointed in them. She stood in the attic and then went to the spot where the folding staircase was secured. She opened the trapdoor an inch and listened, then lowered the staircase to the second-floor hall.

She descended and walked along the second-floor hall to the upper landing of the spiral staircase from the foyer. The neoclassical statues and the paintings were gone. The natural light from the windows in the vaults above the ceiling shone on bare hardwood floors. The strip of sockets along the crown molding for the spotlights above the portraits had no lights connected anymore, and the wall mountings that had held the portraits now held nothing.

Elle reminded herself that never on earth had anything remained unclaimed for long. Somebody inherited, bought, or stole it. The art had been moved out after Nick Kavanagh died. He had been a gallery owner, so most or all of the paintings in the house had undoubtedly belonged to other people. He had merely been storing and selling them for the owners, who probably had them now.

She swiveled her head. The rosy-skinned French demoiselles she didn't miss. She stepped into the short bare hallway to the master bedroom.

The room was transformed. The windows overlooking the garden were shuttered and fastened. The nautical paintings that had given the room blue skies, white clouds, white sails, and sea spray — the illusion of a panoramic view of the world — were gone. Now the room was four bare walls with more fixtures where nothing was hung.

The furniture was still here, moved to the center of the floor unchanged except for the big bed. The mattress and springs and the blood-soaked sheets and pillows were gone, and the bed had been dismantled. The spattered headboard was now clean, leaning against the tall, heavy dresser with the similarly cleaned footboard.

The whole house was dead now, part of a man's lifetime that had ended and must already be half forgotten, replaced by a scandal. She had seen cleared-out places before and had been prepared for the change. She was not a person who let herself be surprised over and over by things she should have expected.

She had taken a risk coming back to the scene of the murders in the hope that the ornamentation would be gone and whatever remained here would be unhidden and undisguised and help her learn something. She wandered around the room, making sure that the floor where she walked had no dust that would retain an imprint of her shoes.

When she saw the pinhole camera she knew she had found the thing that had gone unnoticed before. The white power strip along the top of the crown molding extended to all four walls. On it were sliding white plastic covers that were to be moved aside to bare a socket or pushed back to cover it, depending on whether an artwork was to be lit. She ran her eyes along the white power strips and saw that each of them had a couple of small white squares with tiny white glass dots in the center.

She had never seen one of these devices in her life until the previous day in the shop in Sherman Oaks. She had bought ten of them herself. The man who had handled the sale had said they were the best pinhole cameras available. And they were certainly very good. She had nine of hers watching the office near the airport right now, and the images were clear and crisp.

As she considered the situation she made sure she showed no reaction. She could be on camera right now. Was on camera. She knew that. She just didn't know whether there was still anybody on the receiving end, watching or recording the house, now that the owner was dead. She kept the thoughtful, empty expression on her face as she turned and walked out of the room to the upper landing of the spiral staircase. She turned to move along the hallway. Were there other pinhole cameras in the power strips out here?

Yes, there were. She saw one, and that was enough to make it unnecessary to look for more. Nick Kavanagh's assurance to Valerie McGee Teason came back. He'd said the whole place was wired with alarms to protect the paintings he brought home. That must have been what the installers told him the power strips were for — that they provided current to the small spotlights over the paintings, but they also provided it to alarms that went off if a painting were removed or tampered with. And it was probably true. But the strips could also provide power to pinhole cameras and microphones. If he'd known that, he obviously hadn't given it sufficient thought.

She took out her phone and held it to her right ear as though she were making a call, waiting for someone to answer, but she was recording a movie of the power strip above her as she walked toward the hallway where the staircase was. She said, "It's me. No message," and put the phone away. She remembered the blond woman, Anne Satterthwaite Mannon, saying, "How did you even know we were here?" Now Elle knew how.

The security company had known because it had watched more than just paintings. Maybe the killer hadn't been in a hurry to have the camera that Elle had taken from the bedroom, because it was one of many. If Elle had known how many there were, she might not have bothered either.

Out. She had to get out of this house. She had no idea what else the security company had installed, but the whole building might be bugged, booby-trapped, or anything else. Security people could be watching her right now on computers in their building near the airport, or even on computers in their cars. She had an impulse to unplug the power strips, tear out the cameras and microphones, but that would only let them know she knew. It was better if they didn't. They might make some defensive move or decide killing her was urgent.

She scrambled up the attic steps, pulled up the stairs, closed the trapdoor, and stepped to the window to raise it enough to crawl out. She went out and closed it, but then she realized that they might already have noticed the window was open a crack, so she opened it again. As soon as she was out on the roof she began to feel less trapped. The faint breeze through the tall trees beside the roof cooled her face and hair. She crawled backward, lowering herself to the edge and down to the lid of the black trash can. She had to be more light-footed than she'd been on the first two trips, because there was nothing in the trash can and it wobbled a bit. She jumped off it to the patio.

She jogged along the driveway to reach the sidewalk at an angle, so if a person hadn't already been watching her he wouldn't be sure she hadn't come across the drive instead of down it. She ran at her usual pace and minded her running form, so if anyone saw her there would be no mystery about her. A person's only possible credential as a legitimate runner was being good at it.

She reached her rental car, got in, and drove. She kept going at the best speed she could manage without being noticed and then threw in a few turns and evasions. Then she realized she was only acting out of long practice as a burglar. But right now she wasn't really a burglar. She was an investigator, and this was a chance to prove one of her theories. It required that she take one more chance. She turned and drove back toward the Kavanagh house along the quiet streets south of Sunset. She and the various Mercedeses and Jaguars and BMWs of Beverly Hills braked at the four-way stop signs on each intersection and waited to give each other the chance to go first, then proceeded with caution. It gave Elle the chance to look both ways at each stop to spot the enemy.

She was almost back at Kavanagh's house when she saw the first black Tahoe. It was moving south from Sunset, and it came fast.

Elle saw it race into the first intersection, where three other cars were being hesitant about who should go first. The Tahoe settled it, not even slowing down as it sped through. About three seconds later she saw another black Tahoe, flashing past on a parallel street.

Now she was positive. She could swear to it. This wasn't just some "security company" that had put the cameras in the Kavanagh house. It was the same one that had been searching for her, the one that had cleared out Tim Marshall's apartment, and the one that had killed the two young burglars.

She swung back up to Sunset, turned right to get to Crescent Heights, made the turn to the left, and headed up into Laurel Canyon. She drove to the Valley, went to Burbank Airport, and turned in the Honda CR-V. There was no reason to think that the small SUV had been noticed, photo-graphed, or associated with her, but it might have been. She rented a silver Acura to replace it and then drove south toward LAX. The car had a little more power and it handled well, so she was satisfied for the moment.

On the way, she stopped at a giant office supply store and bought the next set of sup-plies: a stack of computer discs, a few thumb drives, a printer, and a ream of paper. Then she returned to her hotel room and went to work on the security company.

She had not seen anything connected with the company that had a logo or a name on it. The black Tahoes, the black suits the employees wore, the equipment, and the building were all plain and anonymous. She turned on her computer, signed on to the site set up to receive the signals from her pinhole cameras, and began to speed through the surveillance footage. Hours and hours of it showed nothing but people sitting at desks through the night shift. Finally she happened to see the plump woman in the uniform walk past a desk, appear to hear something, pick up a phone, and speak into it.

Elle stopped the recording, backed it up, and played it at normal speed. She heard the phone on the desk ring. She watched the woman pick it up and say, "Nemesis. How can we help you?"

Elle stopped it and went back. She turned up the sound to be sure she'd heard it correctly. The phone rang. The woman picked it up and said, "Nemesis. How can we help you?"

Elle let the recording run. At least she'd established that. The company had a name, and now she knew it. She settled into a routine to find out more.

Elle left her room only once a day when the maid came to clean it. She took with her the laptop computer and discs in the computer carrying case. She would lock the case in a locker and spend two hours in the hotel gym and the pool and the restaurant. Then she would go back upstairs to work.

Over the days she learned more about Nemesis. There were thirty-seven employees. Ten were clerical and administrative, like the ones she'd watched on the night shift, and twenty-six were listed on the board in the hall as three shifts on patrol duty. The last one was not listed as anything, so he must be the boss, Edward Ransom.

She made an effort to study the online presence of Nemesis. The company had been in existence for ten years in Los Angeles and had a history in Virginia before that. The website seemed to imply that the Virginia office was still in business, but when she tried to use the internet to come up with an address, she found none. There was also no current telephone listing. There was a paragraph about the services that the Virginia-based Nemesis offered, which said the firm was available for "overseas posting" and provided "expanded mobility for executives" and "protection of assets and personnel wherever they are needed."

She suspected that the office in Virginia was defunct. It claimed to act as an employment service for bodyguards and mercenaries who had U.S. or NATO experience. Elle was aware that there had been a number of companies like that during the early years of the wars in Iraq and Afghanistan, but she'd heard little about them in recent years. Maybe the demand had dried up.

She created more and more files on the company. She lifted multiple photographs of every person who came in range of her hidden cameras and made a personnel file for each. She listened for names on the sound recordings and enlarged images to read any print — such as the name scrawled on a notebook or gym bag. The best source was the whiteboard duty roster that was updated each shift.

She began with the roster for the night shift on the night when she had broken in. Hernandez had to be the woman who was in the radio room acting as dispatcher. She was the only Hispanic employee that night. That left Littvak as the old white man and Daly as the younger black man. Whenever she saw a person on her recordings reaching for a telephone it was worth going back and turning up the sound. Sometimes the person who answered the phone said, "Nemesis, this is . . ." and then his name. Sometimes after he hung up he would say, "That was Walters," or mention some other name.

Soon Elle was able to fill in blanks through a process of elimination. If the name "Miller" was on the whiteboard for the day shift, she could figure out who Miller was because she knew the other employees' names. Two names listed for "Car 3" were probably the two who left together or came in to punch out together.

Within a week she had files containing the names, a few photographs, and fragmentary information about all thirty-seven employees. She had their work schedules for that week, and she was able to use independent online sources to find addresses and other personal information. She liked the day shifts because there were more people coming and going and talking — both chatting and reporting things to each other.

After a few more days she knew a great deal about the company and its office operations and all the people in the building. She kept monitoring what went on, but she was more skillful now at judging when she should be listening closely and when she could do other things. Now it took only an hour or so to go through a day's recordings.

She began to devote more and more time to studying the information she had acquired about the triple murder, the victims, and their families. She had assumed from the start that what had caused the three murders was off-limits sex. Somebody's husband found out she cheated and was jealous enough to kill her, then interrupted her in the act and killed all three. The theory fitted the visible facts, the timing, and the way human beings acted. But that worked only for a while.

Nothing she had learned after the first few days seemed to fit that theory. The husbands must have learned from the police what had been happening at Kavanagh's house. There was no reason to think either one knew about any affairs while his wife was still alive. Nobody had left or been kicked out of the house. There had been no divorce suit filed, and neither husband seemed to have been comforted by any female friends who were suspiciously prompt to arrive. And usually when there was a murder because of jealousy, the crime was over. The killing of the unfaithful one wasn't the beginning of a crime wave. But this time it had been the first of a series of related crimes.

Sharon and Peter were killed in Sharon's apartment, just a short walk from LACMA. And Tim Marshall had done his best to strangle Elle on the beach in Santa Barbara. The man who had killed the three at Kavanagh's house had certainly been the one to kill Sharon and Peter. The only reason he would have bothered was that he thought Elle was staying in Sharon's apartment. And the only reason he could have known that, or that Sharon was her best friend, was that the three people from Nemesis — the blond woman and her two partners — had gone to Elle's haunts asking questions about her. And they were the same three who went to clean out Tim Marshall's apartment in Riverside. Elle now had files on the three: Charlene "Shar" Bonner, Michael Flanders, and Miguel Escobedo. But why had Nemesis been interested in killing anybody?

Elle had never conducted a murder investigation before. She didn't know how much evidence she needed to collect. It would have to be enough to convince some homicide detectives that she knew what she was talking about. After them there would be an assistant district attorney, usually a person who would not charge anyone with murder until he was persuaded that there was no chance whatsoever that he could lose the case and mar his record.

Elle would have to give him enough to convince a jury of twelve that there was no reasonable doubt that the suspect had done a killing. If she counted all the events she'd need to account for, it seemed to be an awful lot of evidence. She had seen documentaries on television in which the defense attorney would say something like, "Why not a stranger looking for an easy score? Maybe a burglar? How did you eliminate that possibility before you made up your mind that my client had done it?"

She didn't know how all the questions could be answered or how all the standards could be met. So she kept collecting information, tirelessly and methodically. Her files on the Nemesis people were growing steadily because she kept everything, including their profiles on dating sites, with heights, weights, and supposed romantic histories.

The pictures she had taken of the papers in Valerie Teason's files had now been transferred to her laptop and to discs, and she had read her way through half of them at least. She'd done the same with Santo Teason's notebook and begun to correlate Valeric's civic committee meetings with the appointments and production meetings and script readings Santo had jotted down. She had searched the financial information she could glean from the papers she had photographed in Tim Marshall's apartment for some kind of coherence, some sense of how his services had been solicited and paid for. She couldn't assume that anything was irrelevant, so she kept it all.

She was particularly attentive when she found anything that illuminated anyone's connection with Nemesis. She had already seen that Nick Kavanagh's security service was Nemesis and tested the theory by watching the black Tahoes converge on his house after her last visit. She had seen and recorded two Nemesis teams capturing and killing the two burglars at the Teason house. When she had explored the Mannon house, she had needed to leave because an armed, black-suited watchman had arrived to check the place with a flashlight. Now that she had seen her recordings and made still shots of all the Nemesis employees, she knew that the man had been Randolph McNulty Jr., aged forty-three. She had a file on him. She was now sure that all three victims were clients of Nemesis.

What else had the three victims had in common? In the prelude to the group murder, Kavanagh had said they were all in the same social set and that the two women were the ones whom anyone would have chosen to take to bed. The women seemed to agree with both assertions, so that settled it. But what did that mean?

A "set" was a vague term to Elle. Probably it meant people whose kids went to the Bremmer School, people who were members of the philharmonic or at least season ticket holders and donors. They supported the Museum of Contemporary Art and probably the Huntington Gardens. The Norton Simon, the Broad, and the Getty museums had been founded on very rich men's fortunes, so Elle didn't know if people donated to them or not. But the set was that kind of people. She knew she had to try to identify a few of them.

She studied the directory of the Bremmer School families, since both the Mannons and the Teasons had enrolled their kids there. She looked at other documents for repetitions. She scanned donor lists from the organizations Valerie Teason supported and guest lists for receptions and parties. It wasn't surprising that one of the repeated names was Nicholas Kavanagh. Valerie had seating charts for the Hollywood Bowl season ticket holders, and Elle looked at the names in the same section, the front quarter of the stadium taken up by box seats, and then the identical seats on the opposite side of the bowl, and the ones just ahead of the Teasons and the Mannons. She had almost forgotten that she'd come across a drawer in the Mannon house that contained invitations to social events. She had photographed a number of them, and now she added those names.

When she had finished, she had a list of twenty-eight surnames that had been mentioned repeatedly with the Teasons and Mannons in social contexts and cultural contexts. Most of the names belonged to couples. After a bit of sorting and crossing off duplicate mentions of women who used maiden or professional names as well as married names, Elle had a sense of the social set. She spent a few minutes creating a file of social contacts. As she filled in addresses, she had a moment of regret that she couldn't jog by a few of the houses some morning looking for a way in.

She noticed a few that she thought she remembered from the meetings of the museum directors' group, so she went back to Valerie Teason's LACMA files. She was right. There were a few who had turned up on the list of people who had attended meetings.

There was also a set of two sheets in the file that had apparently been misfiled. They didn't seem to be related to the minutes of the meetings. She caught the name Nicholas Kavanagh along the top, but it was printed like the stationery of a business. Because it was an image, not a physical document, she couldn't feel the paper, which looked stiff and thick. It occurred to her that she was probably at fault for mixing these sheets with the meeting minutes. She had simply been snatching up files and papers and clicking her phone's camera over and over. But this was intriguing to her.

The sheets had a list of paintings the Kavanagh Gallery had obtained and transferred on a commission. There were thirteen paintings obtained and held for Valerie Teason, and there appeared to be twelve for Anne Mannon. Each painting had the name of an artist, a title, and a date. Elle cut and pasted the list into the file where she kept the connections between Kavanagh and the two female friends. He had bought paintings for their collections. They were customers.

23

Why had Elle never seen all of these paintings? She should have noticed so many paintings if they had been up in either of the two women's houses. Elle had worked mostly in the dark at Mannon's, but she had visited the Teason house in daylight. Maybe the paintings hadn't been delivered yet. It wouldn't be crazy to postpone taking delivery on a painting until it was added to the family's insurance policy. She looked at the prices on the invoice.

The paintings weren't very expensive, really, at least not one at a time. There were some that weren't much more than the paintings that hung for sale in Los Angeles restaurants: $3,000; $2,800; $6,000. There were only a few that were above $10,000. The date on the invoice caught her eye. It was over two years old.

She stared at the list of paintings and then looked up the names of the artists online.

One was named Aaron Wilbertson. His biography said he was born in 1821 and died in 1906. A member of the Hudson River School, he had studied in Düsseldorf, where the style and methods of the Hudson River painters Bierstadt, Church, Hart, and Brown originated.

Like Thomas Moran, Wilbertson moved west before the turn of the century and applied the Hudson River aesthetic to the dramatic scenery of the American West. He was famous for having moved northeastern rocks, rivers, and mountains into some western paintings to achieve pleasing effects. He was quoted as having said, "God had His joke with us when He hid Niagara Falls among the busy thoroughfares of men. And He made the forests of the civilized East thick and impassable, while leaving much of the West bereft of green and growing things."

The paintings Anne and Valerie had owned were *Sunlight in the Sierra* (1885), *Desert Rhapsody* (1889), *Wind on Bristlecone* (1891), *The Willamette Valley* (1880), *On the Santa Fe* (1891), *Winter on Shasta* (1887), *Gateway to the Columbia* (1888), and *Mojave Spring* (1890).

The second painter Elle looked up was Albert Stolkos (b. 1898, d. 1976). He was referred to in the article as a significant abstract painter of the postwar period who was heavily influenced by a strict Japanese school of thought that eschewed any reference to real objects with three dimensions. His work was known for its jagged lines, which were often compared to colored electrocardiograms. He was a close friend to and considered an equal of the great Western abstractionists of his day.

The paintings were *Jazz Dream/Jetstream Nos. 8, 12, 15,* and *22* (1962–3); *Juicy* (1964); *De-Composition Nos. 18, 44,* and *49* (1968); *Awkward Sensation* (1972); and *Both Ways* (1971).

The third painter was a woman, Sarah Marie Prestmantle (b. 1881). The article said she was born to an upper-class English family that was connected on the male line to the gentry of Yorkshire and on the distaff side to several of the oldest families of France. She was sent at the age of twelve to a boarding school in Rouen, where she studied painting under a master named Valedon, who is not known in any other context. Sarah Prestmantle was obsessed with painting and produced a body of juvenile portraits of her classmates. When the paintings were discovered in a tower of the school, the headmistress and teachers declared them "scandalous" and burned them in a bonfire in the churchyard of the thirteenth-century chapel. Her expulsion from the school presaged her later disownment by her family and repudiation by their connections.

Her fascination with the human form grew and flourished. Today she was seen as a forerunner of and an influence on the great art deco sculptors and designers Claire Colinet, Bruno Zach, and Ferdinand Preiss and was rumored to have been a model for some of the female figures in their work. Her paintings had the same lively poses, graceful forms, and frank realism. She was different from them chiefly in her emphasis on nude pairs and groups of both sexes.

Her works on the purchase list were *Epithalamium* (1913), *The Nymph's Birthday Party* (1915), *The Bower of Bliss* (1916), *The Rites of Spring — Nijinsky* (1913), *Untitled Five Figures* (1917), *Pas de Deux* (1919), and *Eighteen Unbound Sketchbook Sheets for a Study After Aretino* (1921).

Elle started a new file and copied the invoice into it and then the descriptions of the various artists' work and their histories. She promised herself that at some point she

386

would do a serious search and get a look at photographs of the paintings themselves instead of reading descriptions. But for the moment it didn't seem to be a priority. What she needed to know was something that would explain the motive for killing Kavanagh, Mannon, and Teason.

She rubbed her eyes and then used the tips of her fingers to knead the spots on her forehead where her headache had settled. She was tired.

She had been at her research for a couple of weeks, relieved only by her daily exercise break and the five or six hours she spent rehashing the evidence in a feverish half-consciousness that had to serve her as sleep. Elle was tired of staying in the hotel room working, and she wasn't sure that she was getting anywhere.

Elle couldn't just give up and pretend to believe that the man who had killed Sharon would get caught automatically. Maybe he would, but if the cops got him and convicted him five years from now, they'd think they had won. So far the police had made none of the connections, even the obvious ones. There had been no announcement that the deaths of the three rich people were connected with the deaths of Sharon and Peter, even though the methods were identical and the shootings took place a week apart. No spokesman had even announced that a comparison of the bullets had been conducted. Where was the cop who said, "You know, this scene looks a lot like the one in Beverly Hills"?

If there was a cop like that, he hadn't made any noise about it. Elle would have to keep working with the information she had stolen and the illegal recordings she was making in the Nemesis office, and hope she caught somebody before anyone caught her.

Another four days and nights passed while she worked. She was watching the recordings of the previous twenty-four hours on the fifth morning, when she noticed a change that had taken place during the night shift. Hernandez the dispatcher had been on a diet for two weeks now, and she was in the dispatch room looking in the mirror at her uniform trying to detect a change. The pants and the belt still bound a barrel-shaped torso, which had only a slight variation near the top where her breasts must be. The waist of her marine-pressed uniform shirt was no narrower than the shoulders and might even be a bit wider than her hips, in spite of the fact that Elle had been watching her ingest nothing but black coffee during that time.

Just as Hernandez stepped out of the dispatch room and stopped in the kitchen for more coffee, there was the sound of engines outside. A few seconds later the double doors on the airport side of the building swung open hard enough to hit the wall. Behind them were the boss, Ed; and then the two men who had been in the burglars' van the night the burglars had been murdered. A few moments later came the blond woman, Shar, and the two men who usually rode with her, Flanders and Escobedo.

They were all in a jovial mood, laughing and talking over one another so Elle couldn't distinguish individual sentences well. She heard Ed tell someone, "Nice assist."

"He was the last one, wasn't he?" That seemed to come from McNulty, the one who had interrupted Elle's visit to the Mannons.

"Right." This was from a male voice, but Elle couldn't tell which.

"Then that's that."

The boss stopped and blocked the others. He looked back at McNulty. "That is never that. As long as there's money on the table, somebody will be trying to get at it. Nothing's changed." He went into his office and closed his door behind him.

The others stood for a few seconds and then they began to make their way to the bathrooms. Shar had her own because she was the only woman besides Hernandez, but the men all went in rapid succession into the other one.

Elle didn't think they all had to pee at once, like passengers getting off an airplane. They were all using their first chance to wash their hands. They had done something. They were washing off the gunshot residue or the blood spatter or some other evidence. She was sure of it.

She waited as they all emerged and turned their attention to the next thing. Some of them looked at the duty whiteboard to see if the assignments beside their names had changed, or maybe just to refresh their memories of what had been up there at the start of the shift. Three of them went into the break room to pour themselves Styrofoam cups of coffee and fit lids on them.

Shar ducked into Hernandez's dispatch room. She stayed only fifteen or twenty seconds and then came back out. Elle had noticed before that the only two women made a point of talking alone once in a while. She didn't think their bond was close, but they couldn't ignore each other.

Within a few more minutes both teams were on their way back out. Elle transferred the footage to a new file and went back to studying the paperwork she had photographed during her burglaries.

It was not until days later that she thought about the quiet celebration at the Nemesis office again. It began during her break to let the maid clean her hotel room. She did a more strenuous version of her daily workout that morning — more time in the gym on the weights, the bars, and the machines; a longer run; and then more lengths in the pool. When she had finished and dressed again she went to the hotel restaurant and read the *Los Angeles Times* while she ate lunch.

She noticed the article right away. It wasn't at the top or in the long column on the left. It was in an inferior position, a square in the lower right corner, but that was still on the front page. "Curator's Death Ruled a Suicide."

She turned to the body of the article, several pages inside. As she found it she was wondering why she had known instantly that the news meant something. It seemed to be an item that was so close to what she had been thinking about that it must be connected. The article had a byline: Christopher Mainz, the *L.A. Times* art critic.

Jeffrey Arundel Semple, world-renowned scholar and popular pillar of the Los Angeles art scene, has died after seventeen years as a senior curator at the Los Angeles County Museum of Art. His influence on the growth and development of the institution, its collections, and the city's position in the world of art and connoisseurship would be difficult to overstate.

Mr. Semple received his bachelor of arts degree and his PhD at Harvard University and then spent several years serving internships and holding junior positions at a succession of European museums, including the Prado and the Louvre, before coming to Los Angeles at the invitation of museum director Aldous Pernell.

Police spokesperson Lieutenant Jennifer Bolt said his death took place between Saturday afternoon, when he spoke before a group of more than two hundred museum members at a reception, and Sunday evening, when he failed to attend a dinner with friends, who found him deceased. The coroner's office has ruled the manner of death to be suicide. A memorial will be announced by family and friends at a later date.

Elle had begun to work the information into the facts that she already had. She had never heard of this man, but she had assumed there was such a man, or, more likely, a dozen or more men, as always. Each institution of civilization was always attributed to the bold vision of one person, but the long-term process of making these organizations real came from years and years of work by people who knew how to build and operate them. A museum couldn't exist without experts any more than a power plant could.

She instinctively felt sorry for this man, but she had a suspicion about him too. The revelations of her past few weeks began presenting themselves in her memory in different combinations, and her mind was trying to see how they could all fit together with his death.

Elle signed for her lunch and made her way upstairs to her room. It had been cleaned meticulously as usual, the tip she'd left was gone, and her personal belongings were undisturbed. She opened her laptop computer. She didn't know everything yet, but she was fairly sure that some people at Nemesis would have read the article and reacted to the announcement of Semple's suicide. They would probably be thinking of it as a victory. On Saturday night, they had come back elated, having done something that made them all think it was prudent to wash their hands. And now she thought she understood one of the jokes she'd heard. "Nice assist" had seemed to be a sports reference then, but it sounded different now that what happened to Semple was being considered a suicide.

24

Elle decided to make it a habit to check on the name of the dead curator, Jeffrey Semple, once a day to see if there was any new information on his case. There were a few things that she knew would be done during the next few weeks. One was that the authorities would be trying to make sure the coroner was right about the manner of death.

Semple had apparently been a respected man who was well liked by plenty of important — meaning rich and generous — Los Angeles art lovers. The marriage of art and money provided an outlet for various kinds of snobbery. One was the belief that the superbly educated and well bred stopped killing themselves in Roman times. The authorities would have to be ready to persuade Semple's defenders that he hadn't been murdered. Elle didn't know much about the man yet, but she did know quite a bit about certain other people, so for the moment she too had trouble accepting the suicide theory.

Once the suicide theory was established — correctly or not — there would be multiple investigations of what had prompted him to kill himself. She was betting that there was a suicide note. If you wanted to fake someone's suicide you would almost certainly supply one. That way, any law enforcement professional who wasn't already calling it a murder could accept the suicide, sign off, and go to lunch an hour early.

For now Elle spent her time going through the connections among the victims. She used Valerie Teason's minutes from the LACMA meetings to establish the dates and times when the two women and Semple were all together. In the instances when it was clear that Mr. Semple was at a meeting for a particular professional purpose, she noted the topic on which he spoke.

Next she consulted both women's files for the guest lists of receptions, exhibition openings, fund-raisers, parties, and other events to see which ones had included Semple and the women. There were quite a few topics on which Semple was an expert. The museum's website listed twenty-two

"Curatorial Areas," ranging alphabetically from "African Art" to "South and Southeast Asian Art." Semple was curator of "American Art." That appeared to have also made him a stakeholder in "Contemporary Art," "Modern Art," "Decorative Arts and Design," "Prints and Drawings," and "Photography" and knowledgeable on the whole topic of museum management, collections, and exhibitions.

Elle had an urge to see what he had looked like, so she searched the internet for photographs and found a few. He was tall and thin and wore glasses with frames that were transparent and flesh colored, like those many men wore in the era of World War II. The newspaper said he was fifty-one when he died. Elle studied his appearance for clues. She knew that if he had not found himself in Los Angeles he would have worn tweed jackets. As it was, in most pictures he wore a crisp white shirt with a tie. He had a long, narrow nose and a noble brow — handsome for a man his age. That meant she couldn't rule him out as a romantic partner of one or both of the women just yet. He was professorial, but the kind of professor who had once been a famous cricket player or mountain climber but never mentioned it. In the photographs he was often shown in a group of other people, nearly always smiling broadly enough to reveal a row of even upper teeth.

She ran out of information about him in two days, but she did manage to find another stretch of recording from her spy cameras at the Nemesis office that she thought was worth keeping.

Shar the blonde, who seemed to be the kind of woman who couldn't help flirting with the boss, came in at the beginning of the evening shift carrying a copy of the *Los Angeles Times* folded under her arm. She walked into Ed's office, held it up, and then released two fingers to let the paper unfold to show the announcement of Semple's death.

"Saw it two hours ago," Ed said.

"Anything you'd like conveyed to the troops?"

"Tell them to get to work."

Elle made sure the short conversation got into the Semple file and Shar's file. She knew it didn't prove anything by itself, but she steadfastly refused to make any decisions about the information she had been finding and storing. Drawing conclusions was a part of the process that was somewhere in the future. Right now she was focused on finding and storing everything.

She was pretty sure she was, at some point, going to have to tell this story to somebody, but she couldn't do it until she knew what the story was. This new killing, she was sure, was part of the story.

25

The website of the Los Angeles County Museum of Art featured a new notice. It said that special requests to view or borrow works from the permanent collection would be held temporarily because the collection was undergoing an inventory.

Of course, Elle thought. She had read a few times over the years of curators and other museum officials getting caught after quietly stealing art or artifacts from public collections. She was sure she had never heard of it happening at a major museum. Usually it happened at a small college or privately endowed collection whose directors didn't know the value of something a donor had left them in his will — a series of paintings or rare books or a decorated triptych from a medieval church. The official would get caught trying to sell it, but sometimes the crime would be hushed up because the institution didn't want other potential donors to become spooked.

The LACMA permanent collection was not some small-time operation. LACMA was the largest collection west of Chicago. The site said the permanent collection was about a hundred thousand items.

The museum couldn't be completing an inventory just because a curator with an unblemished reputation had killed himself. It was a massive job that would require the attention of the surviving twenty-one curators and an army of trained personnel. Could the police have found some work from the collection in his house? No. That would have been the lead item in the news reports about his death.

Elle had always known that nobody but an idiot ever tried to steal art from museums. When a theft occurred it was always an inside job. And if a curator took something, it would have to be a special situation where he believed he was taking advantage of some weakness in the system, some temporary opportunity. He would have to be able to conceal the theft. Maybe he would remove the item from the museum's records or provide a written explanation of where the item went. "What happened to *Don Augustino Reviews His Troops on Parade*?" "This notation says it's in Vienna for the exhibition of sixteenth-century martial paintings. The show opens this fall, and then the exhibition will tour for five years."

But that kind of story didn't fit any of the facts that Elle had uncovered. Valerie Teason and Anne Mannon were on the board, but that didn't make them insiders. A curator like Jeffrey Semple wouldn't have needed, or even benefited from, their help in a theft. And if he and they had stolen something, it wouldn't have gotten anybody killed; they'd just be arrested.

In spite of the fact that Elle liked art museums, she was no art expert. What she was an expert at was stealing. Nobody with a functioning brain stole art. It made even less sense for an insider to consider stealing anything. He would know that great paintings were too famous to sell. A man like Semple knew that the sudden shift of a van Gogh or a Jackson Pollock to a new owner would be known around the world in an hour. By the second hour the talk would be about why the former owner would have considered accepting any offer for it. And soon there would be a hold on the curator's passport and people pounding on his door.

And then Elle knew. The knowledge was simply a rearrangement of the information she had been collecting for weeks into a different configuration. It was like a slight turn of a puzzle piece that made every piece fit. First she didn't know, and then she knew.

She wasn't in command of every detail yet, but she knew that a great many details were in her possession. She would just have to look at each one and see what it told her now that it was part of a picture. What mattered was that already she knew the main fact. The main fact was that there was no money in stealing paintings from a major museum's collection. The money was in buying paintings that were underappreciated, and therefore undervalued, and making them better appreciated.

She worked her way to a formulation that made sense. Jeffrey Semple had not been taking things out of the collection and selling them. If he had been doing something, it was helping Valerie Teason and Anne Mannon to add paintings to the museum's collection.

Elle's professional sense of how dirty money was made allowed her to grasp the potential instantly, and her weeks of research had told her just where to look for specifics. Two years ago Valerie Teason and Anne Mannon had bought twenty-five paintings from Nick Kavanagh, or, more accurately, through Nick Kavanagh. The paintings had cost between $3,000 and $10,000 each. If Valerie and Anne managed to get one painting each by Sarah Prestmantle, Aaron Wilbertson, and Albert Stolkos included in the permanent collection of LACMA, what would they be worth? Quite a bit more than they had been.

What if the respected curator Jeffrey Semple then began the process of giving the paintings a bit of publicity? He might plan an exhibition and give them a walk-on role. He might, for instance, have a large-scale show drawn from the museum's American collection and presented in a historical context. He could start with paintings from the colonial and revolutionary period, with Benjamin West, John Singleton Copley, Gilbert Stuart. Then he could move to the turn of the nineteenth century and the regional schools, including the Hudson River School with Thomas Cole, Moran, and Wilberton, who would be an ideal figure to lead into the westward movement from George Catlin to Frederic Remington. Semple could put in the European-trained and sophisticated John Singer Sargent and James Abbott McNeill Whistler, taking the story to the turn of the twentieth century. He could segue into the next generation of sophisticates with the art deco movement, including the naturalized American Sarah Prestmantle, and then the jazz age, the Depression, and the public art sponsored by the WPA program. There could be a grim pause for World War II, and then the postwar modernists, including de Kooning and Pollock and Stolkos, and on to the likes of Jasper Johns, Barnett Newman, and Mark Rothko and to the most recent works by living artists.

Semple could write a brilliant introduction to the catalog, because that was what the first rank of art historians did. They were trained to do it on demand. And in this catalog he would mention the usual two hundred names in their historical places, only this time it would be two hundred and three names.

It would be even better if the exhibit traveled. Assuming the three artists weren't atrocious, they would soon begin picking up converts — people who would find the new old artists refreshing and people who felt they should. People in smaller cities with less influential museums might be inclined to accept what was presented to them from afar.

Elle estimated that it wouldn't take more than a couple of years of unobtrusive advocating to bring an artist from utter obscurity to being known by the elite. After that, it was an easy transition to the point where not knowing the artist would make a person's claim to knowledge seem shallow and suspect.

Even if other critics and scholars disliked the paintings, called them unworthy or derivative imitations of something better, as soon as they mentioned a painting, it was in the record. It was more than just art, it was art history.

At that point, the question that would arise was where one could see more of the artist's work or obtain an example of it. And the answer would be that there were a few astute private collectors who had seen and purchased the best pieces years ago. For these three artists, there would be Valerie McGee Teason and Anne Satterthwaite Mannon.

Elle was sure that she was right about the outline of the scheme. She knew that Anne and Valerie, the two close friends, had conspired with each other to get their friend Nick Kavanagh, the gallery owner, to buy for them a significant number of paintings by three artists of different periods who were not widely known. Maybe he was in on the scheme from the start. And then she guessed that somehow they had conspired with Jeffrey Semple to get one or two works by each painter into the museum's permanent collection.

There was only one way to check her theory. Elle went back to the LACMA website. She went to the museum's listing of works of art in the permanent collection. In a short time she found that the institution owned one work each by Wilbertson, Prestmantle, and Stolkos.

This scheme was not crude or violent, with apelike men using razor blades to cut paintings out of their frames at night and escaping in a van. It was a scheme worthy of a group of people who were educated, well connected, sophisticated, and at least moderately rich already. As far as Elle knew it wasn't even a crime. Nothing would be taken from the museum. No money would disappear from its endowment or operating budget.

The museum had, in fact, received three authentic old paintings, probably through a transfer or donation of some kind. Elle was sure of that, because museums received things that way all the time. They liked to stockpile their cash for the rare bidding wars for any of the genuine world-class masterpieces that came up at auction now and then. The museum's three works would become important, then essential, and they would gain in monetary value the more they were mentioned. The museum would gain and then keep gaining.

But Elle's lifelong study of ways money was made dishonestly didn't tell her what each person in the scheme actually had done, if anything. Nick Kavanagh had served as broker in the purchase of the twenty-five paintings that were going to be held in reserve and sold after they were worth enough. But was he aware that the purchase was a scheme? Elle guessed instinctively that he wasn't in on the conspiracy on the day of his death. Someone would have mentioned it while the three were alone, and nobody had.

It was possible that the real reason the two women were willing to have a threesome with him was to induce him to join and help them in the rest of the plan. They had needed him to remain discreet and loyal. While sex didn't have a perfect record of ensuring loyalty, the hope of more sex could accomplish wonders.

They needed his silence, if nothing more. If you had a collection of paintings that was going to skyrocket in value, you wouldn't want anyone to know you had it until you were ready. If getting the three artists accepted into the museum collection required voting money for them or engaging in some form of advocacy, owning the artists' works could discredit you. It would actually be best if, when you sold, your broker could handle the sale without revealing your name. Auction houses often kept people's names secret, both bidders' and sellers'.

It was even more difficult to be sure of the role that Jeffrey Semple had played in the whole operation. Elle thought she knew what a curator would need to do to get the paintings into the collection, but she didn't know whether he had done it, or didn't need to do it. She didn't even know if he was a paid helper or a partner. It was possible that he had been seduced by one of the two women in order to get him involved, but it was also possible he was an absolutely innocent bystander.

Elle knew everything, and yet she knew nothing. She went back to her computer to scan a few hours of recordings from the Nemesis office. When she was finished, she planned the next phase of her murder investigation. The people at Nemesis were so prolific that it was difficult to keep up with the list of people they had murdered. Tomorrow she would begin to make studies of the two dead burglars, and of Jeffrey

Semple, and of anyone else whose fate might tell her something.

26

Elle woke up in the dark, glanced toward the screen of her computer, then sat up fast. The screen had gone black. In place of the nine small squares showing what her pinhole cameras could see, there was a single black square, like an empty blackboard.

She scrambled out of bed and stared at the screen, then moved her hand back and forth over the pad, but the computer hadn't gone to sleep. She clicked on the BBC news site and it came up clear and bright. She clicked on CNN and watched the face of a newswoman talking and the headlines scrolling across the red stripe at the bottom.

She went back to the screen with the images from the pinhole cameras. Still black. She retyped and connected to the address of the site she had created for the recordings and then repeated the setup procedure. The attempt to reestablish contact with the cameras and microphones brought her the

411

same black screen.

Elle went to the closet and took out her night burglary outfit and dressed — belly band with the Rohrbaugh R9 and ammunition, black pants, shirt, socks, shoes, baseball cap, and denim jacket. In about five minutes she was out the door.

She got her car out of the hotel garage and drove toward the Nemesis building. She worked on calming her heartbeat and her breathing. She had been preparing herself for this moment since she had planted the cameras. At some point, somebody in the bugged building was going to find the mics and cameras, and apparently this had been the night. Even stupid people saw things. She kept her phone on the site and set it on the seat beside her. Now and then she would look again, but the screen stayed black. She put her earbuds in to listen for the sound from the microphones, but she heard nothing.

It had been inevitable that somebody in the kitchen would open a cabinet that wasn't right by the sink and see a white insulated wire or a pinhole camera. They had lasted a long time, much longer than she'd had a right to expect. When she'd found the pinhole cameras that Nemesis had installed at Kavanagh's house, she had seen immediately that they were the same as hers. Any Nemesis person who saw hers would know what they were.

That was almost certainly what had happened. She had to know, for several reasons. She wasn't a great computer person. She didn't know if the Nemesis people were capable of tracing the signals of the cameras to her site. If they could do that, could they trace the signal to her hotel? She thought they couldn't, but they were the sort of people who might be much more sophisticated than she was. Being wrong might mean being dead.

In spite of her fear she had another hope. If the cameras had gone off because someone at Nemesis had found them and taken them out, she might be able to fool Nemesis by putting in new ones. It was something people like them would never expect her to do. They would assume that because they'd solved the problem it would stay solved. Spying on killers was a crazy, risky thing to do. Would anybody try to do it twice? Nemesis people might even see a lens or a wire and assume it meant nothing because someone in their organization had already neutralized it. She still had a pinhole camera in her jacket. If the first ones were destroyed, maybe she could at least install the spare.

She parked beyond the deserted building where she had parked the first time. She knelt by the dumpster, pulled out the metal sheet she had left beneath, and took it with her. She walked along the back of that building to the high chain-link fence that separated the airport's empty acreage from the civilian buildings along the road, then across two lots toward the Nemesis building. She stared at the building from the airport side. She counted eight Tahoes parked there. As she moved closer, she could see the building's double doors. They were black. There seemed to have been a power failure. Maybe they hadn't found her cameras after all.

She kept going until she reached the corner of the building, then watched and listened for a time, trying to see if anyone was in evidence. The eight Tahoe SUVs parked in the lot didn't look like a sign of life. Nobody was near them. She looked up at the surveillance cameras on the corners of the building and wondered if they were off too. She noticed that in the field across the highway there were three black SUVs parked, but they didn't look like the ones Nemesis used.

Elle made her way along the building's side wall to the spot where she had cut a hole to enter. She knelt beside the hole and examined the plywood sheet she had spray-painted white and left as a cover. Nobody had moved it or nailed it shut or done anything else to it.

She moved the sheet and crawled in through the opening, then pulled the sheet back toward her to cover the spot again. She was now inside the empty cabinet space beneath the kitchen counter. Farther along the counter, she remembered, were the sinks and the U-shaped drainpipes. She quietly crawled a few feet and felt for the sockets where she had left pinhole cameras and microphones plugged in. She could see through the cracks at the cabinet doors that there was near darkness in the room. She remained still and tried to understand what was happening.

She had assumed that the reason her transmission was interrupted was that the Nemesis people had found the cameras and torn them out, but here they were, still plugged in.

A voice Elle recognized from the recordings as Hernandez the dispatcher said quietly, "I should have known something like this was going to happen. I just didn't get it."

"What are you talking about?" It was the

other woman, Shar.

"They were watching us. I found a pinhole camera in a corner of the hall aimed into the communications room about a week ago."

"Why didn't you do anything?"

"At first I thought I should run and tell Ed. I actually got up to do it, and then I realized I was doing what stupid people do."

"What do smart people do?" said Shar.

"They leave the camera there and pretend not to see it. Then they do the best work they can do. I thought the one who was watching us was Ed. I did two months of paperwork in about one week, and I was sweet to everybody I talked to, came in early, and left late. I was showing him what a great worker I was. I figured he might even give me a raise."

A male voice from outside the doorway said, "I told you two not to talk. So shut up."

"What are you going to do, shoot us?" Shar said.

"Just one. Then the other won't have any reason to talk. Who is it going to be?"

The two women fell silent. Elle began to crawl as quietly as she could toward the sink. She knew it was dangerous to venture far from the exit she had cut, but the place was dark. There were no windows, and the only light seemed to be coming from the glass doors at the far end of the hall, which admitted the dim glow from the airport taxiways.

She slithered under the U-shaped pipes beneath the sink and reached the end of the counter. She heard Hernandez say, "Do you think he would shoot?"

Shar said, "Probably. They're from the Virginia office, and they're pissed. They might make an example of somebody before they take over."

Hernandez fell silent again, but the fact that the two had spoken meant the man was out of earshot.

Elle opened the cupboard door a quarter inch and peered out. The two women were sitting in two of the steel chairs that had been around the third table. Now the chairs faced the wall, and they both appeared to have their ankles duct-taped to the legs and their arms pulled behind them and joined.

Elle crawled out of the cupboard and closed the cupboard door, rose to her feet and crouched at the doorway. The man had moved on, but she could hear other noises in the darkened building. From the front doorway she heard a man snarl, "Hands up." There were grunts and the sound of

417

the impact of a body being hurled against a wall. "Get his wrists."

Elle turned the other way and hurried to the one place she thought would be empty — the ladies' room. It was at the end of the hall with the men's room on one side of it and Ed the boss's office on the other.

She pushed the door in only a few inches because she had noticed on her recordings that when it was pushed all the way in, the spring-restrained closer squeaked. When she was inside, she let the door close slowly so it wouldn't flap.

On her first visit she had not tried to go this deep into the building. Now the room was pitch-black. She turned on the screen of her phone and was surprised. This wasn't just a sink and a couple of stalls with toilets in them. It was a locker room with a two-fixture shower and a large mirror above the three sinks. There were two rows of lockers, eight lockers in all, with two benches for sitting down to tie shoes.

The two women seemed to have taken full possession of the place. There were two hair dryers and a curling iron on the shelf above the sinks and under the mirror, each with its own extension cord, and bottles of shampoo and lotion and cans of hair spray. Some of the lockers had white adhesive tape with the women's names on them — two lockers each.

She turned from the mirror to the left and oriented herself to the door. The boss's office had to be past the lockers and on the shower end of the room. The showers consisted of a plastic shell with two showerheads on the wall about a foot above it.

Elle stepped into the shower and put her ear to the wall. She heard rumbling voices that belonged to men, but the sounds could not be separated into words. She was about to go back the other way when she saw something peculiar in the light from her phone. It was a well-chewed piece of pink bubble gum stuck to the side of the wall just above the upper edge of the white shower shell. She looked hard at it and thought it was disgusting that some woman — either one of the two tied up in the kitchen or some earlier one — would stick her gum there.

It also made no sense. It was stuck — not to the shower, as though somebody had wanted to keep it and then came to her senses — but to the painted wallboard above. Elle picked up one of the benches near the lockers, brought it back, and stood on it so her eyes would be level with the gum.

She took out her knife and popped the gum off the wall. She could see a faint glow and realized she was looking into the boss's office. She quickly put her phone away. The spot the gum had covered was a small hole drilled in the wall. Either some voyeur had drilled it so he could watch women in the shower, or some woman had drilled it so she could spy on the boss.

Elle took out the pinhole camera she had kept in her jacket pocket. She carefully pushed the tiny camera lens into the hole. Next she stepped to the row of sinks, unplugged a white extension cord from a hair dryer, and brought it back with her. The power to the whole building seemed to be off. Apparently the people taking over had turned off the main circuit breaker to throw the occupants into confusion so they could be overpowered.

But when Elle had come in she had noticed that on the ceiling there was a three-inch pill-shaped device with a red light on it glowing steadily. The smoke detectors in the building were apparently hardwired into their own circuit, and that circuit was still working. Elle put her bench under the smoke detector and used her knife to pry off the cover. She could see that the wiring consisted of a pair of wires coming from above the ceiling spliced with twist-on insulation caps to a pair of wires from the smoke detector. She stepped down and picked up the extension cord. She used her knife to cut off the plug end, sliced the two wires of the cord to separate them, and bared an inch of copper on each.

She climbed back up to the smoke detector, disconnected it from the power wires, used the twist-on caps to splice the extension cord to the power wires, and then restored the cover. She used the adhesive tape from the door of an unused locker and cut it into short strips to tape the white cord along the ceiling to the raised side edge of the shower stall. The cord ran as far as the bottom of the shower, where it ended with a socket.

She took the white insulated wire of her pinhole camera and ran that along the raised top edge of the shower and then down to the socket at the end of the extension cord. She held her breath while she plugged the camera into the socket. The plug didn't fit the socket very well, but she got it in most of the way. Then she picked up the bench and took it back to the lockers where she'd found it. She sat on the bench and turned on her phone again.

She connected to the website that received

and recorded the images from her pinhole cameras. There was a signal and a clear picture of three men in the office on the other side of the shower wall. The room was still dark, but there was a tactical flashlight sitting on the desk that threw a bright circle on the ceiling and lit up the room. One man she recognized as Ed, the boss of this office. He was bound to a chair with wire and duct tape, as the women in the kitchen had been. The other men she had never seen before. They both looked big and athletic. One was young, with the build and bearing of a wrestler. The other was much older, at least sixty. He no longer had the beefy look of the other man, but had a trim, erect body and a hard face.

She put on one of the phone's earbuds so she could hear what they were saying.

The older man was apparently the leader of the intruders from Virginia. He began to pace in front of Ed, who seemed to interpret the pacing as a prelude to something unpleasant and physical.

"I swear, Mr. Caine," Ed said, "all you would have had to do was call me up and ask, if you wanted to talk in person. I've always agreed to that. I would have come to you in Virginia."

Hearing him speak made Elle's stomach

sink. She had detected in the voice a false friendliness that didn't work, because there was a weakness in it. She could see that the man he'd called Mr. Caine had heard the same notes and was savoring them.

"Then you're getting what you want, Ed," said Mr. Caine. "This is it. This is your face-to-face meeting. Maybe you think it was too dramatic to show up here with more men than you have — better men — and remind you how easy it is for me to walk in and push you around. Is that what you think?"

"No," Ed said. "This is mostly your company. You could have done that any day. I always knew that. I was just telling you that you never had to. I had everything in control, and I was going to tell you everything as soon as it was final."

"All right," said Mr. Caine. "This is your chance. Start at the beginning and tell me everything that happened."

"Sure. I want to. I'm just saying you don't have to keep me tied to a chair."

"That will depend on what you tell me. Start now."

27

Elle heard a radio voice that must be coming from the communications room. She turned off her phone to listen. "This is Car Seven, come in HQ." There was no response. She assumed the person who should be answering was Hernandez, who was tied up in the kitchen. "This is Car Seven. Car Seven calling HQ." Still there was no answer. Finally, Elle heard heavy boots coming at a trot. After a moment a male voice said, "Give location, Car Seven."

"We're done with the stop in West L.A. It was a false alarm. We're driving west on Santa Monica Boulevard."

"Then come in to headquarters now. There's an important meeting."

"We didn't hear anything about a meeting."

"You will when you get here."

"Where's Flora?"

"In the ladies' room. Get here as soon as

you can. HQ out."

Elle heard the man leaving the communications room, and he didn't seem to be coming her way, so she returned to the website that received her recordings. The voice she heard was Ed's.

"We always assumed there must be a limit, but we didn't know where the line was going to be drawn, so we tested. People weren't very protective of their privacy, and we got better at our pitches. Nobody can ever have too much security. We sold people more and more small cameras and bugs, added transponders to their wives' and kids' cars. In a year or so we started going back to customers we already had and updating their systems. The richer people, the ones with things to protect — coin collections, serious jewelry, antiques, art collections, important musical instruments — all had lots of insurance, but they didn't want to get robbed in the first place. The insurance companies wouldn't even insure a lot of that stuff without high-end alarm and electronic surveillance equipment. They inspected the houses and told the customers what they had to have. Whatever it was, we supplied it. When we could we talked people into more protection than the guidelines recommended, and the insurance inspectors were delighted.

"We started the next phase almost accidentally, just using the links we had installed to check our equipment. Do the camera feeds work in somebody's hallway? Turn them on in the middle of the night when the customers are asleep and see if we get a clear image. We started doing that for whole sectors, and we began to pick up things — conversations. People said and did things that they didn't want known. We came to know it, and we had recordings. I'm not saying that we switched from security to blackmail. We kept up with the parts of the business we always had.

"We put most of the spy equipment in the richest people's houses because they could pay for it. When we did, we could do a better job of protection. We caught burglars, a lot of them. We started to get more and more business from the people in places like Beverly Hills, Bel-Air, San Marino, Malibu."

Mr. Caine interrupted. "You're stalling. I know all this. I invented some of it. I want to know how those three people got killed in that house in Beverly Hills."

"I'm sorry, Mr. Caine," Ed said. "I was coming to that. The first one of those people I came across was the woman named Anne Mannon. Her husband owns two restaurants, one in Beverly Hills and one in Malibu. One look and you knew she was a special woman — beautiful, with light blond hair like kids have. She was lively, interested in things, and smart. Her husband was away at the restaurants from early morning to late night, six days a week, and maybe half-time on the seventh."

"So what?"

"She had to spend most of her time without him. She had a lot of friends from her various interests. She was out most of each day at other people's fancy houses, museums, charity offices, places like that. She was never alone. The kids got taken to school by a driver. As soon as they were gone she would be out to breakfast at someplace like the Beverly Hills Hotel with friends. She was on the boards of a lot of civic organizations, so there were meetings. She had a whole duplicate life."

Mr. Caine watched him, his own face expressionless, not yet showing him whether he was doing well or sinking. "So what?"

"There were men, sometimes at her house in the afternoon when the husband and kids weren't likely to show up. One of them was named Jeffrey Semple. He worked at the art museum, the big one on Wilshire Boulevard by the tar pits. And as I said, she was smart too. Some days, after the sex, they talked a lot about all kinds of things.

"What we learned was that she and a close woman friend of hers had been working with Semple to pull a scam. They had bought up a bunch of paintings by three dead artists that Semple knew about who were pretty good but not super famous. Semple was going to get paintings by the three of them into the permanent collection of the museum and help them get a lot more famous."

Elle heard car noises coming from beyond the wall beside her. She took out her earbuds again and listened. The side wall of the ladies' room, she realized, faced toward the road and away from the parking lot. She wondered if what she was hearing was another of the patrol cars arriving. She listened for a few seconds, but the one car was the end of it. She listened to the phone again. It was still Ed's voice.

"Jeffrey Semple was an expert, and he had never done anything that was even questionable in his whole career. He was one of a few male friends she saw at meetings and parties and had sex with once in a while. To him she was a miracle, the love of his life. And she was a woman who wasn't above noticing that she could control him if she wanted to.

"So things went on this way. Anne and her friend Valerie Teason bought twenty-five paintings by these three painters through their friend the dealer Nicholas Kavanagh and then bought three more in a secret sale. They planned that, once the three painters got better known and more expensive, they would have Kavanagh sell the paintings."

"How much did they expect to make on the sale?"

"They had no way to know, but when they talked on the recordings we made in their houses, they always used the term 'millions.' Meaning each painting, not all together. Part of the game was that they would wait until they could sell one for a lot of money, and each one after that would be more, building the going rate as they went along. So the tenth one might be many times as much as the first."

"They expected this curator to just slip the paintings into the collection?"

"No. What they did was take advantage of one of the ways the museum acquires things. They were both on the board. In April every year there's an event called the Collectors Committee Gala. The Collectors Committee is a bunch of rich people who each give around sixty grand for an invitation. Most of them also donate bigger money besides that. It's a fund-raising event. That year the committee was eighty-seven couples. During the gala weekend each year the museum's curators show them about a dozen to fifteen artworks that the curators have approved. The committee members vote on each work to determine if it should be bought and added to the museum's permanent collection. It's a yes or no, so the committee can't vote something into the museum that's just crap."

Elle heard the entrance door swing open, and instantly there was a commotion at that end of the building. She turned off the sound and pocketed her phone, then pressed her ear to the door. She heard, "Freeze! You heard me. Down on the floor!"

There was another male voice. "In case you haven't made up your mind, you should know I'm behind you. That's better. Down. Put your hands behind you."

There were more footsteps as the two who had been ambushed and captured were taken away. It sounded as though they went into a room about halfway down the hall. She turned up the phone again to hear Ed.

"Albert Stolkos's *Crimson Twinge,* Aaron Wilbertson's *Mississippi Canyon,* and Sarah Prestmantle's *Caligulan Fantasy.* Most of the nominated works got bought, including those three, so they were on the way to being better known.

"I don't know if the two women lobbied the eighty-seven couples for those paintings or if lobbying was necessary. These women probably knew a lot of the eighty-seven couples socially or through things like the philharmonic or some charity. There was probably some 'I'll vote for yours if you vote for mine' going on. But Semple was a big deal, so maybe he was all it took. And from the conversations we recorded, I know that the two women had paid for the three paintings and donated them anonymously. It was a yes-or-no deal with no reason to say no."

Caine said, "Did their scam work?"

"So far it's worked fine. I checked about two months ago to see if they'd sold any of the twenty-five paintings yet. They hadn't, but a couple of others were sold by people in other parts of the country, and they were worth about ten times what they were once. They've gone from thousands and tens of thousands to hundreds of thousands. They may keep going up, or they may go back where they started, now that Semple and the women are dead."

"Why are they?"

"It's a complicated story," said Ed. "When

we watched the scheme work its way through its steps, we realized that it really might make these women a million a painting over a few years' time. So we —"

Elle heard a lot of heavy footsteps in the hallway outside the women's locker room. People were coming. She turned off her phone as she took her first step toward the lockers.

She opened the door of one of the lockers that had no name on its tape just as she heard the door of the bathroom squeak open. She pivoted inside the locker and silently pulled it shut.

These lockers were the kind she'd had at her junior high school. The handle was on the outside and slid up and down. It was attached to a sliding piece of steel inside the door that had two holes in it to fit over two rounded hook shapes. When someone slammed the locker, the slide would go up and the hooks would engage. To open the door from the inside she could simply lift the slide a half inch and push.

She knew these lockers well, because she was small — just the kind of girl that boys liked to put into lockers and close the door on. For her the door was just as easy to open from inside as outside. As soon as the "damsel in captivity" act got tiresome to her, she would shift to the "I can't breathe" act or pretend to be having a seizure. If the boy opened the locker she would jump out at him. If he ran off to get a teacher she would just open the door and disappear before he and the teacher got back.

She was inside, and the room was pitch-dark again. She could hear through the half dozen horizontal slits at face level. She slowly pulled her R9 pistol out of the belly band and held it. If the locker opened, somebody was going to die.

In a moment she could see a bit. Some-body had turned on a flashlight. The two women came into the room and then a man carrying a small automatic weapon like an Uzi or a Skorpion.

She recognized Shar's voice. "You don't have to come in with us. You guys have all the weapons and phones, and there aren't any windows we can use to escape. You could wait outside."

"Just go," he said. "You said you had to go, so do it. Close the door to the stall, and I'll keep my distance."

Hernandez hurried into one of the stalls as though she was afraid he'd change his mind. Elle heard her pee. Elle supposed Hernandez had been in special distress, because she never seemed to take anything in but coffee. After a few seconds, Shar went into the other stall.

Suddenly Elle heard the distinctive sound of a locker's slide moving up and the door swinging open. The man aimed his flashlight into one of the lockers, and Elle used her thumb to disengage the safety on her pistol.

Shar called out, "What are you trying to find in my locker?"

"Guns," he said.

"Knock yourself out."

He looked in the other locker, which must have belonged to Hernandez. One toilet was flushed and then the other. The two women emerged from the stalls, went to the sinks, and washed their hands. Elle couldn't see them through the slits in her locker door, but she could tell that the man had stopped walking about two paces behind them. She heard the ladies' room door open with a squeak and swing back and forth once before silence returned.

Elle lifted the slide in her locker door, opened it, and came out. She sat on the nearest bench and turned on her phone again, put in her earbud, and then tapped her finger on the website.

She heard Ed still talking. "Anne said, 'You have recordings?' and Shar said, 'Enough of them. I think we could get your husband to kill you.'

"I told her I knew that she and her friend Valerie were going to make a lot of money on what they'd already done — started to make the twenty-five paintings they owned much more valuable. I said that was history, and they could keep it. All she and her friends had to do was find three other painters and do the same for us."

"What did she say?"

"What anybody would say — 'I can't do that. It's impossible to do it more than once. It was a onetime opportunity that's gone. Trying again will get us all sent to prison.' "

"Was it true?"

"No. I don't think it was even illegal. I said, 'Just try. Not trying will lose you your husband, your kids. Your husband is an old-fashioned guy with international connections, and he runs the businesses. What you think you'd get in a divorce will disappear.' The two women finally agreed.

"It was just like a stock market pump-and-dump scheme. You buy something, you run the price up, and then you sell. Only it wasn't against the law. I told her we wanted it done once, and then as long as there was absolute secrecy we'd leave them alone forever."

"And they bought that?"

"They had no choice but to try. They found the paintings for us, and we bought thirty — ten by each artist."

"So what went wrong?"

"Them. At some point they decided to cheat."

28

"I was planning to work the night shift that night, so I was at home trying to get some sleep. I always sleep with my phone next to my head. It rang and it was Shar. She had called to tell me that something unexpected was happening. The two women were double-crossing us. She and McNulty had found out completely by accident."

"What was the accident?"

"They weren't spying on Anne or Valerie. They were just checking the reception and clarity of the cameras and bugs in the security system at the house of another customer of ours."

"Which one?"

"Nick Kavanagh. I told you a little about him. He was the gallery owner who bought the paintings for the two women. They were all part of the same bunch of people who went to each other's parties, ate at Mannon's two restaurants, sent their kids to the same schools, lived in the same parts of town. Kavanagh's gallery was near the Design Center. He was rich, originally from a career in finance in New York.

"It used to be that if you went to New York you'd run into these assholes who were in finance and making huge salaries. Now they collect huge fortunes while they're in their thirties and get out of that business, so you meet them here. They're usually investing in a music company or trying to get into the movie business. But in Kavanagh's case the money and the connections gave him a leg up on the art gallery business. He knew a lot of rich people who had art collections. He also knew a lot of people who wanted to be out every night, and gallery openings were good for that. So he made a lot of money running the gallery too. You know when you buy a painting at a show in a gallery what the standard commission for the gallery is?"

"No."

"Fifty percent. Half of the purchase price goes to the gallery. It takes a real idiot not to make money, but plenty of them don't. He did. When Shar and McNulty called in and told me the two women were at Kavanagh's house in the afternoon looking at paintings, it occurred to me what they must be doing. They had used up Jeffrey Semple, so they were in the process of replacing him with Nick Kavanagh."

"Just like that?"

"He wasn't a stranger. He was part of the same social scene they were in. He had already handled their anonymous purchase of the first twenty-eight paintings. He had bought the paintings for Nemesis too. We were even more anonymous, because he thought he was buying for the women again. He might not have the historical knowledge of a guy like Jeffrey Semple, but he must have had taste and a sense of which paintings were better than people knew. They had already trusted him and he hadn't let them down. All they had to do was get him really committed to them."

Elle heard more heavy footsteps coming up the hall toward the ladies' locker room where she was hiding. She put her phone in her pocket and prepared to slip into the locker again, but they were approaching too fast. She heard the squeak of the door opening, and the footsteps coming in. She realized she couldn't get inside the locker in time. She dropped to the floor and slid under the bench beside the lockers where she had been sitting. She was just short enough so the top of her head and the soles of her sneakers barely touched the two solid supports of the bench.

She heard two men walk past her toward the toilet stalls. "I don't think we're supposed to be in here. This is the ladies' locker room."

"I don't think they'll be needing it. They're all tied up at the moment. And I'm not using that men's room. Too many guys have been in there taking a piss with the lights out."

Elle heard the two men urinate into the two toilets and then flush. The sound of the flushing worried her, because it was loud enough so she couldn't hear their footsteps as they passed her bench, but in a moment she heard the water running at the sinks and then paper towels being torn off a roll. The door squeaked shut and then flapped once. Elle listened to the silence for a count of a hundred in case they hadn't both left or there were more men coming in. Then she turned on her phone and went to her recording site.

"It wasn't a party. It was just the two women and Nicholas Kavanagh looking at paintings that he'd brought home from work and hung. If you'll free my hands I'll show you the recording."

"Sit tight where you are. Vic will do what

you tell him."

Ed sighed. "Okay. Turn the laptop toward Mr. Caine and wake up the screen." There was a pause. "Now bring up the folder 'Kavanagh,' comma, 'house.' Click on the final file in the folder."

Elle looked at her phone screen again to verify that the file was what she thought — the company's recording of the conversation, sex à trois, and murder. She concentrated on the faces of the three men in the office. She assumed that they would be consumed with interest in what they were seeing. But Ed, like Elle, had seen this a couple of times, so he was primarily interested in watching the face of Mr. Caine, who must have been evaluating the evidence to decide whether Ed was an asset or a liability. The young man Mike squinted at the screen as though he thought he might be hallucinating, then got the idea. At the moment, he seemed to be seeing Nick Kavanagh as the luckiest man in the world. That would change shortly, she thought.

Caine was unreadable to her. He was clearly Ed's boss, the decision maker, and he and his men had come here from the Virginia office in an unfriendly mood. He glanced at the screen a couple of times but had no interest in the proceedings. He was just waiting for the recording to end. From the sounds she could hear, the sex part was reaching its peak, but Caine looked impatient. Elle decided that she would never understand men if she lived to be a thousand. They all seemed obsessed with sex, but when there was business going on, they weren't interested.

Finally she heard the shooter arrive. Nick Kavanagh said, "Uh," in surprise. Anne said, "How did you know we were here?" and Valerie said, "Don't."

Caine said to Mike, "Stop it. Now go back." He pointed. "Who's that guy — the shooter? Is that you?"

Ed said, "It's not even a guy. It's Shar. You know, the tall blond girl you guys have tied up in the kitchen."

"Did you tell her to kill them?"

"She recommended it, and I said yes. We realized those three had done all they were going to do for us without cheating us or —"

"Yeah, I get it," Caine interrupted. "Why does she shoot that well?"

"It's just her thing. She practices a lot. Maybe she figures that she's got to be better at that because she can't fight like a man. But she's an odd person. Sometimes I think she does these things because she wants to impress me, and sometimes I think what she wants is my job. For now, I guess it doesn't matter."

Caine had stopped listening. "So you killed them before they could turn on you and — I don't know — tell the cops or get caught."

"That's right," said Ed. He was beginning to feel optimistic. "I figured it was my duty to you to be cautious. The three artists they'd gotten into the museum for themselves were rising in value. The three they'd done for us were now part of the permanent collection too. So without the women we would be okay. If our paintings went up only a little, we'd make a profit. But we couldn't trust the two women anymore. They had lost their fear."

"What do you mean?"

"Maybe they'd never had any fear. They were born with a huge head start. They were beautiful and educated and smart. They had married rich men. Their experience for their whole lives was probably that even when everybody got caught, they would be the ones who got let off, because they weren't the kind of people who do bad things, so they must have been victims. They knew that the game with the paintings wasn't illegal, so if they got caught nothing much

443

would happen to them. If we got caught, we had committed some crimes. So we decided to quit while we were a little bit ahead."

Mr. Caine said, "I've listened to your story. What else do you want to tell me or show me?"

"It also occurred to me that since they hadn't sold their twenty-five paintings, and almost certainly hadn't told anybody about them except Kavanagh and Semple, there was a great chance we could get our hands on them. I mean, the purchase prices were small enough so they could easily have handled the transactions without telling their husbands about them. And how could they have told them? All these arrangements with other men would have been too obvious."

"I can tell by looking at you that there are problems you're still worried about. Tell me now what they are."

"Well, at that point there was a little bit of trouble. The morning after the killing, a young woman came into the house and stole a recording of the afternoon that Nick Kavanagh had made. I don't know why he did that. I don't think he imagined he would be making a sex tape, because he couldn't have known in advance that they were going to seduce him to tie him into a new scheme. It's possible he just ran the camera whenever he was going to talk about art. He was a salesman, and that kind of practice might be useful. Or he could have left it going by accident, after he took pictures of the new paintings. The camera was in plain sight. The girl just showed up the next morning, broke in, and found everything."

"Why? What was she?"

"A burglar."

"Shit. Why didn't Shar kill her too?"

"The girl wasn't around until hours later, when Shar was long gone."

"Did you hunt her down?"

"We've made an effort. Shar found out the friend's house where she was staying, but only the friend and some guy were there, so Shar had to kill them and leave. And every night Shar and Escobedo and Flanders went out looking for her. I think she knew we were looking for her."

"Did she leave town?"

"No. We hired a guy, a freelance pro we had used once or twice. He was good at finding people, and especially women. He found her at a big, nice hotel in the Valley. He was a really good-looking guy, and he managed to talk to her and then take her out. He was going to take her to Santa Barbara, kill her quietly, and dump her in the ocean."

"So? Did he?"

"The next day they found his body in the Santa Barbara harbor between two boats. He had a lot of stab wounds."

"Jesus," said Mr. Caine.

Ed watched while Caine stared at him. He seemed to be getting more and more uncomfortable. Finally he said, "I've told you everything I can think of."

"Have you? You bought a bunch of paintings with Nemesis money, which is mostly my money. How many again?"

"Thirty." He brightened, but his voice was hollow. "I can show them to you. They're in a storage place. And we found the twenty-five paintings the women bought. They were locked in the strong room at Kavanagh's gallery. Now those are in our storage place too. You have to feel good about that. We paid nothing for them."

"You know what I would have felt better about?"

"What?"

"If you had called me and come to Virginia and told me you were doing this. And you would have brought photographs of the paintings and a key to the storage place. That would have shown me that you at least

446

thought this was a good use of my money and that you weren't just robbing me to set yourself up to get rich."

"Oh my god," said Ed. "It never occurred to me that this would look that way to anybody, much less you."

"Too bad," said Mr. Caine.

"I'll give you those things right now. You'll see the paintings and have a key to the storage unit."

Mr. Caine said, "Okay, Vic. You can cut him loose in a minute, but first let me state the conditions. Ed, if you make an aggressive move, you'll die. And I'll have my guys go through this building and shoot everybody else in the head."

"Of course," said Ed. "I'd never try anything like that."

"And you will get rid of this witness, this burglar girl. You'll find her and kill her, not make an effort to kill her."

"Yes. I'll be sure," Ed said. "I've just had a lot to do. After the first three and the burglar's friend and her date, we had to get rid of Jeffrey Semple too. We made it look like he'd hanged himself because Anne Mannon had died."

"I don't want to listen to any more excuses about anything."

"No more, I promise."

"All right. Cut him loose, Vic. We're going to this storage place."

29

Elle turned off her phone and put it in her pocket. The crisis that had made the Virginia squad turn the lights out and overpower everybody was ending quickly, and she would have to get out before the lights came on again. If they caught her here she was dead.

She was sure Shar and Hernandez, the only two people likely to come into the women's locker room, were once again tied to chairs in the kitchen under the eye of the man with the automatic weapon, but they wouldn't be there forever.

All the regular Nemesis employees in this building were in different rooms, disarmed and probably manacled with plastic ties and duct tape. There would be at least one man from the Virginia contingent at each doorway with a short-barreled automatic weapon to keep them under control.

She went to the door of the ladies' room.

She checked and saw that for the moment all the men with machine pistols were out of the hallway, still watching the people they had captured and disarmed.

The very slight light streaming into the hall from the double doors at the far end was enough for her to make her way to the kitchen door. She slowly leaned her head into the room and surveyed the scene. The guard looked a lot like the man Vic who had been in the office with Caine and Ed — broad shoulders, thick neck, big arms. He was sitting at his own table watching the two women with his gun resting on the tabletop. The women were back in their chairs, facing away from him. All of these men seemed to be former soldiers. They knew how to keep a prisoner from doing anything to reverse an advantage or escape.

Elle knew she would not have much time to do what came next, so she didn't hesitate. She stepped in through the doorway and along the wall to her left, knowing her feet had to make no noise whatsoever. If the man heard anything he would turn to see what it was. When she reached the counter she dropped to the floor, opened the first cabinet door, crawled inside, and then very slowly pulled the cabinet door shut behind her.

Moving the few feet she had just traveled in perfect silence was an enormous accomplishment, and now the fear and relief settled on her at once and made her lightheaded and terrified in retrospect. If the guard or the women had simply heard a faint sound or felt a displacement of air, she would already be dead.

She was invisible for the moment, and she felt reluctant to move again, afraid to make a noise or bump something in the dark.

Then she heard the office door open in the hallway. The voice of Mr. Caine called out, "At ease, everyone. This has been a successful drill. Los Angeles people, stay right where you are. Do not turn on any circuit breakers or lights, or leave the spot where you are. Someone will be around to release you. Wait for them."

Right away Elle heard heavy booted footsteps coming along the hall from the office doorway. As the footsteps reached the communications room she heard other boots come out and follow, and then the man in the kitchen got up and joined the group as it moved along the straight corridor; then came more boots.

She could tell from the sounds that the final two pairs of feet were shuffling; probably these two men were walking backward to be sure none of the former captives came out of their rooms. Then the double glass doors opened and seemed to stay open for quite a few seconds, before everyone was out and she heard them swing closed again.

Hernandez said, "I've never been so scared in my life."

"I was scared for a minute because I thought they were the FBI or the police," said Shar. "Once I knew they were guys from the Virginia office, that went away. They might have been mad at the boss, but they had no reason to hurt us."

Elle heard some tearing noises and realized it was Shar pulling the duct tape off her wrists and then her ankles.

"What's the matter with you?" said Hernandez. "What are you doing? They said not to do anything or turn on lights."

"I'm not turning on any lights. I'm going back to the locker room."

Elle heard her footsteps move off to the hallway and turn toward the locker room. She waited for Hernandez to follow, and after a few seconds she did. Elle began to crawl along under the counter. She made it past the sinks and drainpipes to the place where she had opened the wall from the outside. She pushed the sheet of plywood aside and then the corrugated metal, and slithered out behind the plain metal sheet she had placed over the outside wall.

Once she was out of the building she lay still, breathing the cooler night air. After a short wait she saw the three big, dark SUVs pull away from the lot across the street. She waited for their taillights to disappear down the highway before she got to her feet, put the white-painted sheet back against the outer wall, and began to walk.

After about a hundred feet of controlled walking she passed the next building, so she knew she was out of the field of vision of the cameras on the Nemesis building. The adrenaline that had been rising in her for the past hour seemed to release itself and course through her bloodstream. She broke into a run.

Shar reached the locker room and stepped inside. She found her second locker from memory in the dark, opened it, and took out her purse, then her spare burner phone, which she turned on. Now she could see well enough to take out some street clothes and a towel. With the power turned off, it had gotten hot and stuffy in the building. She glanced in the direction of the shower.

The lights were still off, but the dim light of her phone screen let her find her way.

She took off her black work clothes and stepped into the shower.

She hadn't told Hernandez, but she was feeling good. Ed had lived through the visit from Caine. That meant the scheme to sell the paintings was still on. Ed and Shar and McNulty and Flanders and Escobedo were going to be millionaires. Probably Hernandez wouldn't get rich just for sitting at a radio console every night, but she would get the raise she had been hoping for.

Shar had an odd feeling that something was different. What was it? Her wad of gum was gone. She had put it there a year or more ago to cover the mysterious hole she had found. It had looked like a peephole from Ed's office. Of course she didn't need the gum now. The whole building was dark except for the little light her phone screen threw.

She grasped the handles and turned on the water, then adjusted the temperature and stepped under the stream. The water felt wonderful, pouring down and washing the sweat off her skin — sweat from the lack of air-conditioning, sweat from the fear that she had told Hernandez she hadn't felt. She turned her whole body around to look up into the spray.

Shar thought about the peephole and

about Hernandez. Maybe Hernandez was right. If you learned you were being watched, the smartest thing to do might be to pretend you didn't know. The smart thing might be to give Ed a peek at what could be available if he was nicer to her. If she gave him something to think about, it was possible that in time she would get twice as rich.

As Shar showered, the water collecting in the basin of the molded plastic shower floor pooled deeper. It made her feet feel clean. It rose to her ankle bones and then closer to the rim of the shower floor.

Shar didn't notice the white extension cord that ran from the smoke detector on the ceiling beside the shower to the pinhole camera cord near the floor. When the water was ankle-deep it reached the spot where the camera cord's two prongs were only partially pushed into the extension cord socket to draw power. There were bright sparks and a loud buzzing sound as a new circuit completed itself. Shar's muscles tightened spasmodically and stayed clenched, because the new circuit ran through her body, paralyzing and heating her muscles until it killed her.

Two miles from the airport the three black

SUVs pulled over at the side of a street. The first one separated from the others and drove around a block to the entrance of a storage building, pulled in, and parked. At this point the vehicle appeared on the storage facility's surveillance cameras. A man went inside the building to the office. After a few seconds of discussion with the night guard, the man came back out.

He and his two companions entered the building and took the elevator to the third level. They went to the large storage space that the man had rented about a year earlier. They took a number of flat objects of different sizes — all tightly wrapped in thick paper jackets — and put them into the elevator and then took them outside to load into the SUV. Then the SUV pulled out just in time for the second SUV to take its place. Each of the three SUVs was loaded with wrapped paintings and then drove off. The man who had rented the storage space a year earlier, paying for three years in advance, didn't emerge from the building.

30

Elle had committed so many burglaries over her career that sometimes it seemed as though the walls of a house were made of butter. This time the locks were a model that she had admired when it first came out. She had bought one at a beautiful hardware store catering to designers and architects and practiced for days picking it until she could do so in a couple of seconds. It was even pretty — a handle instead of a knob, done in a dull nickel finish without unnecessary decoration. That was why so many really tasteful homes — like this one — had it.

She was feeling a bit off-balance because of the backpack on her shoulders tonight. She went to the nearest couch, sat down, slid the weight of the pack off her shoulders, and stood.

She took inventory as she unloaded the pack there. She took out the 26 numbered thumb drives, 48 computer discs (also numbered), and 116 pages of computer-printed storytelling containing everything she had been able to find out about the case. There were references, like footnotes, to act as a guide to the particular recordings that proved what she had written. A reasonably smart person could use her narrative to pick which recordings to watch and in what order and know who was on each recording, without spending more than a day or two with a headache. A slower or more thorough person could watch many more recordings and read many more pictures of documents and end up with the same impression, but with many more days of headaches.

She set the backpack beside the pile of records, then went up the stairs from the foyer like smoke floating upward into the hallway. She found the man's bedroom, stood in the doorway, and looked at him asleep on his bed. He slept on a bare sheet in a pair of boxer undershorts.

She studied his position carefully. He had one arm in the middle of the bed at about the level of his head and the other stretched out so his arm bent at the wrist and his hand hung over the edge of the bed. He was bigger than she had imagined him from his pictures — at least six feet two inches and about two hundred pounds — and from here most of that looked like lean muscle. Her plan could be done, but if she made a mistake, all she could possibly do was shoot him.

She watched and began her approach. As she moved she thought about cats. Because she had spent so much time in other people's houses at night she had learned to watch their cats. They would sit in a shadow unmoving until they became a part of it, and then they seemed to dissolve and flow into the next place of deep darkness, usually not in a straight or direct course, or even continuously, but from one shadow to the next when they felt the urge. She imitated what they did on her trip to the bed.

When she arrived beside the bed, she was already kneeling with her head below the level of the mattress. She gauged the distance from the wrist to the steel frame of the bed. It was too long for the chain of her handcuffs to reach.

She spent ten seconds pulling the cuffs open and mentally practicing the order of necessary movements so they would be fast. Then she reached up for his wrist. She closed one handcuff on his wrist and in a single motion drew the other downward far enough to click it shut on the steel bed frame. Then she threw herself backward fast, so he couldn't leap on her before she was out of the danger zone.

She stood in the center of the big bedroom, her legs tensed and ready to make a run for the stairs.

He wasn't awake. He was just lying there, his breathing still deep and untroubled. Finally she adjusted her ski mask and switched on the overhead light.

"Wake up, Sammy!"

He stirred and blinked his eyes. "What? What's wrong?" He seemed to sense the inappropriateness of what he'd said. He tried to sit up and noticed the handcuff. He rattled the other cuff against the frame and looked over the bed at it. He finally performed the only maneuver he could and lifted himself off his stomach, turned, and sat. He squinted at her. "Are you a girl?"

Elle smiled through her ski mask. "Boy, if you had guessed wrong on that one, some guy would be kicking your teeth in about now. But yeah, I'm a girl."

"Are you here to rob the house or something?"

"No, Mr. Zucker, I brought you a gift. I found out you're the one in the DA's office who's been assigned to the murder of the people at the Kavanagh house. I'm here to tell you I've solved the case and bring you all the evidence you could want to prove it. I left it all downstairs on your couch."

He said, "You know, you could go to jail for a long time just for being here like this."

"I'm not going to hurt you or rob you. When I leave, you can go down and pick up the goods and spend the next couple of days on it. You'll be a hero."

"Why didn't you give it to the police?"

"I tried with the first stuff I acquired, but they don't seem to have done anything. Maybe they haven't watched it yet. I may even have given it to the wrong police force. But you're the right prosecutor, correct?"

"Correct. But you've broken a lot of laws already tonight. You may not like the next time you see me."

"Don't get hung up on legalities."

"I'm a lawyer. It's what I do."

"In the morning go downstairs, look at the evidence, and be a human first. I've brought you the whos and hows of about eight violent deaths, with proof to convict somebody of each one. This is your chance to do something for law and order — the real kind. Most people don't deserve to be murdered. I'm trusting you because I looked into who you are and I think you're the one to do this. You're clean, honest, smart, and good at your work. I'm some of those things too, but I'm handing it over to you."

"Who are you?"

"The evidence fairy."

"Nice name. Good costume too. Why are you doing this?"

"You'll figure out how I fit into this when you've seen the evidence. I don't think you'll figure out who I am, exactly. The discs, drives, papers, et cetera are all copies I made for you while wearing surgical gloves. If you do figure out who I am, you'll see I'm not the one you want." She turned away from him.

"Wait." He rattled the handcuffs.

"I'm sorry about the handcuffs. But you're bigger, stronger, and faster than I am, and you would have overpowered me in the first few seconds. You'll have to dismantle the bed, and that should take you long enough so I can get out of here." She looked at him. "Maybe not by much."

He nodded. "I suppose. But I'll probably see you again."

She said, "I hope not. In case you don't, have a nice life." She stared pointedly at the empty side of his bed. "And find yourself a nice woman. You're a catch." She turned and walked quickly out of the room.

As he pulled the mattress and then the box springs off his bed to get to the steel frame, he listened for her running footsteps and then for the sound of a door or a window so he could tell the responding officers a direction, but he heard nothing.

When he had painfully loosened the two nuts at the end of the frame with his fingers so he could disconnect the horizontal pieces, he hurried downstairs and found her gone. He also found the printed narrative, the discs, and the thumb drives.

He knew he shouldn't delay calling the police to pick her up, but as he looked at the things stacked and arranged on his couch, he had the feeling that hunting for her was not a higher priority than getting dressed. She was, at most, a witness, not a killer, and she was sure to have left a print or DNA somewhere on this much stuff.

He went to his home office, found the box with the handcuffs and the gun that the City of Beverly Hills had issued him when he'd been formally sworn in three years ago. He tried the key that had come with his handcuffs and unlocked the set she had put on him. Then he took his laptop out of his briefcase and carried it out to the living room.

31

Denny Wilkins heard a knock on his apartment door. At first the sound was very faint and tentative, but then it was hard and loud. He hurried to open the door and find out what was so urgent. He swung it open and standing before him was L, the woman he had been thinking about for a couple of months. Her beautiful face was smiling at him.

He said, "L! Hi! What are you — I'm glad to see you. What a nice surprise."

She was still smiling. "Yeah, it is. Of course it's not a surprise to me, because I was the one who came here." She stepped back and looked up the street and down and even behind her. "It looks good in daylight."

"I thought you were avoiding me," said Denny.

"Well, yes and no, to tell you the truth. You and I had sort of an unusual start. And

464

then for — whatever it was — five weeks?"

"Seven, I think. It was a Thursday night, so seven yesterday."

"For seven weeks and one day I didn't get a call from you. I mean, I may not be the best and most beautiful person you've ever been with, but you have to admit I did my best to be pleasant."

"Pleasant?" he said. "You *are* the best and most —"

"Shhh!" She winced and shook her head.

He continued. "I somehow lost your number off my phone that night. I went back to the bar the next couple of nights, and I found Ricki at a table, but she knew nothing, and then Sal, who was able to get me your number for two hundred bucks."

"Sal? My friend Sal charged you two hundred bucks for my phone number?"

He nodded. "And it was real. It always went to voice mail but the recording was your voice. So I kept trying."

"It's okay," she said. "I had thought, *Wow. I went to bed with him just like that because he was brave and a gentleman, and we were a really good match, compatible and neither of us weird or creepy, but no call the next day? No attempt to get in touch? Despicable.* But I recently got access to that old telephone again, and I listened to all the messages you

465

had left. One a day, huh? And some really nice compliments too. So I thought I'd stop by and see how you are." Her smile reappeared. "How have you been? Do you have a girlfriend yet?"

"No," he said. "When you said it would just happen, it sounded true, so I haven't rushed it."

"Then I'm free to answer your messages. Yes, I will go to dinner with you. And the movies. And the beach. And we can drive down the coast a bit for a picnic. And go running up in the hills. And to a Dodger game. And —"

"Is there any of those things you'd like to do today, right now?"

"No. Right now I'm just stopping before I go out of town for a while. Maybe for a week or two, or maybe a month if it's still hot here then. My suitcase is in the car. Trust me, we all still love the three hundred sixty-five days of good weather in L.A., but near the end of the summer like this it can get to be too summery for human life, you know? You see mirages in your own driveway. When I get back I'm going to be looking for jobs."

"What do you do?"

"I've mostly been living off what I inherited from my grandmother. Obviously that

466

can't go on forever. I'll start trudging from office to office applying when I get back and it's cooler." She paused. "You look so sad. Do you want to come with me?"

"Yes!" he said. He looked wide-eyed, either because he hadn't expected the invitation or because he was surprised to hear his own answer. "Yes. Definitely. Can you come inside for a few minutes while I pack?"

"Sure. In fact, I'll help you. Men don't know how to fold things. They get to a nice hotel, take a shirt out of a suitcase, and it looks like old aluminum foil." She stepped inside and closed the door.

A minute or two later an observer might have been able to see her small, delicate-looking hand move the edge of the front curtain a half inch to check for pursuers, but there were no pursuers and no observers. Within ten minutes the pair were miles away and gaining speed.

ABOUT THE AUTHOR

Thomas Perry is the bestselling author of more than twenty novels, including the critically acclaimed Jane Whitefield series, *Forty Thieves,* and *The Butcher's Boy,* which won the Edgar Award. He lives in Southern California.